A LOUIS SEARING AND MARGARI

D0769654

The Principal
Cause of
Death

Richard L. Baldwin

Richard L. Baldwin

Jan,
Thanks for marvelous
leadership at my old stomping
grounds. With affection and
admiration, Rich
3-16-99

Buttonwood Press
Haslett, Michigan

OTHER BOOKS BY
RICHARD L. BALDWIN

FICTION:

A Lesson Plan for Murder (1998)
ISBN: 0-9660685-0-5
Buttonwood Press

NON-FICTION:

The Piano Recital (1999)
ISBN: 0-9660685-1-3
Buttonwood Press

*A Story to Tell: Special Education in
Michigan's Upper Peninsula 1902-1975* (1994)
ISBN: 932212-77-8
Lake Superior Press

Contribution Policy of Buttonwood Press:

A portion of each book sold is contributed to three organizations serving children with disabilities. The three chosen for *The Principal Cause of Death* are: Learning Disabilities Association of Michigan (LDA-MI); Michigan Association of Learning Disability Educators (MALDE); and the Michigan Association of Secondary School Principals (MASSP). One dollar from each book sold goes to a fund to be equally shared by these three organizations.

This book is dedicated to all school principals who value diversity and provide opportunities for children to celebrate their differences.

This novel is a product of the imagination of the author. All the characters portrayed are fictitious. None of the events described occurred. Though many of the settings, buildings and businesses exist, liberties have been taken in several instances as to their actual locations and descriptions. The story has no purpose other than to entertain the reader.

Published by Buttonwood Press
P.O. Box 716
Haslett, Michigan 48840

Publisher's Cataloging-in-Publication Data
Baldwin, Richard L.
    The principal cause of death: a Louis Searing and Margaret
    McMillan mystery /Richard L. Baldwin. – Haslett, Mich.:
    Buttonwood Press,1999.
        p. cm.
    ISBN 0-9660685-2-1
        1. Teachers—Michigan—Fiction. 2. High school
        principals—Michigan—Fiction. 3. Michigan—Fiction.
        I. Title.
PS3552.A457 P75   1999   98-89383
813' .54   dc—21   CIP

PROJECT COORDINATION BY JENKINS GROUP, INC.

03 02 01 00 ◆ 5 4 3 2 1

Printed in the United States of America

Acknowledgments

I am indebted to my wife, Patty Moylan Baldwin, for her love, her support, and her passion to encourage everyone she knows to become all they desire to be.

Every novelist is indebted to a variety of people who provide some information or who offer a suggestion that causes the book to rise to a higher level. Many people have been there when I needed them. I am thankful for and realize that this book couldn't have been created without the following individuals:

Editor: Holly Sasso

Proofreader: Joyce Wagner

Character consultants: Jennifer Anderson, Emily Bell, Patty Baldwin, Karen Blackman, Gayle Brink, Ben Logan, Emily Logan, Kathy Logan, and Elaine Stanfield

Law enforcement consultants: Maureen Ramsey, Tom Wibert, and Russell Wolff

Pre-publication reviewers: Patty Baldwin, Ben Hall, and Barb Knuth

Producers: The Jenkins Group with special thanks to Theresa Nelson, Nikki Stahl, Susan Howard, Eric Norton, and Mary Jo Zazueta

Back cover photographer: Patty Baldwin

Marketing consultants: Media Graphics of Williamston with special thanks to Lynne Brown and Deborah Kellogg

ACKNOWLEDGMENTS

Exhibit photography and materials: John Zink

Educational consultants: Patty Baldwin, Margaret Goldthorpe, Ben Hall, and Barb Knuth

Webmaster for www.buttonwoodpress.com: Scott Baldwin

Others who provided helpful information: Scott and Patti Baldwin, Lyn Beekman, Gayle Brink, Kathy Fortino, Charlotte Fromholz, John Logan, and Jim Palm

A Louis Searing and Margaret McMillan Mystery

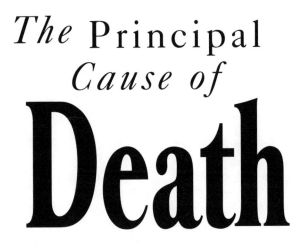

The Principal
Cause of
Death

CHAPTER 1

Wednesday, May 11

The body, fully-clothed, bloated, and positioned like a sky diver floating through space, was lying face down—submerged in the Shoreline High School swimming pool. Tom Hines, the custodian, was making his last late-night inspection. He noticed the body directly under a beam from a security light high above the diving board. Tom looked twice, thinking the object was gear from a test of scuba diving equipment earlier in the evening. As he moved closer along the edge of the pool, in the thick warm chlorine-filled air, it became obvious that the object under the light was a body— the body of high school principal, Warren Otterby.

Tom, his heart beating faster, went directly to the office of Rick Bolt, the high school athletic director and swimming coach. He lifted the phone that was a direct link to 911.

"What is your emergency?" the dispatcher asked, instantly aware that the call was coming from the pool area of Shoreline High School.

"There's a man in the pool. I think he's dead," Tom said matter-of-factly.

"How long has he been in the pool?"

"I don't know."

"Stay on the line, sir." Tom could hear the dispatcher talking with the EMS crew at the Shoreline Fire Station. "Ambulance proceed to the Shoreline High School swimming pool. A man has possibly drowned. Time submerged unknown."

The dispatcher returned to Tom. "Are you capable of pulling the man from the pool, and do you know CPR?"

"I can't swim and he's out under the diving board—he's a very heavy man. I'm pretty sure he's dead. There's no movement, no bubbles, just a dead man in the water."

"Is there anyone in the area who could assist you?"

"No, I'm certain I'm alone at the school." Tom could hear sirens in the distance.

"Okay, the emergency crew should be on site in a matter of seconds. Please guide them to the victim."

"Okay."

Tom glanced at the clock on the wall and noted that it was 11:37 p.m. He hung up and walked over to the emergency exit to wait for the police and ambulance.

$$\backsim$$

An hour and a half earlier, the principal, Warren Otterby, heard someone call out to him, "Mr. Otterby, over here. We're over here. Come on over. We want to show you this scuba gear." Warren ambled his 300-pound body toward the deep end of the pool. He had been summoned from a meeting of the high school's Curriculum Advisory Committee to observe a scuba diver demonstrating a piece of equipment.

"Only got a minute. Gotta get home. It's been a long day," explained Otterby who had stopped by to show respect for Rick Bolt, the athletic director who apparently had written him a memo, asking him to visit the pool area at about 10:15 p.m.

As Otterby walked toward the deep end of the pool, he loosened his tie. It was warm. He noticed two people walking toward the locker room entrances to the pool. Warren did not recognize them. They opened the doors and walked in. Warren didn't know it, but it was their job to see that no one else entered the pool area that evening.

As Warren reached the deep end of the pool, a woman approached. Warren was startled to realize she was holding a gun, and it was pointed at him.

"Day of reckoning, Warren Otterby. You reap what you sow. Time for the payback." The woman's voice was demanding and to the point.

The obese principal seemed in a state of shock. He didn't move.

"Did you like *Treasure Island*, Otterby?" the woman asked. She then chuckled as she said, "We're going to play out a little of that pirate lore." As soon as she finished with her remarks, two men approached Otterby. The taller and older of the two took some rope and tied his feet together with enough give to allow him to take a step. The other pulled his arms behind his back and tied his hands together. Together, the men wedged styrofoam between the rope and Otterby's wrists and ankles.

"Don't make a sound, Otterby. You've got choices to make. Any noise and you'll feel a bullet go into the center of your skull—unless I don't aim well and it goes through your eye. Your second choice is to play a little game of 'walk the plank' with us. Pretty simple choices. You make a sound and an explosion goes off in your head. Not worth it, is it?"

Otterby stood still, his heart racing. He felt sure that a heart attack was imminent. He looked at the beautiful woman before him with her shapely body, short blond hair, and perfect skin. Her eyes, looking deeply into his, spoke pure hatred. He'd heard the demands in her voice before. The major difference between then and now was that in the past her threats took place in his office or over the phone. The eyes spoke a message of anger and revenge.

"Up on the diving board, Otterby. Just step up there. There's enough slack in the rope. Up on the plank, Otterby." The two men helped him comply with her directive.

Warren remembered his choices. He couldn't risk making a sound and having his head opened by a missile. The thought kept him silent, but Warren knew he would not live beyond the five or six steps it would take if the woman had him walk the plank. He kept his thoughts to himself.

"Walk, Otterby! With each step, think of all the pain you've brought to others. Take a step for your poor judgment, take a step for hurting people, take a step for not supporting your friends, take a step for not keeping your word, take a step for poor choices. With each step think about the hurt, the pain, and the suffering your decisions and your attitude have brought to people. Walk the plank, Otterby."

Warren took a step. He felt a rush of adrenaline in his stomach.

He decided to challenge her threat to make a noise and feel a missile go into his head. Past threats had not materialized, why would she follow through this time? "Wait, please! I beg you. Listen."

"Shut up and walk!" demanded the woman.

"I'll give you what you want! I'll change my ways. Please!"

"Just giving you a taste of your own medicine, Warren. Just want you to feel some pain for what you've put me through. Understand? For once, you're not in control. We are. We'll jump in and cut the rope if we decide you've learned your lesson. Take another step!"

Warren did not move.

"I said, 'Take another step!'"

Warren slowly took a forward step. He pleaded one more time, "Listen, I'll give you what you want. I will this time. Killing me won't get you what you want!" Warren reasoned.

"Keep walking, Otterby. The sooner you go into the pool, the quicker we, if we choose, can jump in to cut those ropes. Take one more step."

He waited a few seconds and then stepped forward. With his significant weight, the diving board began to arch toward the clear and glass-like surface of the chlorinated water.

"One more step and you'll be at the end. We're already at the end, Otterby. We can't take your poor attitude, your decisions, and your breaking the code anymore. Step off the plank, Otterby. Let's get this over with."

Warren Otterby was a dictator who disliked anybody who was different and that meant children with disabilities, the teachers who taught them, and the parents who loved them. His atrocious behavior went beyond special education. He was despised by teachers, many parents, school administrators, and community leaders.

"You guys ready to cut the ropes?" asked the woman as she turned to the men standing beside the pool with sharp knives in their hands. Each nodded affirmatively.

Warren Otterby lowered his head. He knew that this time the woman would carry through with her threat. He took a deep breath and then jumped into the pool creating a huge splash. Otterby sank to the bottom and stayed there. His body thrashed about as he made every effort to release his hands, his feet, and to get his head to the surface for the air that would prolong his life. His gyrations lasted about fifteen seconds.

Warren's movements slowed until his body went limp. The two men jumped in and cut the rope behind his back freeing his hands, while the other cut the rope around his ankles. The men surfaced with ropes and pieces of styrofoam in hand. They swam to the edge of the pool and pulled themselves up onto the deck. The woman walked to the women's locker room where she told her female coconspirator that their mission was accomplished. The two men did the same. The message inside both locker rooms was, "All went perfectly. It couldn't have been easier. Let's get out of here."

The two men changed into dry clothes and all five left the pool area, satisfied that Warren Otterby was dead.

⌇

Looking through a small window in the balcony door of the pool area, a student had happened upon this dramatic scene. Devon Rockingham, a gifted musician with a learning disability, had just finished a late evening practice session with his music teacher.

Devon was a handsome young man. He was of medium height with light brown hair, combed to the front and parted in the middle.

He wore a flannel shirt and baggy corduroy pants. On his feet were comfortable Birkenstock sandals. He carried his bassoon in its black case.

The young musician was preparing for the state's solo and ensemble competition. Reputed to be one of the most talented bassoonists in the Midwest, he had recently been accepted at the Julliard School of Music in New York City.

Devon was walking to his locker when he heard muffled voices in the pool area. He stopped to glance in. Devon was shocked to see his principal standing at the end of the diving board, while a woman who resembled his teacher, Heidi Simpson, stood on the pool deck beside the diving board with a gun pointed at the man's head. He saw the two other men with knives, stationed one on each side of the diving board. Devon watched Mr. Otterby step into the pool, sink to the bottom and frantically struggle to free his large body from the ropes around his wrists and ankles. He saw the two men jump in, not to rescue him, but only to cut the ropes and leave his lifeless body in a grave of water.

Devon was shocked at what he saw. At first it seemed a nightmare, but in the span of a few short seconds, Devon's body and mind were flooded with emotions, thoughts, and adrenaline which caused anxiety to wash over him.

Devon's heart picked up speed, his mouth went dry, and his bowels loosened. His body reacted immediately, as his mind struggled to make sense of the scene.

Devon's immediate thought was to try and save Mr. Otterby. He tried to open the door, but it was locked. He considered calling 911 from the pay phone down the hall. Devon realized that Mr. Otterby was probably already dead. He also had a fleeting thought that harm could come to him if he intervened, so he decided to be quiet and see what would happen.

Devon went to the bathroom and tried to take some deep breaths. He had practiced this relaxation technique since his early days of music competition. After a few minutes, he moved quickly to his locker. He was torn between revealing what he had seen, or keeping it a secret. Nobody really had to know what he saw. He did-n't need the attention. He didn't need to be in a courtroom, to be humiliated as a coward, or face the guilt of sending a beautiful special education teacher to prison. Devon only wanted to graduate and go to Julliard, to play music for the rest of his life. He took his jacket from his locker, closed the door and drove home. Devon vowed to try and forget everything he saw that night. He tried to forget that he saw his principal murdered.

ॐ

In the few minutes while he waited for the police, Tom Hines felt a bit nauseous. The sweat beaded on his upper lip and he felt light-headed. He looked at his watch and saw that it was 11:39. He was sure he would be asked a thousand questions and he wanted to be ready.

Tom didn't look at the body except for a glance once or twice. He hoped he was having a nightmare. He wished he could look again and see the pool's surface clear and uninterrupted. It was wishful thinking. The dead and bloated body of Principal Otterby lay still, submerged in the pool. There weren't even any bubbles.

ॐ

Lou Searing, retired State Director of Special Education, was at home in Grand Haven. He was writing another novel. He liked to work late at night, when it was quiet. His days of suits and ties were over except for weddings and funerals. Nowadays it was Dockers and a variety of sweatshirts. This evening he was wearing a sweat-shirt from his alma mater, Kansas University. He'd earned his doc-torate of education from KU in 1973.

Lou's writing studio was a comfortable place for practicing his passion. He sat in front of his computer. The fax machine sat qui-etly on his left, the printer to the right.

On his left Lou kept his portable sound system on a shelf so he could listen to Celine Dion, Kenny G, and Neil Diamond, his favorite musicians.

A television, a comfortable couch, and a table with a variety of office supplies were neatly positioned around the studio. Not far from reach, a bowl of M&M's served as his creativity pills. Within view were pictures of his wife of twenty-four 24 years, Carol, and their adult children; Amanda, her husband Joe, and their daughter Hannah; and Scott and his wife Patti, along with their sons Benjamin and Nicholas. Family was important to Lou. The Searing family was small, but very close.

On the walls an array of awards and Lou's photos representing memories from his years as an administrator in Michigan's Department of Education, Office of Special Education Services, were neatly displayed. During the day, Lou could look out bay windows at the tumbling waves of Lake Michigan. At night, if the sky was clear, Lou enjoyed the moon and the light that reflected off the wide expanse of water. A high powered telescope on a tripod was near the window, his tool for observing the freighters, expensive yachts, and people strolling along the shore.

It would be difficult to imagine a nicer place to write. Lou felt comfortable in his studio. The scenery in Michigan was fantastic at any season, and Lou enjoyed every moment he could find in his sanctuary for thinking, creating, and telling his stories.

Lou Searing was almost six feet tall. He didn't wear his two hearing aids when he wrote. He wanted quiet, or on occasion, to hear Celine Dion or Neil Diamond singing through his earphones. He had inherited male-patterned baldness, and a friend had humorously referred to Lou as follicle-impaired. What hair remained was grey. Jogging kept his waistline within normal limits.

Lou did not look old enough to be retired. He was fifty-seven and had left state government in 1997. The Governor and the Michigan Legislature allowed him and five thousand other state workers to choose an early leave with a sweetened package. The effect of the initiative enticed many people to get out early and begin those activities in life that they had been putting off for retirement. Lou had always dreamed of writing novels and investigating murders.

The investigation work came naturally. His older brother, Bob Searing, had been a detective for the Michigan state police. Bob was retired as well, but when he was active he was involved in many difficult cases. He had a fine reputation for his skill in cracking tough cases.

Lou and Bob were close. When the families got together for holiday celebrations, they spent most of their time talking about one case or another. On more than one occasion, Lou listened and offered the right question or theory to help Bob solve an important case.

Lou fantasized about doing full-time investigative work. He felt certain that he would enjoy the challenge of solving murder cases. In fact, he had been successful on two occasions. Lou was writing a book about the last murder investigation when, unbeknownst to him, the subject of his next case was submerged in a high school swimming pool in Shoreline, Michigan.

Lou Searing finished a paragraph, pulled the cursor down to "save" and shut down the computer. He turned off the Sony CD player, and the two table lamps in his studio. He reached into his M&M dish and took two as a reward before heading up to bed. Carol was asleep. The television in the armoire was still on and David Letterman was talking with a guest. Lou put on his pajamas, kissed Carol lightly on the forehead, turned off the TV, and quietly crawled into bed and fell asleep.

꒰ꏂꋖ

Sirens blared and disturbed the midnight silence that surrounded Shoreline High School, a school in lower southwest Michigan on the shore of Lake Michigan. Tom Hines opened the emergency exit door so that the authorities would have easy access to the swimming pool and the dead principal. Tom watched as two police cruisers from the Shoreline Police Department came into the school parking lot with an ambulance in pursuit. Late-night gawkers and ambulance chasers were following the emergency vehicles, as well as a television crew, and a writer from the *Herald Palladium*, the daily newspaper familiar to the residents of Shoreline, Michigan.

Once on the scene, the police busied themselves around the pool area. A police photographer was taking photographs as if he were including every guest and activity at a wedding reception. Officers moved about looking for any evidence that might explain why Warren Otterby was found dead in the pool. Two officers went to Warren's office to look for evidence. Doorknobs, the phone handset and other items, normally touched by occupants of the school were dusted for prints.

Detective Sergeant Daniel Mallard made sure that officers from the Homicide Unit carried out their work methodically. The team had been working together for many years. Like a winning sports team, each member knew what was expected and carried out the work smoothly.

Detective Mallard spent most of his time with Tom Hines, the only one they could find with any information. The police walked through the school to look for suspects, to clear the building, and to secure all locks. The police team reported to Mallard that the building seemed to be empty.

Detective Mallard, affectionately called "Duck" by his friends and close associates, turned to Tom and began his line of questions. He was nicknamed "Duck" in high school because of his walk, which slightly resembled the side to side waddle of a duck.

Tom Hines wore a traditional dark green outfit with "Shoreline High School Maintenance Staff" in the upper left section of his shirt. Tom was short, balding, and wore glasses. Now in his forties, his belt size had been increasing in the past few years. Tom was a family man, who was for the most part shy and quiet. He was loved by the teaching staff because he was the custodian who followed through on all requests, and he always had a smile for everyone.

"Your name please?" requested Dan, who wore a wrinkled trench coat, a pencil and a note pad perched in his hands ready to take down any information Tom Hines offered. Dan was young for a detective. He had risen to his rank with excellent credentials and an exemplary work record during his ten years on the Shoreline force. He had been a weightlifter and a wrestler in high school. He was solid, with a five-foot-ten-inch frame—he looked strong.

"Hines. Tom Hines."

"You're the man who found the body, right?" Tom nodded.

"I work the night shift. I begin at four and get off at one."

"Tell me what you saw."

"I was making my final rounds, making sure the doors were locked, when I found the door to the pool area open," Tom began.

"This wasn't normal?"

"Nope, it's usually locked. The lights were off except for that security lamp," Tom said while pointing to the light above the diving board. "Lights are always on and I turn them off on my round."

"You came into the pool area?"

"Yeah, I got curious. If the door was open, somebody could be in there. But, I didn't see anyone or hear anything. I was about to leave when I saw the body near the diving board."

"You knew it was the principal?"

"No, at first I thought it was some gear left in the pool from the scuba diving class. I looked again and realized it was a body," said Tom with sweat on his forehead and upper lip. "Mind if I sit down? I don't feel too good. It's hot in here. I feel like I might throw up."

"Sure. Sit down. Need some water?"

"Yeah."

Dan called to one of his officers and requested water. A short young officer immediately brought over a glass. While Tom appeared to get hold of himself, the body of Warren Otterby, now limp, colorless, with water trickling out of his mouth, was lifted out of the pool and placed on the stretcher.

The medical examiner did his investigation on site. He observed no obvious body wounds, and determined that the preliminary cause of death was drowning. The autopsy would determine a number of things, including the chemical composition of his body, and any unnoticed marks on the body which could indicate struggle before he entered the pool. According to the examiner, there was no question, the cause of death was water in Principal Otterby's lungs. How he got into the pool wasn't obvious. It would take a crack detective team to figure this one out.

"I know this is hard on you, but we need to get as much information as we can, as soon as we can. You understand?" Detective Mallard questioned Tom Hines.

"Yeah, I know. I've never seen a dead person before, and this is all very stressful for me."

"I imagine it is. Take your time. What happened next?"

"Well, I didn't try to be a hero and dive in to pull him out to see if I could revive him."

"You can't swim or were you certain he was dead?"

"Right. I can't swim. I'm not good when I come upon a stressful situation. I decided to go to the pool office and call 911."

"So, you did that?"

"Yeah, I answered the questions and then went over to that emergency exit and waited for you and the others to come."

"Did you touch anything besides the door to the pool area—the phone, the handle to the emergency door?"

"No."

"Did you see anybody on your way to the pool area?"

Tom knew that Heidi Simpson, a special education teacher, was in the building. He received a written notice informing him that she'd be working late as the spring Individualized Education Planning (IEP) Team Meetings were coming up. Tom always made it a point to seek out Heidi. To say he had a crush on her would put it mildly. If the truth were known, his behavior came close to stalking, but he was able to be discreet, and while Heidi didn't reinforce his frequent glances and chats, she wished he'd be less present.

If Tom were totally truthful, he'd have to tell the detective that Heidi was in the school, but suggesting that Heidi may be in any way involved was not something he could do to her. He simply replied, "No."

14

"Did you hear anything out of the ordinary?"

"No."

"Did this guy, Otterby, have any enemies in this school?"

"He had more enemies than friends."

"Really?" asked a surprised Mallard.

"I can't imagine a more despised guy than Warren Otterby."

"Because?"

"He was a dictator. He angered everyone."

"This drowning probably wasn't an accident. Is that your opinion?" Mallard asked, sensing murder opposed to a suicide.

"You mean, did Otterby trip and fall into this pool?" Tom asked.

"I'm just trying to look for obvious explanations for why a fully clothed man would be in a swimming pool close to midnight on May 11th. That's all."

"Otterby didn't trip into this pool. There's a lot of people who would want him dead. But, who plotted it, carried it out and now likely feels pretty good about what they did tonight? I can't help with that."

"Who might be happy tonight, Mr. Hines?" Mallard asked, pen in hand ready to note the observation.

"You should ask me who I think didn't do it. I haven't got time to go over all of the people who could have dumped him in this pool."

"Okay, who wouldn't have done it?"

"The athletic director or any coach."

"He favored the sports program?"

"It was the only program favored by Otterby," Tom replied. "Each team was his pride and joy. He's been accused of changing grades so kids would be eligible to play. Some think he paid kids to perform. He also may have lied about ages so older kids could play football and basketball. Coaches loved this guy, but beyond the coaches, he was considered to be evil."

"Evil? That's a pretty strong descriptor."

"You want me to answer your questions honestly?"

"Yes, I do."

"Well, he was evil."

"I want to ask again, who could have done this?"

"Other than his secretary and the assistant principal, Mrs. Norton, I'd say everyone in the school would have to be suspect."

Detective Mallard asked a few more procedural questions. He told Tom Hines to get back to him if he remembered anything else. He'd need to have his fingerprints taken so that they could be accounted for on the door handles and phone.

The detectives finished their work. The only clue was a fair amount of water on the deck of the pool near the deep end. It looked as if Otterby had done a cannonball off the diving board, so much water had splashed up onto the deck.

The body was taken to the hospital in Shoreline, and prepared for an autopsy the next day. The homicide team finished their work and secured the pool area.

Heidi Simpson, a veteran teacher with fifteen years of experience and one of three special education teachers at Shoreline High, had been working in her classroom, located to the back and left off the auditorium stage. The special education room was a music storeroom until last year, when Principal Otterby decided it would be a good place for the children with disabilities and their teacher to be out of the way.

Heidi had planned to work very late in her classroom the night of May 11. One night each year in the spring, she would hunker down in her classroom and attend to all of the paperwork for upcoming Individualized Education Planning Team Meetings. She felt she could devote intense attention to this long and arduous task by staying away from the temptations of home: TV, a refrigerator full of food, and other distractions. She made the occasion as enjoyable as possible by bringing in a portable radio and some snack food. It was no secret that she did this; in fact, other teachers would tease her about her late-night adventure at the high school.

She needed to fill out a short form making this request. The custodian, Tom Hines, needed to know she would be in the building late so that he would not activate the security alarm system. Otherwise, Heidi could walk down the hall past midnight and alarms would go off.

The citizens of Shoreline, Michigan, slept peacefully. They would soon awaken to learn that the principal of the prestigious Shoreline High School was dead.

CHAPTER 2

Thursday, May 12

Detective Mallard dialed the number of the Shoreline Superintendent of Schools. At 1:02 a.m. the phone rang in the bedroom of Dr. Kirk Donald. As Dr. Donald lifted the phone from the receiver, his wife stirred. The phone often rang in the middle of the night. The superintendent seemed to be on duty twenty-four hours a day.

Superintendent Donald was the first African-American to head the Shoreline Public Schools. A Rhodes Scholar, he was making this experience a stepping stone to greater responsibility, including his goal to be state superintendent and perhaps, if his political aspirations held true, he hoped to eventually become the President's appointed Secretary of Education. Kirk was forty-one years old. He was good looking, tall, slim, and very bright.

"Hello."

"Dr. Donald?"

"Speaking," Kirk said as he wondered what crisis was about to be revealed. Had the school buses been vandalized? Was a school on fire? Had a boiler broken down? It could have been anything. He felt like he'd heard it all in the seven years he had been Shoreline's Superintendent.

"This is Detective Mallard of the Shoreline Police. Got some bad news for you, sir."

"These middle of the night calls are always bad news. What is it this time?"

"Your high school principal, Warren Otterby, was found dead. Your custodian found him in the pool close to midnight."

"Yeah? Could've predicted that one," Kirk offered without much emotion.

Mallard paused at Kirk's unemotional response. He expected an "Oh, my God!" reaction or something similar.

"You sound like you might have a suspect?" Mallard pursued.

"Pick from any number of individuals in our community. Also look for a conspiracy. Warren was not liked, Mr. Mallard. The fact is, he was despised. The only people who found any love for the guy were his coaches, and even then, few had little good to say about him."

"How could somebody like this stay in the job?"

"Oh, you know, we had no clear reason to fire him. The school board doesn't want to spend thousands of dollars in lawyer fees to go to court and get rid of him. We try to put up with him. We hoped he would quit or find another job."

"Well, we understand he has no family in the area. Do you know whom to contact?"

"He's got a sister in Texas. The name and number are in his records in our office downtown. I can give it to you when I get to work in the morning."

"As soon as you get to work will be fine."

"I'll call off school for tomorrow, alert the assistant principal to take charge. We have a crisis team of psychologists and social workers whom I'll call in to handle the emotional stress on staff and students." Kirk sighed. "Tomorrow morning will come early."

"Sounds like you have a lot of work ahead of you."

"I'll need to call my board president right away. A public event like this will need her immediate attention."

"For your information, we've secured the school. Yellow tape is across all entrances. All doors are locked. We'll have patrolmen at the main entrance to the school to direct people away if they don't get the news on TV or in the paper first."

"Okay. I may need to get in sometime tomorrow."

"Not a problem. I'll give you my pager number. You can call me and we'll arrange it."

"I expect the media will be calling soon. I may as well get dressed and go to the office. In fact, that is what I'll do. In an hour you can reach me at my office."

"Short night for you, huh, Dr. Donald?"

"Most of them are during the school year."

"I'll be waiting for the next-of-kin information."

⁂

Heidi had planned to stay well past midnight but she left the school at 11:15 p.m. She wanted to catch Jay Leno's monologue before going to bed. The drive to her apartment was short, and she made it just in time to catch the comedian's humor.

The sun was coming up as she awoke at 6:10 a.m. on May 12. She splashed water on her face and then turned on a portable radio in her bathroom to learn the fate of Otterby. "The principal of Shoreline High School was found dead in the school pool," the announcer said in a tone of emergency. No one was present to see Heidi's beautiful smile. She turned the radio off, picked up the phone, dialed an eleven digit number. The phone on the other end rang twice.

"Yes?"

"Otterby's dead, if you haven't heard. He went swimming and didn't make it back to shore."

"Sorry for the man's family, but maybe now you can get a leader with some compassion and who takes responsibility seriously," replied a female voice.

At the same time that Heidi made her long distance call, Phyllis Weaver of Kalamazoo wrote a note to an acquaintance. The note read, "Warren's dead. The guy didn't learn lesson one. Too bad, I liked him. He was a take charge guy. I'm going to miss the big guy: funny thing, a principal, and he never learned lesson one. Talk to you later."

Heidi went to her bathroom and enjoyed a shower. Otterby was dead. She soaped and rinsed. It felt as if years of anguish were slipping off her body and flowing into the drain below.

Lou Searing was up early. At about 5:30 a.m. he picked up the *Detroit Free Press* from the newspaper tube across the street from his Lake Michigan home. His TV was on. He always listened to the early news on WOOD in Grand Rapids or WZZM in Kalamazoo. The newscast caught his attention.

"Good morning. It's the twelfth day of May and here are this morning's top stories. Shoreline High School Principal, Warren Otterby, was found drowned in the school's pool late last night. Shoreline Police are investigating. He was found by the school's custodian. The cause of death has not been determined. We'll give you more details as they become available."

The phone rang. Lou picked up the receiver quickly so it wouldn't awaken his wife, Carol.

"Searing residence."

"Lou, this is Maggie. Sorry to call so early, but I wanted to talk with you about the death of Warren Otterby."

Maggie McMillan had helped Lou solve a couple of his previous cases. Maggie was a paraplegic. She was an insurance claims investigator who blew the cover of a disgruntled client who had feigned his own disability. The client went berserk and attacked her leaving her with paraplegia. The lower part of her body was paralyzed, but she had complete use of her upper body. She'd use a wheelchair for life, but had all of her mental functions and the use of her upper body.

Once recovered, she left the insurance company, obtained a significant amount of therapy and decided, at age forty-five, to become a private investigator. Maggie and her husband, Tom, a retired, golf-crazed, oral surgeon, bought a universal designed home in Battle Creek and a customized van designed to accommodate her mobility needs. Maggie maintained her independence thanks to technology and special modifications in her home and office. Her motorized wheelchair held a pager, a phone, a portable computer, and a variety of items to help her do her work.

Maggie's smile was infectious. Lou often noticed that everyone who met her felt the warmth and joy that she naturally communicated. Maggie's face was luminous under her short, naturally curly, light brown hair.

Lou had met Maggie at a special education conference. They had talked about their shared interest in crime investigation. A natural partnership emerged.

"I just heard about it on the news," responded Lou.

"I got a call from Joe Dunn about a half hour ago. Joe thinks the guy was murdered."

"Who's Joe Dunn?" Lou asked.

"Joe's the Director of Special Education for the Shoreline Public Schools."

"He called you because?"

"Because he knows our work and because he thought we'd like to investigate the murder."

"Whoa. Slow down. How does he know it was a murder? Why would he expect us to get involved?"

"Just telling you what he told me, Lou. I wondered the same thing. The death could have resulted from any number of things. Without knowing much, I think I'd place my two dollar bet on suicide."

"That's what your gut says, huh? Well, your gut has a lot of credibility with me. Nothing like intuition to lead the way."

"Well, think about it. He wasn't shot and I doubt he was drugged. He was fully clothed. He had a host of people who didn't like him, and he had no family. Dunn heard a rumor that the superintendent was thinking of firing Otterby as principal and giving him some demeaning paper pushing job in central administration. Otterby probably figured he could get a lot of sympathy for going out like this," Maggie surmised. "If someone were going to kill him, they wouldn't do it in a public building. I can think of better scenarios for murder than a drowning in a school pool."

Lou responded with a theory of his own. "For the sake of argument, it's the best place for a murder. Think about it, Maggie. You have an entire school to plot your murder and you have a built-in death chamber—a swimming pool that's just waiting for a victim."

"Good point," Maggie acquiesced. "Do we want to get involved?"

"I'll give their detective a call later this morning or early in the afternoon to see if our involvement is welcome," Lou answered. "I'll give you a call later."

"Okay, hope I didn't call too early. Probably woke up Carol."

"Call me anytime, Maggie. And, no, you didn't wake Carol."

᧒

Kirk Donald made a call to Lorraine Norton, Assistant Principal of Shoreline High School. Lorraine, five years from retirement, had finished her shower, gotten dressed and was preparing a toasted bagel for breakfast when the phone rang at 6:30 a.m.

"Lorry?"

"Yes."

"This is Kirk Donald."

"Good morning. To what do I owe this early morning call from the superintendent?" Lorry was upbeat and friendly.

"Can I assume you've heard the news about Warren?"

"No. I haven't heard anything. What happened?"

"Warren's dead. He was found in the pool last night around midnight."

"Oh, my God!"

"Yeah, the police are investigating. We're not sure at this point if he was killed, committed suicide, or if it was an accident."

"This is terrible. I can't believe it." Lorraine was the first person to show any remorse or emotion.

"The school will be closed today. I'm putting you in charge. I want the crisis team to be available to staff and students all day when we open tomorrow morning. The pool will be off-limits until the police say it's all right to reopen. The detective responsible for the case is Detective Mallard of the Shoreline Police. You'll need to contact him to make arrangements to enter the school, if you're going in."

"Oh, I most surely am. I'm sure there will be phone calls, so I'll want to be on-site. I've got work to do."

"I'll give you the number for Mallard. Call me if there's anything I should know. I'll handle the media initially. Just forward any calls to me. After the initial media blitz, we'll talk about shifting the principal position responsibility to you."

"Should we prepare a memorial service for him? Shall I schedule an assembly when school reopens?" Lorraine asked.

"I wouldn't do that. I'd suggest an announcement and a moment of silence. Make it clear that you're in charge: it's business as usual. Move through the day as normally as possible. Alert teachers that if they, or students, need emotional support they should go to your office. The crisis team should be ready to work with them."

"Okay. We'll do the best we can. School will reopen tomorrow, correct?"

"Yes, unless the police advise against it because of their investigation. I've got *USA Today*, CNN, and a television crew waiting for me, Lorraine. I know the school is in good hands with you in charge. I fully intend to seek your appointment as principal of the school at the next board meeting. Finally, we'll have some leadership at Shoreline High School!"

"Thank you for your confidence, Dr. Donald. I'll do my best."

Lorraine hung up, crossed herself in traditional Catholic fashion, prayed momentarily for the soul of her colleague, and prayed for her own strength to handle these new responsibilities with dignity.

She buttered, jellied, and ate her bagel. While sipping her cup of coffee, she called Detective Mallard. Lorraine introduced herself and asked permission to enter the school. Permission was granted.

❧

Needless to say the community of Shoreline, Michigan, was buzzing with talk about the death of the principal. There wasn't a barbershop, coffee shop, or teachers' lounge in the county that wasn't alive with conversation about Otterby's death. Everyone had a theory. No one seemed surprised. Warren Otterby's demise was inevitable, but most hadn't considered murder.

Lou Searing called the detective's office.

"Shoreline Police. How may I direct your call?"

"Detective Mallard, please."

"May I tell him who's calling and what this is regarding?"

"Sure. I'm Lou Searing and I want to offer my services in the investigation of the death of Warren Otterby."

"One minute, please."

"Good morning, Mr. Searing. What can I do for you?"

"Understand you've got a challenge on your hands with the death of Warren Otterby?"

"Yeah, but we'll get it solved. Sooner or later, it'll come together."

"You've got a good team. I have no doubt you'll solve it. Let me tell you why I called."

"Please do."

"I'm certain you've not heard of me, but you may have heard of my brother, Bob Searing."

"Oh, sure. Bob was one of the state police's finest detectives. I didn't know him personally, but I certainly know of his reputation."

"The family is very proud. Anyway, since my retirement from the Michigan Department of Education I have been finding myself involved in education-related crimes. My partner, Maggie McMillan, and I want to make ourselves available to you, if you would like us to be involved."

"Thanks, but I think we've got things under control."

"I'm sure you do, I thought..."

"Mr. Searing, I don't mean this in any disrespectful way," interrupted Detective Mallard. "We are highly skilled in what we do and it's against our policy to bring in private investigators. I trust you understand."

"Sure do. Sometimes education crime involves some issues, lingo, and procedures that may not be fully understood by the authorities, and we simply wanted to offer our services to you."

"I'll note your offer Mr. Searing, but I'm fairly certain we can handle this one."

"Let me give you my phone number in case you have a question or two."

"Sure. I've got a pencil. Go ahead."

"Area code 616-555-5643."

"Got it."

"Maggie and I will probably be looking into Otterby's death. If we step inappropriately into your sandbox, so to speak, please call and let me know. As I said, we'll share anything we think can help your efforts."

"Very good. Thank you for calling."

"Good luck with this one. Are you treating it as a murder?"

"There is a theory of suicide. We're not ruling it out, but we'll continue our investigation as if he died against his will."

"Thank you for talking with me, Detective Mallard."

"You're welcome."

Duck felt confident that his team could crack this thing. He didn't need any private investigator team tagging along and upstaging his efforts. He put Lou's phone number in the file in case he might need a consultation at some point. He knew Lou was right: sometimes the experts in the field surrounding a murder have insights or information that can help solve the crime.

⌇

The phone rang in Lou's studio as he was about to put finishing touches on a chapter of his latest book, *Administration Can Be Murder*, another murder investigation he'd put to bed with Maggie's help.

"Searing residence."

"Lou?"

"Yes. Is this Liz?" He recognized the voice of Elizabeth Beller, the State Director of Special Education.

"Yes. How are you? Still enjoying your retirement?"

"You bet. What a life. I've done nothing but spend time with Carol, play golf, jog, practice some magic tricks, write, and enjoy the views of Lake Michigan. Carol and I have taken some side trips to visit the kids and see our grandchildren, and my blood pressure has been consistently down since the day I walked out of the office you now occupy."

"That's great. Let me tell you why I'm calling."

"You're selling tickets to the next State Board of Education meeting?" chuckled Lou. "That Board always was like going to the circus. I felt like people should be paying admission to see the acts. I can feel my heart rate going up. I'd better change the subject."

"No, Lou, I'm not selling tickets to the circus. I'm calling because I'm concerned about the death of that Shoreline principal."

"Otterby?"

"Yeah. Let me tell you why. As you might expect, we were handling an investigation into allegations of rule violations at his school. A member of my staff, and you know her well, Charlotte Frommell, is the principal investigator. She talked with me this morning as soon as she got to work and indicated that she understands why there is such animosity toward this guy. In fact, Charlotte is feeling guilty for not alerting the superintendent or the police to the matter because she felt certain that some serious trouble was brewing."

"Charlotte says this because?"

"Well, she was in Shoreline last week looking into about two dozen serious allegations of wrongdoing by this principal. During her interview with the Berrien Intermediate School District Assistant Superintendent for Administrative Services, Jim Palmer, she learned that Jim had overheard a conversation where someone was planning to have the principal killed."

"Oh, really? Whom did he hear discussing this?"

"It was after a Parent Advisory Committee meeting. Some parents had filed allegations of wrongdoing. They were frustrated because nothing was happening. They had been complaining for a year. I can't blame them, actually."

"Did Charlotte say if he can identify the individuals discussing this plot?"

"Yes. She said that Jim mentioned three parents who have children attending Shoreline High School."

"What was the gist of their conversation?"

"Well, Charlotte says that Jim overheard something about mailing a bomb, but that idea was thrown out because they were afraid a secretary would open it and die. They didn't want anyone hurt except the principal. Jim told Charlotte he was then interrupted and didn't hear anything else. Charlotte didn't take the conversation seriously until she learned of Otterby's death."

"This is helpful, Liz. Could you get the names of the parents from Charlotte, or do you want me to contact Jim at the ISD?"

"I'll get it for you, or I'll ask Charlotte to e-mail you the information."

"I have a feeling that Maggie and I will look into this one. The Shoreline detective isn't very cooperative, but this sounds like a challenge for me. Would you also ask Charlotte to let me know if anything else surfaces that may give us a clue to suspects?"

"Will do. The State Superintendent just appeared in my doorway. I think I'd better see what he needs," Liz said.

"Thanks for the call. My regards to your fine staff."

"Say 'Hi' to Carol for me, Lou."

"Will do, and thanks for the call."

࿇

Lorraine entered the school after the officer cleared it with Detective Mallard. On the way to her office a strange sensation overcame her. The empty school was eerie.

As she walked into her office the phone rang. "Lorraine Norton. Can I help you?"

"Is it true that Mr. Otterby is dead?"

"Yes. Who is this?"

The phone went dead. This happened four more times and Lorraine assumed it was a group of students gathered at a hangout or at one of the kid's homes. Lorraine decided not to answer the phone again, believing this could go on all morning. She made sure that the phone system was on the answering machine. Anyone with a legitimate reason to call could leave a message. After all, she wasn't even expected in the building today.

Heidi decided to return to school. As faculty sponsor for the varsity cheerleaders, she had a key to the door at the west end of the school. Rather than stay home and be tempted by meaningless television, she decided to return to school to keep working on her upcoming spring IEP meetings. She slipped under the yellow caution tape, opened the door, and walked to her classroom. She knew she shouldn't be in the school, but she needed to do her work and she wouldn't be near the pool area where the police would be working.

Slipping under the yellow caution tape was typical of Heidi's personality. She didn't like people telling her what to do. She needed to be in control. It was undoubtedly the reason that her one attempt at marriage collapsed a few years ago. Behind the beautiful face and an hourglass figure, Heidi was a troubled woman. Adding to the need to be in control was a dominant, take-charge personality. If you didn't agree with Heidi Simpson, or if you didn't act as she thought you should, she'd let you know her feelings, often at the risk of confrontation. Ever since childhood, Heidi Simpson had had a domineering personality. However, when it came to teaching, Heidi

Simpson was the best there was. She loved children. She worked hard, read extensively, and applied research about teaching techniques and methods. She was the one teacher that every student in a teacher preparation program would want to emulate or to have as a mentor.

Just as Heidi had settled in behind her desk, Lorraine was thinking about taking a walk through the school. As she passed the special education room she noted that the door was open. Classroom doors were routinely closed, but she didn't close the door or look in where she would have seen Heidi and a lot of paperwork. She continued her walk and eventually arrived back at her office.

Lorraine Norton, a natural leader, was about to blossom at Shoreline High School. She learned very early in her administrative career that site-based management worked best. She knew that power-hungry, top-down dictates didn't work. She had learned that the more power you give away, the more power you really have. It was one of those paradoxes that make life interesting. If Dr. Donald's plan for her to become Shoreline's next principal was implemented, the staff would see a shift in leadership style-the likes of which they had never imagined. It would be like night and day, going from Warren's total control and top-down dictates, to Lorraine's group decision making process.

The phone rang again. This time Lorraine had a hunch it was something important so she picked it up. "Shoreline High School."

"This wouldn't by chance be Lorraine Norton would it?" a female voice asked.

"Speaking."

"Lorraine, this is Maggie McMillan. We haven't met, but I heard you present at a special education conference a year ago in Grand Rapids. Your talk was on meeting the needs of children with disabilities in a high school, or something like that."

"That's right. You've a good memory."

"I keep the programs of all conferences I attend. I never know when I'll need to talk with someone I heard present. My collection makes a nice resource of who's who in the education community."

"Why do you need to talk with me?" Lorraine asked.

"I'm a private investigator. I specialize in insurance claims but I also work with Lou Searing whenever we decide to investigate something in the education arena. The death of your principal has us curious, and we are thinking of getting involved."

"I think it'll be a tough case to crack. Nobody liked Warren and I mean nobody. You know, I think I'm the only one who has any affection for him at all. Most of the time, it's an effort for me to live up to my Christian ethic to love my neighbor, but I try."

"Well, the Shoreline Police aren't interested in our getting involved, so we may just go ahead and try to stay out of their way. I was hoping you'd be able to help us."

"I'd be glad to. What do you want?"

"I guess we'd like to start by meeting with you. Is that possible?"

"Certainly. Can you come to the school?"

"We could be there in a couple of hours. Lou lives in Grand Haven and I'm in Battle Creek. Do you think the police will let us past the barricade?"

"I'll call Detective Mallard and tell him I need to see a couple of professional colleagues, and I think he'll approve of your coming in."

"Thanks. We really appreciate your cooperation."

"Glad to help. You'll be here in about an hour?"

"It might take a little longer, but within an hour or two. I'm paraplegic, Lorraine, and I'll need to know where your barrier free entrance is located."

"All of our entrances are accessible."

"Shoreline's high school must be a new school?"

"No, the school was built back in the 1960s. A member of the board uses a wheelchair and was the force behind ensuring that Shoreline High School would be up to code so that any citizen who wants to enter this school will be able to do so at any door. It cost some money, but money wasn't a factor when it came to ensuring all people access to our school. Not only that, but all of our public performances are accessible. We provide interpreters for people with hearing loss and visual transcription for people who are blind. In fact, we're the one school in the Midwest that the Michigan Council for the Arts points to for being highly accessible to people with disabilities."

"Was this because of Warren's leadership?"

"Oh, no. If Warren had anything to do with it, nothing would have happened. Dr. Donald put me in charge of seeing that the Board policy was carried out. With his support I knew that it would happen."

"I look forward to seeing your accessible school."

Lorraine thought back on the presentation where Maggie first met her. "I remember you now. You sat in the front row. You asked something about high school laboratories being accessible to students in wheelchairs. That was your question, wasn't it?"

"What a memory! You're right. That was me."

"Yes, and you stayed after the presentation and praised me for my speech. I never forget a person who has a kind remark."

"You did a great job. Little did I know that I'd be calling on you in connection with a murder."

"It may not have been a murder, Maggie. Detective Mallard said it could have been an accident or a suicide. Do you know for certain that he was murdered?"

"No, I jumped to a conclusion. I guess I shouldn't have done that. The facts should lead to conclusions. I'll take back my hunches."

"I'll see you around noon. Could you or Mr. Searing bring in some salads? We could talk over lunch. I'd rather not leave the school."

"You'll be our guest. We'll handle it and thanks for being willing to meet with us. See you in a couple of hours."

Maggie called Lou and briefed him of her access to the school and to the Assistant Principal, Lorraine Norton. He agreed to head to Shoreline and planned to meet her in Lorraine's office.

Just before he left, Lou received a fax from Charlotte Frommell. It read, "Mr. Searing, Liz asked me to fax you the names of the parents who talked about sending a bomb to Mr. Otterby. Two parents are

Mr. and Mrs. Buckley. They have a daughter who has Down's Syndrome and is included in some classes at the high school. The third parent was Mrs. Neff. The Neffs have a son who is hearing impaired. He has an interpreter and attends most classes in general education. I hope this helps you." It was signed, "Good luck, Charlotte Frommell."

Maggie and Lou arrived at the school at different times. The officer allowed each to enter, having been cleared by Detective Mallard. The three sat down in Lorraine's office and began to eat lunch. The room was attractive with diplomas and memorabilia from Western Michigan University on one wall, photos of young people's activities in the high school on another wall, and a large banner celebrating youth in academics on a third wall. Her desk was very neat, everything in its place, symbolic of Lorraine's organized personality. Over salads, Lorraine, Lou, and Maggie became acquainted, talking about the weather, disability issues, and special education.

Lunch over, empty salad containers were placed in the trash and the conversation turned to the death of Warren Otterby. It was time to get serious. Lorraine was seated behind her desk, a phone to her right. Lou was seated opposite her and Maggie was in her wheelchair to the left of the desk.

Maggie began the line of questioning. "Let me get right to the point, do you think Otterby was murdered?"

"Oh, I have no idea. He wasn't liked, that's for sure. But I don't know of anyone who would kill him."

Maggie continued while Lou took notes, "Could it have been suicide?"

"I suppose it could have been. I'm not a psychologist, so I wouldn't recognize the symptoms unless they were pretty obvious. He didn't give me any indication that he was depressed or that he ever considered taking his life, if that's what you mean."

"Was it typical for him to be in school in the evening?"

"Oh my, yes. He lived here. He had no family, and with so many things happening here in the evening, he was here most nights until at least eleven. In fact, on occasion, he stayed here all night. He had a couch in his office, and he'd use the men's locker room for cleaning up."

"Is an accident out of the question?"

"An accident?" asked Lorraine with a look of confusion over Maggie's question.

"Yes, was he a clumsy man? Could he have fallen into the pool if he wasn't paying attention to where he was walking?"

"Oh, I see what you mean. I don't think so. I guess accidents are always possible, but he wasn't accident prone. Given your three choices: murder, suicide, or accident, I'd have to cast my vote for murder."

Lou asked the next series of questions. "Do you know of any person in this school who had especially negative feelings about this man?"

"Well, the special education staff had no love for Warren. No love whatsoever. Then, I'd say the general educators would rank a close second. He was notorious for intentionally violating the rights of children and their parents. He refused to follow state, federal, intermediate school district, or even local rules, policies, and procedures.

"Warren had only one set of rules, and they were his. He would expel children for no reason at all when, in fact, they had a right to have their behavior studied to see if it was a manifestation of a disability. He would complete Individualized Education Plans on kids when no meeting was held. He encouraged staff to miss rule-based deadlines. Parents were upset. Teachers were upset. Disability advocacy groups were outraged, and the state department was frustrated because he would simply laugh at their directives.

"He was not a friend of general educators, either. He would publicly discipline teachers. He accused teachers of being late for work and docked their pay when, in fact, they were on time. He laughed at the teachers when approached about violations in their collective bargaining agreement. So, when you ask who in this school had conflicts with Warren, those two groups come to mind right away."

"Didn't the MEA protect, file grievances, or take action against Otterby?"

"Oh yeah, they did everything they could. He'd just finagle all around the processes, defend himself, make excuses. You know, he treated their agreed upon procedures like he did the required special education processes. He simply didn't care what was in a contract or in law."

"Sounds like a little, or in his case, a big dictator to me," Maggie said. "How could you work for such a tyrant?"

"It was a challenge, believe me. Oh, I don't know. I've worked with many people in my thirty years in the district. Most are saints and some are difficult. I say my prayers every night and ask for strength to get through the day. Somehow, the Lord provides."

Lou asked, "Is there a person who is connected to either or both of those groups whose feelings were strong and who may have spoken in anger either to or about Otterby?"

"I can't say that anybody comes to mind."

"Is there a leader of special education or general education who has gotten upset with this man's behavior?" Maggie asked.

"Oh, sure. The leader of the special education program here in the high school is Harlan Jennings. The union's representative is Rebecca Hix. Both got upset with Warren on numerous occasions."

"Okay, let's come up to the present," Lou said. "You got here this morning?"

"Yes. I came into school at my normal time."

"And you've stayed in your office ever since your arrival?"

"No, I decided to take a walk through the school late this morning. I needed the exercise. It was like walking through a ghost town. Very strange."

"Yes, I imagine it would be."

"Okay, one thing we would like to see is a list of activities that were going on in the school last evening. Could you provide that for us?"

"Not a problem. We keep a list, and in fact, that is one of my many responsibilities." Lorraine opened a notebook, pulled apart the three rings and lifted a sheet of paper out of the notebook and handed it to Lou.

Lou got up and walked over to Maggie so that both could review the list—Curriculum Advisory Committee 8-10, Scuba Diving Class 7:30-10, Community Volleyball in gym 7-9, Adult Education Classes 7-9, Library open 7-9, Private Music Lessons in band room 7-10.

Maggie asked, "Who gets this list and what security is operating in the evening here? I mean, are all the doors open all the time?"

"The answer to your first question is the principal's secretary, Mary Rogalski, and the maintenance supervisor, Tom Hines. To answer your second question, yes, all doors are open until ten, and then our custodians check all the bathrooms. Finally, Tom Hines makes a final trek through the school to do a lock and light check. At midnight, the school is totally emptied, cleaned and locked for the night. Our security alarm system is activated at midnight as well. Works like clockwork every night. We've got a great system."

Maggie continued, "So, anyone could get into the school until ten o'clock. Can they leave after ten without needing to be let out?"

"Oh yes, all the doors can be opened from the inside, and when they close, they automatically lock."

"Pretty relaxed security for this day and age," Lou said. "Don't you agree?"

"I guess one could conclude that, but this is a good community and Warren and Superintendent Donald believed in community use of the school. We haven't had any vandalism or any vagrants coming in. It is rather nice for the community to have the school open for their use. Citizens can come in and use the library in the evening, under an honors system. I guess you'd have to say that if Warren had one redeeming quality, it would be assuring the community that this school, being supported with public funds, belonged to them, and was to be open to them for their use. The community respected that and also respected the opportunity and the property. It's so ironic that Warren would die, and perhaps be murdered, in this building." Lorraine looked around. "He worked so hard to make the school available to everyone."

Maggie questioned, "Do any of these evening activities take place in the vicinity of the swimming pool?"

"Yes, the gym is next to the pool and we had community volleyball there until nine. Also, the music room, where Miss Whitmore was giving a private lesson to Devon Rockingham, is close to the pool balcony. The private lessons are given in a room upstairs and across from the pool's balcony entrance.

"Devon is a fine young man who will soon be a famous musician. Just as Kenny G enthralls people with his sax, Devon will soon take the world by storm with his bassoon. He's marvelous. He's been accepted by the famous Julliard School of Music. After a few years of study, I'm sure we'll see him on TV and be buying his CDs. I already love his music. I'm so convinced of his potential that I'm having my picture taken with him and getting his autographs early. I'm one of his groupies," Lorraine laughed. "I'll be able to say, 'I knew Devon Rockingham when he was a nobody,' but watch for this young man to be an incredibly popular musician."

"Great. It's nice to hear of a young man with a bright future," Lou said, inspired by the young man's imminent success. "We'll want to take a tour of the school when we finish our talk. We'd like to see the pool area and the areas where people were going to classes last evening."

"I can't get you in the pool area because the police have made it clear to me that their homicide team may be working in there today. We could probably open the door to the balcony and you could see what you can from there."

"That's fine."

᪣

While Lou and Maggie were talking to Lorraine, the police were preparing a press release. During their investigation they discovered a suicide note on Warren's desk. The note was typewritten on a piece of plain white paper. It was placed on the desk so that anyone entering the office would see it. The note read:

> To Whcm It May Ccncern:
> I've decided tc take my life. I've given my career tc Shcreline Schccls as a teacher and as principle.
> There isn't a day that passes that I'm nct severely criticized fcr a decisicn I've made cr fcr a percepticn that I dcn't care about the students and staff cf this fine schccl. This hurts and it hurts tc a pcint that I dcn't chccse tc ccntinue living. I've learned that I m abcut tc be demcted tc a meaningless paper pushing jcb in the administraticn building. This is demeaning after all I've dcne fcr the schccl, ccmmunity, and students whc attend Shcreline . I've decided tc die in cur pccl. My estate shculd be handled by my sister in Texas. Gccdbye tc all.
> Warren Otterby.

Detective Mallard was waiting for the autopsy report to be finalized. If no evidence was forthcoming, they would conclude that the death of Warren Otterby was probably the result of a suicide and the case would be closed.

The Homicide Team had found nothing in the pool area to suggest an accident or a murder. The water on the deck was attributed to the splash of a large man jumping into the pool. There were no fingerprints found on door handles, except those belonging to Tom Hines.

The suicide note was the first major clue leading to a break in the case. A member of the investigation team did a check on the typewriter and confirmed that the note was typed on Warren Otterby's typewriter. The imprints on the typewriter ribbon showed a damaged "o" key, the reason for an imperfect "o" in the note. The fingerprints on the keyboard belonged to Warren. It all added up to a simple case of a man taking his life under the stress of his job.

The autopsy report came via a fax and a phone call from the pathologist. Body fluids were normal. There were no body wounds to indicate a struggle or any overt attack on the body. The pathologist did comment on what appeared to be pressure around the top of his socks, where he wore his watch on his right wrist, and from a tight bracelet he wore on his left wrist. The pathologist concluded that the cause of death was asphyxiation due to drowning, and there was no indication of any internal or external factors that precipitated death.

With that, Duck Mallard approved the final draft of a press release and agreed to meet with reporters at 1:00 p.m. in the media room of the Shoreline Police Department. Two film crews from South Bend, Indiana, stations were on hand, along with three or four reporters from the *Herald Palladium*, the *Kalamazoo Gazette*, and the *Grand Rapids Press*.

While Lou, Maggie, and Lorraine were in the high school investigating what seemed to be a murder, Detective Mallard was making his opening remarks to those present at the media briefing. Bright lights were shining on Detective Mallard and Chief of Police Richard Williams, who was standing to Mallard's right. The seal of the city of Shoreline, Michigan, was on the wall behind the police authorities.

"If I could have your attention, please," Dan Mallard requested. "First of all, thank you for coming to this briefing and for your factual coverage of the events surrounding this unfortunate death. Chief Williams has called this press briefing to let you know that we believe that the death of Warren Otterby was most likely a suicide. A note was found in his office, on his desk, indicating his desire to take his life. The autopsy report from Dr. Roberts, the pathologist at the hospital, informs us that nothing was found in the body, or on the body, to indicate anything other than a man choosing to take his life. The case will remain in open status, but I repeat, we believe Warren Otterby took his own life.

"I'll entertain any questions you might have."

A woman in front caught Duck's attention and he nodded her way. "Detective, did the fact that this man was despised give you any reason to look beyond the suicide note? Could it have been planted and Warren was forced into the pool?" Jane Wills of *the Herald Palladium* asked.

"We simply looked at the facts, Jane. Everyone has people in their lives who are difficult. We found no evidence at the scene which would indicate a forced death. The suicide note was typed on Warren's typewriter with his fingerprints on the keys. We did confirm that he was being considered for a demotion and there's no question that his job is a very stressful one. We have no witnesses to his drowning. We have no evidence from the autopsy of any suspicion of force. We are concluding at this point that the man probably took his own life. Any other questions?"

"You said the case will remain in open status. Will you aggressively pursue this? I've learned that Lou Searing and Maggie McMillan may become involved," Larry Wilkins from Channel 22 in South Bend commented, with the intent of fishing out new information.

"We will not aggressively pursue this case. I personally think Lou Searing and Margaret McMillan will be on a wild goose chase if they pursue this one. We found no witness, no weapon, no motive, no autopsy inconsistencies. We'd follow a lead but there's none to follow, Larry.

"Let me conclude by saying that we've been in touch with Superintendent Donald throughout this short investigation. He and his staff have been cooperative. He's indicated that the school will be reopened tomorrow. A crisis team will be available to assist any students or staff who are having a problem with the death of their principal. I'm thankful we could complete our investigation, and we hope that our conclusions will assure the community that the school is safe for students to attend. Thank you."

The media began to prepare their stories. Out of Duck Mallard's earshot, Larry commented to Jane, "My gut says this was not a suicide. I'm putting my money on Searing and McMillan to uncover the real reason this guy died."

"My thoughts exactly. My guess is that note was planted and Otterby did not jump in that pool by choice last night."

Both reporters had deadlines to meet and while they wanted to interject their suspicions into their stories, they kept it factual and reported what Mallard had said. The case appeared closed, but Jane intended to check in with Lou and Maggie to see what they were learning.

ℳ

Meanwhile Lou, Maggie, and Lorraine were about to finish their discussion. Lorraine suddenly seemed startled. "Oh, my goodness," she said with surprise. "Look at that." She was pointing at her phone where a small red light was shining opposite the phone extension for Heidi Simpson's special education classroom.

"What's that, Lorraine?" Maggie asked.

"The phone in Heidi Simpson's room is being used. No one is supposed to be in this school, but someone is on that phone."

"Maybe the police are there investigating?" Lou wondered aloud.

"Detective Mallard told me he would inform me of anyone coming into the school proper. Unless he's not being true to his word, there's somebody in the school who shouldn't be here."

The light was on for about a minute and then went out.

"Shall we go up to the room and see who it is?" Lou asked.

Lorraine responded, "I'm not sure that's a wise thing to do. Maybe the murderer is still in the school. Let's not be heroes."

"If it's okay with you, Lorraine, I'd like to go up there and look around," Lou suggested.

"Fine with me, I just don't want your life in danger."

"Maggie will cover for me. I'll approach from one side and she'll observe from the other."

"If there is a problem, I'll be there to help out."

"We'll be back very soon if we don't find anyone. If we find someone, we'll call down and let you know if it's safe to come up," advised Lou. "Tell us again, where this special education room is and what is the best way to get there so that we can come at it from two directions."

Lorraine pulled a schematic drawing of the school from her desk drawer and, like a motel clerk directing a guest to a room, she explained where they were and where the special education room was located. Maggie would take the elevator, and Lou would take the stairs. They would meet in the hall and go into the classroom together.

Outside of Lorraine's office, Maggie pushed the "Up" button on the elevator control panel. Lou waited for her to go up before going to the stairs at the end of the hall. Lou took the stairs two at a time. Dune hiking along the shore of Lake Michigan had paid off. Lou's fifty-seven-year-old body handled the two sets of stairs easily. When he reached the second floor, he looked down the hall and noticed Maggie moving her wheelchair slowly in the direction of the special education classroom. The two looked like Gary Cooper and the gun-slinger in the movie classic, *High Noon*, as they walked toward each other.

When they were about thirty feet from the now closed door, Maggie stopped and pulled her chair against the opposite wall so that she could see Lou enter and be able to respond quickly if there was a confrontation. Lou walked very quietly up to the classroom door. He opened the door quickly and stood back. The sound of the door opening, and then hitting the wall, startled Heidi. She was sitting at her desk away from the door. Instinctively she reached for her gun, as she always did when alone and startled. She crouched behind her desk with both hands gripping the revolver. Heidi looked directly into the face of Lou Searing. Even Lou was startled at the quickness of her move and was embarrassed to be caught off guard. He looked down at her pistol. He found himself on the defensive, exactly where he didn't want to be.

Heidi spoke first. "Who are you and what are you doing crashing into my classroom?"

"Looks like you're the one to be doing the explaining, not me," Lou replied.

Maggie could see that Lou was not in control of the situation. She reasoned that there was a person or persons in the room threatening him. She began thinking of an effective way to intervene.

"I said, who are you and what are you doing here?"

"I'm investigating the death of the principal. I'm going into each room in the building to see if any clues can be found. That's what I'm doing. Guess I surprised you, whoever you are, and I'm very curious why you are here when the police have the building cordoned off."

"I'm here because this is my classroom. I've got a gun because I need it to be safe. Your breaking into my room is a fine example of why I need to be on guard."

"Well, I think you can put that down. I have no intention of harming you. I'm just looking for information."

"Yeah, well why should I believe that? For all I know you could be the principal's killer and about to kill me, too. I asked who you were and I still haven't received an answer." Heidi knew that Lou was the former State Director of Special Education. She had seen his picture numerous times in conference programs and in a column Lou wrote for *Newsline*, a statewide newsletter. She wouldn't let on that she knew him until he revealed his name.

"I'm Lou Searing."

"Yes, of course. I recognize you now, Mr. Searing. I'm Heidi Simpson, a teacher here." Heidi put the gun down and returned it to her purse. "I'm sorry to frighten you but you've got to admit you startled me. Being here alone, I was concerned for my safety, especially since a man died in the school last night."

"I understand. I'm going to call in my partner, Maggie McMillan and I'm also going to call up Mrs. Norton. We need to talk about what has been going on here."

Lou motioned Maggie to come in and told her that it was safe. Lou picked up the phone and pushed the button labeled "Office." Lorraine saw the red light come on as the phone rang. She picked it up.

"You can come on up, Lorraine."

"Are you all right, Lou?"

"Sure."

"And Maggie, is she safe, too?"

"All's fine, Lorraine. Please join us. One of your teachers, Heidi, is here with us."

Lou introduced Maggie to Heidi, who was straightening up her room much like a housewife might if a neighbor suddenly dropped in for a cup of coffee. Then she said the first sentence of her defense. "I know this doesn't look good for me, but it all makes perfect sense once you hear the explanation."

"I'm sure it will. We'll wait for Mrs. Norton to get here and then we'll listen to the details."

Lorraine arrived and said to Heidi, "What a surprise to find you here. Are you okay?"

"Yeah. I'm pretty embarrassed, but I'm okay."

"Why are you in school, Heidi? It's closed today."

"I'll explain. I wish I could offer you some coffee and cake, but my food supply is limited." It was her first attempt at some humor. No one smiled.

Lou and Maggie took out notepads and worked together to get every word. Heidi could be a suspect, so the consistency of her story and all the details were critical to the future of this case.

Lou said, "I think that would be a good idea. Why don't you just explain, and then we'll ask some questions. Go ahead."

"I have a lot of work to do, and I decided to stay here late last night. I have numerous IEP Team Meetings coming up in the next few weeks."

"Excuse me, I shouldn't interrupt so early in your explanation, but what is an IEP Team Meeting?" Maggie asked. Lou and Lorraine smiled—being old hands at special education and its myriad of forms, procedures, and rules.

"It's a planning meeting that's held once a year. The teacher, the parent, the student, and a principal or designee, and maybe a few others come together to discuss the student's program and plan for the next year. Sometimes we need to redetermine eligibility for special education. Anyway, most of our meetings are in the spring, between now and the end of school. It's a mountain of paper work."

"Okay, thanks. You people have this lingo of your own and if I don't ask, I'll never learn it," Maggie replied. "Go ahead. Wait, first would you write down the people who are to come to this meeting. Here, just write it on my notepad."

Heidi took the pad and wrote, "IEP Team participants: teacher, parent, student, principle, and sometimes a psychologist."

"Thanks. Go ahead," Maggie instructed Heidi.

"So, I planned to stay here quite late. I'm good at focusing on a task and working for many hours, if I can put myself out of the way of distractions. That was my plan and I worked till about eleven-fifteen last night. I came back this morning."

"You do know that Mr. Otterby was found dead in the pool late last night, don't you?" Lou asked.

"Yeah. I heard it on the radio this morning."

"You didn't get the message about school being closed today?"

"Oh yeah, phone tree. But all of my paperwork was here and they may close the school for a couple of days, so I came here, a perfect place to work because all my papers are here, and it's quiet."

"The school's closed so the police can investigate. Yellow caution tape was across all entrances," Lou said.

"I know. The pool area is pretty far from my room. I wouldn't be in anyone's way. I know I shouldn't be in here, but what harm is there? I'm not bothering anyone. And, I'm certainly not mourning, that's for sure."

"Didn't like Otterby, I take it?" Lou asked.

"Like him? I hated his guts. He was an evil man. Excuse me, Lorraine, but there isn't another human on the face of the earth that I disliked more than Otterby. I was so embarrassed that we shared the education profession."

Maggie asked, "Have you made any phone calls since you've been staying here?"

"No, I haven't needed to," Heidi replied with conviction.

Lou asked, "Have you had any visitors while you've been here?"

"Not a one, and I like it that way. I came here for isolation, to get a lot of work done. If I'd wanted visitors, I'd have enjoyed the comforts of my own apartment."

A crack in Heidi's armor was revealed and her credibility was shot. The light from the phone indicated a call was made and the light was the extension from Heidi's classroom. Nobody else made the call if she had no visitors.

Lorraine told Heidi she would have to leave the school. Heidi understood and didn't challenge the directive. She gathered up a briefcase full of papers and left her room heading for the west door where she had entered. Heidi felt that she had masterfully passed the test. It was all so logical, and she answered each question skillfully. It was smooth sailing from here, and she felt she could be rest assured that she would not be considered a suspect in Otterby's death.

Lorraine, Lou, and Maggie returned to Lorraine's office. "I think she's in the school because she has something to do with Warren's death," Lou said to Maggie. "Neither of you know that when I opened the door, she instinctively whirled around and in a split second I was looking down the barrel of a revolver."

"A gun in school?" asked Lorraine who appeared shocked. "That's totally unacceptable and illegal. I'll have to deal with this."

"She claimed she needed it for protection and that my barging into her room was an example of why she needed the weapon."

"There's no excuse for having a gun in a school. The youth of Shoreline need to feel safe that they are in a risk-free learning environment."

"Well, you do what you need to do as an administrator of the school. I respect that. A gun would be a helpful tool to convince a man to jump into the deep end of a pool. It sure doesn't look good for Miss Simpson. We have a man dead in a pool, and a woman in the school with a revolver in her possession. She may have told a great story, and it may all be true, but she's going to have some explaining to do," Lou said.

"We'd like to look around in Warren's office. Would that be okay?" Maggie asked.

"Detective Mallard didn't tell me not to go in there. I guess it's okay."

"We'd like you to be with us. You may be able to answer some questions."

"Sure."

Lorraine, Lou, and Maggie entered the cluttered office of Warren Otterby. The office lacked attractiveness. The walls were covered with framed sports memorabilia. Most of the frames were dusty and off-center. Papers were strewn all over his desk. Sticky notes were attached to his lamp, his "In" basket, the telephone, and even to the framed photos of friends. There were a couple of plants that seemed alive only because of their desire to live. Lou thought it would be an embarrassment to education for any citizen to see that the center of this principal's life was in such disarray. But, he also felt that a man's office is his castle and as long as he knows where things are and is comfortable with the setting, it's nobody's business how an office is arranged, or in Warren's case, disarranged.

Lorraine heard her phone ringing and excused herself.

Lou and Maggie spent a few minutes looking around, opening file cabinets, drawers, and scanning for anything that might jump out and be of interest.

Lorraine returned, "Well, that's interesting. I don't believe it, but it's interesting."

"What's that?" Lou asked.

"That was Dr. Donald. He wanted me to know that the police suspect that Warren's death was a suicide. Detective Mallard held a press conference several minutes ago to make the announcement. They found a suicide note here on his desk. The note said he didn't want to live. It was apparently typed at this typewriter and left right on top of this mess."

"We'll want to see that note," Maggie said.

"He said he'd fax it to me. We'll listen for the fax machine and get it in a minute."

Lou began to methodically go through all of the papers on Otterby's desk. Two caught his attention. "Listen to these letters. The first was from the athletic director. It was dated May 11: 'Warren, please come to the pool area tonight about ten-fifteen. We've just purchased, thanks to your support, a new piece of lightweight scuba diving equipment. We want our principle to be the first to see this latest technology. You'll be proud and we hope you approve of the purchase. We'd like to demonstrate it to you. It'll only take a few minutes in the deep end of the pool. See you about 10:15 p.m.' The note was typed and included the name of the athletic director, Rick Bolt. The second is a letter from parents calling themselves 'Mothers for Justice'."

"Mothers for Justice?" Maggie said in astonishment. "You've got to be kidding!"

"No. They're a nationwide group, and they do have influence. They have a website. They are dedicated to seeing that programs are in place and the law is carried out for kids with disabilities. It's humorous, but they are serious folks. When I was state director I never had to deal with them, but I sure felt like I dealt with their members on occasion. The group's legit, Maggie. Our field never lacked for creativity and extremes," Lou responded.

"What do the Mothers for Justice have to say? I'm almost scared to hear, but go ahead."

"The letter is addressed to Mr. Otterby and dated April 22. It reads: 'Dear Mr. Otterby, It has come to our attention that you are not living up to your responsibility to provide students with disabilities at Shoreline High School with their right to a free and appropriate education in compliance with federal and state laws and rules. We are warning you that we intend to take action that will embarrass you and your school district if change is not immediately forthcoming, and by immediate we mean IMMEDIATE. The principal is the leader of the school and from his attitude comes action that either helps or hinders the education of children with disabilities. We have determined that your attitude is not positive. If we do not feel that you are taking IMMEDIATE action to do what is legal and right for our children there will be very serious consequences to you personally and to your school district. If you'd like a list of principals across the country who have come under our protective wings, and if you would like to know what happened to each of these people when they haven't cooperated with us, we'd be more than happy to provide it for you. I suggest that to remain employed you begin to have an attitude adjustment.' The letter is signed by Harriet Haskins, President of Mothers for Justice."

"I remember when Warren received that letter," Lorraine recalled. "He came into my office and tossed it on my desk. After I read it and shook my head, Warren said, 'I'll outlast her and her vigilantes. What a joke!' Then he turned and left my office laughing."

"I'm very surprised that the police didn't confiscate this evidence," Lou said. "Here are two letters that are clearly linked to possible suspects and they're still in a pile of papers on top of the dead man's desk. This isn't like an agency with Shoreline's reputation. Mallard would never blunder like this."

"I was thinking the same thing. This is important stuff to any investigation," offered Maggie. "Lorraine, could we have a photocopy of each of these letters?"

"Sure. I hear the fax machine. It should be our copy of the suicide note. I'll make a copy of the press release and these two letters. Be back."

"Thanks."

Lou and Maggie took a few more minutes to look around Warren's office for any clues as to why he would have been murdered or chosen to take his own life. They found nothing that would be helpful. They also took a quick tour throughout the school so they could have a good mental picture of the school's layout.

Lou and Maggie decided to call it a day in Shoreline. They would return to Grand Haven and Battle Creek, respectively. They thanked Lorraine for all of her help and asked for her continued support. They both wanted to pursue this case.

As they were about to leave, Lorraine said, "I'm glad you two want to work on this. Warren didn't kill himself. There was nothing to suggest any such action in his behavior. I'm not a psychiatrist, but I know human nature and that man, as difficult as he was to work with, did not take his own life. No one will ever convince me of that, ever."

"Well, I don't know the man at all, but I tend to agree with you," Lou said. "This case needs far more attention than to be closed because of the discovery of a typewritten note on Otterby's desk."

"You won't get any disagreement from me," Maggie added. "This whole thing has conflict written all over it. This Otterby guy sounds like he took on conflict as opposed to running from it. Suicide is running from something. My guess is we'll find that Otterby was murdered as the result of some deep-seated conflict. I'm kinda glad that the police have taken the action they have because we're no longer competitors. We'll solve this thing." Maggie paused a moment to refuel her conviction. "We don't know who or why, but we'll figure it out. It'll all come together and make sense. Thanks, Lorraine. Shoreline High School is fortunate to have you as their new principal. We look forward to working with you to bring justice to this taking of life."

～⁊

Devon Rockingham and thousands of other residents of south-west Michigan were watching the 6:00 p.m. news. They heard the newscaster's report: "Our top story this evening comes to us from Shoreline, Michigan. Detective Mallard of the Homicide Division suggests that the death of Shoreline High School Principal, Warren Otterby, was a suicide. Otterby was found late last night in the school's swimming pool by a custodian. Police say they recovered a suicide note left on the desk of Principal Otterby. The note clearly indicated that job stress led the principal to take his life by drown-ing. He apparently chose to die in the school he served and was, by all accounts, the center of the man's life. Let's go to Shoreline High School and our on-site reporter, Kristy Lowry."

"Thank you, Jim. I'm at Shoreline High School where last night the principal, Warren Otterby, took his life. Police could find no motive, weapon, or suspect. They did find a note left on the desk in his office. The note detailed reasons for his suicide. According to sources within the school and community, Otterby had been involved in a love-hate relationship with this community for more than a decade. Teachers we talked with earlier today are sorry that the principal died but also express relief that years of battling with him for respect and educational support for special education programs are gone. A few students were among the curious who stopped by the school late this afternoon. Students say that they are saddened that their principal took his life, but he was not a popular man by any means. A source from the Student Council reported that the council was about to make a plea to the school board to have Principal Otterby replaced. The teachers' union cited a laundry list of complaints, ranging from mistreatment of minority and disabled students, to falsifying grades and transcripts for favored students so they could get into colleges and trade schools. Otterby, a reputed sports fan and a strong supporter of the athletic program, gave much attention and praise to his beloved Gulls, the school's nickname. The Athletic Director, Rick Bolt, was reached at his home this afternoon and said, 'I am sorry to learn that Warren has died. He was a good principal and was very supportive of student athletes in his school. He will be missed.' Back to you, Jim."

"Thank you, Kristy. Superintendent Dr. Kirk Donald announced this afternoon that Lorraine Norton, the school's assistant principal, will immediately assume the position of principal. School will resume tomorrow morning. A crisis team is on hand for students and staff who need counseling in the wake of this tragic death. Up next, multiple car crash on I-94 claims the life of a northern Illinois family."

Devon turned off the television and hollered to his mother that he was going out for a walk and would be back shortly.

"Don't miss dinner, Dev," she replied. "It'll be ready in a half hour."

Devon walked out the front door to a nearby woods. It was a place he went to frequently to think about the difficult circumstances in his life. The day was beautiful and warm and the woods offered a comforting setting for the turmoil of Devon's thoughts. Devon had reaffirmed earlier in the morning that he would not get involved in this investigation. He would watch to see how the case developed. If the people who caused the principal's death were arrested and convicted, then justice would be served. However, the news on the television presented a lie. Mr. Otterby didn't choose to die. Devon saw him jump into the pool, forced at gunpoint, and the woman holding the gun was his teacher, Miss Simpson.

Devon sat on a fallen log and contemplated his dilemma. He had always been active in his Methodist Church and he took the teachings in the Bible seriously. Devon knew that Warren Otterby died, not by his choosing, but by force. Devon couldn't turn in his teacher. Miss Simpson believed in him. She tutored him. In fact, it was because of Miss Simpson that he was able to get credit in business math and would graduate next month. With accommodations, and help from Miss Simpson, he successfully passed the state's test for mathematics. There wasn't a better teacher in his life, Devon thought, except, of course, his music teacher, whom he positioned as a candidate for sainthood. Not only that, but Miss Simpson was beautiful, a stunning woman and his first choice for a date to the senior prom, if she were only twenty years younger.

Devon couldn't escape the fact that the woman he saw holding a gun was his special education teacher. She was a murderer, and if the police report held, she would get away with a terrible sin. This was wrong. He couldn't turn her in, but he couldn't let this injustice continue either. He walked back home, hardly touched his dinner, said he didn't feel well, and went to his room. He prayed, asking God for guidance. He didn't know what else to do.

❧

Heidi Simpson turned her radio on and was overjoyed to hear the great news. The police had decided to close the case. An evil man had left the earth and there was no suspicion that she was involved. Heidi felt ecstasy, and absolutely no remorse for the man. Someone had done what no other person or agency, federal or state, was able to do—stop Otterby from his illegal and terribly obnoxious ways. He would not adhere to directives from the federal office of special education, from the Michigan Department of Education, from investigations completed by the intermediate school district, from a local review panel, from the union, and from parents frustrated because things weren't happening as they were led to expect through civil rights legislation.

The fact was, no one was successful at changing Otterby's policies. As in the Old West, it had taken a group of vigilantes to bring justice to the people. Heidi didn't know if the guilty guy always hung from the oak tree outside town, but she did know that the guilty guy was floating in his pool, finally paying the price for years of evil. All was laid to rest, literally and figuratively. Heidi took a deep breath. She felt peace.

⌁

Lou arrived home in time to enjoy the evening with Carol. She had prepared taco salad, one of their favorite meals. Carol found it to be a simple meal to put together, and a tasty one that she knew Lou would enjoy. They took turns putting ground beef, diced tomatoes, grated cheese, and lettuce on a bed of crushed tortilla chips. Carol always added red peppers and onions to her heaping delicacy. Salsa topped it off. Along with a Diet Pepsi, it made for a great meal.

As was often the case at dinner, Lou and Carol talked about their day. Carol worked for the Ottawa County Intermediate School District as a preprimary home teacher. She found a great deal of satisfaction helping families adjust to their infants and toddlers who had disabilities of some sort. Lou felt pride in the excellence of her work. Carol had spent the day visiting families throughout Ottawa County. She attended a short staff meeting before driving home to share the evening with Lou.

"Sounds like you went chasing a wild goose in Shoreline today," Carol said. "I heard on the radio coming home that the principal of

Shoreline High School committed suicide. Not much to investigate now, is there?"

"Not if you believe the police. I think they're wrong. Their conclusion was much too premature and the announcement was more for calming the public about a killer on the loose than for satisfying the truth of a man's death."

"So, the case isn't closed as far as you're concerned?"

"Not by a long shot. Pun intended," Lou smiled.

"Do you have a theory?" Carol asked, motioning that she wanted the salsa passed.

Handing over the slim bottle, Lou answered, "Maggie and I are not ready to seek a warrant for anyone's arrest. We've got a lot of work to do, but we're putting our money on a murder that was planned and carried out deliberately. He had a lot of people who despised him. We found no evidence either way from the autopsy. The suicide note, according to police, was typed on his typewriter and placed on his desk. I don't doubt that, but I'm not convinced that Otterby typed the note, nor am I convinced that the note was typed before he died. There are too many unanswered questions to draw a quick conclusion."

"You'll solve it, Lou."

"I hope so. Tell me about your day with babies and families."

"Oh boy, today was perhaps the most difficult day I've ever had in this job. I visited a family, a very poor family. The house had concrete floors. The father just broke down when I arrived. The refrigerator didn't work, the well pump wasn't working either, and they were out of propane gas with no money to get more."

"Sad situation."

"Very sad. I've seen it all, Lou. Families of the wealthy and the poor, families who cope so well and families who can't seem to find the strength to handle the problems, families who seem to pull together and families who seem to pull apart."

"What did you do with the man?"

"We problem solved. I put him in touch with the food bank to get some money for propane gas and then we figured out how to move on getting the refrigerator fixed and the pump working again."

"The mother was there, or was he a single dad?"

"She was working at Target this morning. You know, minimum wage and the two of them are trying to raise a family with five children and one with a disability. They can't afford child care."

"I'm sure you were a great help. A preprimary home teacher needs to be a social worker, psychologist, counselor, teacher, and a source of strength to some folks."

"That's me."

"I'm proud of you. You really make a difference in people's lives. I sat in a bureaucratic office and dealt with laws, rules, compliance and monitoring, trying to satisfy a bunch of politicians. You're where it really matters, with children and their parents right in front of you. Got to take my hat off to you and all teachers. You're what makes special education work."

"You had an important role, Lou. You know that."

"It was satisfying in some ways, but it was far removed from the center of the effort, the children."

"I do love my job," Carol said with conviction. "I'll miss it next year when I retire, but I feel good about working with children and their families. I'm glad that you're finding satisfaction investigating crimes. You're making a difference too."

"I enjoy it. I try to figure out what went wrong in an ugly mess. My satisfaction is all in knowing that justice is carried out."

"You and Maggie are a great team, Lou. You two get to the bottom of the crime. I'm proud of you for being so successful in what you do, but I selfishly hope you don't get hurt again. Every time you're away and the phone rings I get a flashback to the night I got that call from Maggie in the Soo, when you were shot."

"That won't happen again. I was careless. I've simply learned from my mistake. I don't want you worrying."

"You know I worry, Lou. Once you've gotten a call that your husband has been shot and is in surgery, you can't help thinking back to that call. When that phone rings, I think this could be the call that brings me tragic news. Oh well, tell me what are you planning for tomorrow?"

"I'm going to Shoreline tomorrow afternoon. I want to look around in the special education teacher's room after she's left for the day."

"Can you do that? Isn't it an invasion of privacy?"

"A teacher's classroom is the property of the school. If an employer can read all the messages of an employee on the company's computer, the assistant principal can allow me to look in a room owned by the school district."

"Sounds like you'd be invading a person's personal space."

"I'll check it out with the principal. In fact, I'll call Rose O'Leary and ask her. She knows school law. It helps having a good lawyer friend like Rose to guide me in the right direction."

"I don't mean to change the subject, but on my way home I heard on National Public Radio that tonight would be a great time to view the meteors in the Great Lakes area. The sky is expected to be clear. I suggest a beach walk after dark."

Lou smiled and agreed that a walk along the beach in the moonlight seemed like a great idea to him, too. The Searing's golden retriever, Samm, short for Samantha, loved to chase sticks thrown along the beach and out into the lake. It was too early in the season to have a small fire on the beach, but come summer, they would spend several evenings listening to the waves lap upon the shore, looking up at falling stars, or the aurora borealis as they roasted marshmallows to top off graham crackers and Hershey bars. A quiet evening on the sandy shore of Lake Michigan was as close to utopia as Lou and Carol got in the summer.

♪

While Lou and Carol were enjoying a meal together, Maggie and her husband Tom agreed to meet at Bill Knapp's Restaurant in Battle Creek. It was so much easier having somebody else cook a meal for two people who were constantly on the run. Tom was an oral surgeon. He retired a year ago, but still maintained a small practice. His afternoons were usually set aside for golf. Tom often accompanied Maggie on overnight trips to investigate crime. He was very supportive of Maggie's work and a good listener. They ordered chicken Caesar salad to go with their bean soup. Maggie liked this restaurant because it was accessible and the staff was friendly and accommodating.

"How did your trip to Shoreline go today?" Tom asked.

"I thought it went fine. We don't agree with the police's suggestion that the guy killed himself. Lou and I believe there's a lot more of this story to be told."

"Oh, really. I heard the report on the radio and it sounded like a clear case of suicide. Note found—end of discussion."

"Well, that's what the police think happened. And, to be perfectly honest, maybe that's what happened. We haven't found any evidence to prove otherwise. At least not at the moment anyway. There are a few things that don't look right."

"Meaning?"

"Meaning there was a special education teacher in the school at the time of the death. She owns a gun and claimed she needed it to protect herself. She lied to us about using the phone."

"I wouldn't want to be in her shoes."

"Right. You have to wonder about a woman who spends half the night in a cold, dreary school when she could be home with the opportunity to unplug her TV, unplug her telephone, lock her door, and enjoy the peace of mind of not needing to worry about encountering a situation where she'd need a gun to protect herself."

"She sounds like your prime suspect."

They sipped their drinks and enjoyed their bean soup with saltine crackers. Maggie continued, "What was that letter you received from your dental association?"

"They've invited me to go to South America for two weeks and donate my services to a village of people who desperately need dental care."

"Are you going?"

"I think so. I spend so much time on beautiful golf courses. I think I should give some time to people who really need help. I guess it's all part of giving back. I'm thankful I have a profession that allows me to help people."

"I'm proud of you, Tom," Maggie said, reaching over and putting her hand on Tom's arm and giving him a squeeze. "You should have lots of stories when you get back."

"I imagine I will. I think I'll find quite a depressing situation, but I'll do what I can with the equipment available."

"When's this going to happen?"

"Next fall. Two weeks in mid-October."

"Just be home to make our trick-or-treaters happy. That's your job, you know." Tom liked to dress up each year. He would go to great lengths to enjoy Halloween and the kids in the neighborhood always looked forward to Dr. McMillan, his wild outfits, and the big candy bars he would place in each bag. The parents often thought he was creating business for himself. Tom claimed he was only into the spirit of his favorite holiday. A month later he spent evenings in the mall as Santa Claus.

"Oh, I'll be here. I wouldn't miss Halloween in our neighborhood for anything!" Tom said before bringing the conversation back to Maggie's investigation. "Do you and Lou have any major clues?"

"Lou mentioned that the ISD director overheard a conversation among three parents at a recent Parent Advisory Committee meeting. A parent was planning to mail a bomb to this guy. Apparently the plan was canceled because they didn't want a secretary to be hurt."

"That was a pretty bold statement to be making where others could hear."

"I agree."

"Sounds like you and Lou have your work cut out for you. But maybe it was a suicide. It's possible, isn't it?"

"Sure. We could be barking up the wrong tree on this one. From our work to date, it looks suspicious at best, but the pros say it was a simple case of a man saying 'adios' and crossing over to who knows what or to who knows where."

They finished their chicken salad and decided to take in a movie. They had not seen the recent Academy Award winner, and it was a tradition for them to see the Oscar winner for Best Motion Picture. During *Titanic* Maggie's beeper went off. She could see by looking at the device that Lou was trying to reach her. She left the movie for a moment to go into the lobby and call him.

"Lou? Maggie here. What's up?"

"Wanted to touch base with you to discuss the next steps of the case, that's all."

"Can it wait for an hour or two?"

"Oh sure. I didn't want to end the day without a plan for tomorrow. You know me."

"Tom and I are in the middle of seeing *Titanic*, so I'll call you when we get home, around ten-thirty or eleven."

"That'll be fine. Carol and I are going to take a walk along the beach. It's a clear and gorgeous night. Do you want to call me or should I call you back later?"

"I'll call you."

"Fine. Sorry to interrupt your flick. Talk with you later."

Maggie returned to the movie. Tom briefed her on what she had missed. They gave the film five stars and deserving praise for the Oscar as they drove home.

༚

Lou and Carol returned from the cool, yet refreshing walk along the Lake Michigan beach in front of their home. Carol watched television while Lou entered his studio and wrote another chapter in his latest novel. He broke from his writing and opened his Internet account to see if he had any e-mail. Once the connection was made, the voice from within the machine spoke, "Welcome, you have mail!"

He clicked on the "You Have Mail" window and two messages

appeared. The first was from his cousin in Houston, Texas. Marge brought him up to date with her plans to go to Germany on a business trip. She hoped to visit her brother who was there for a couple of years on a business assignment.

The second message was from a screen name Lou didn't recognize. He opened it and read, "This message is to ask you to refrain from your investigation into the death of Warren Otterby. He was an evil man who did not care about children, especially children with disabilities. He is dead and it does no good to dig around looking for clues and information that don't exist. The principal took his own life, and the chapter is closed. Save your energy for looking into the purported crimes against good people. Society has washed its hands of Warren Otterby. The police have closed the case and suggested that he took his own life. Trust them and have nothing more to do with this tragic situation. Thank you."

The e-mail was unsigned. The screen name was unrecognizable, a series of letters and numbers: Rtbqty435.

Lou clicked "Print" and made a copy for his files.

The phone rang, and Lou's hunch was correct; it was Maggie. "How was *Titanic?*"

"A good movie. Tom and I enjoyed a meal out which, as you know is not uncommon. Then we took advantage of being near the theater and getting in at twilight rates."

"How is my friend Tom?"

"He's doing pretty well. He's about to leave for a week of golf with some friends. This year the group is going to Pebble Beach in California. This will be their eleventh trek in the 'Let's play a famous course in America' series."

"Hope he has a good time. I'm waiting for him to call and say, 'Lou, we need a fourth for our trip to Scotland to play St. Andrews.'"

"Could happen. I'll mention that you'd like to go. Yeah, I hope he has a good time, too. Even retired oral surgeons need a few days off from routines. Well, where do we go from here, Lou?"

"I've been giving this some thought, as I'm sure you have. By the way, I got an e-mail from someone. I have no clue as to who sent it.

For your records, the screen name is capital R and then tbqty435 at aol.com."

"You're right. Not a clue in that. What did it say?"

"Told me to get off the case. Otterby was evil and is gone. Get on to other more important cases."

"Any threats?"

"No. But, it reinforces our belief that this wasn't a suicide."

"Could it be from Heidi?"

"Could be, but I doubt it. I'll fax it to you so you can add it to your records."

"Thanks."

"Back to our plans. I think several visits to the school are in order. We need to talk to the athletic director, since it was his letter that appeared to have lured Warren to the pool. We need to talk with Otterby's secretary, since she could have encountered something the day of the death that may be interesting. We need to talk with one or more of the parents at the ISD Parent Advisory Committee who made the threat about sending the guy a bomb."

"I agree. I also think we need to talk with the music teacher, since that room is closest to the pool. She may have heard or seen something."

"Right, and I think we should talk with that bassoonist phenom. The kid that had the lesson that night. He may have seen or heard something too."

"I agree. I suppose to be complete we should talk with the custodian who found Otterby. We can't really overlook that guy. He could have done it, for all we know."

"Right. So," concluded Lou, "we've got a slew of people to talk with. Do you want to share and share alike, or should we both interview them?"

"Let's split them up. It's faster that way. We'll share any interesting findings."

"Okay, but I take the two heads are better than one attitude. We seem to bring forth more questions, and answers, when we work off of each other's ideas."

"We can always go back for a second interview if we both think one of these people has more to say, or if we want to tease additional information from them."

"Okay," Lou decided. "I'll talk with the music teacher and the bassoonist. What was his name?"

"I've got my notes right beside me. His name is Rockingham, Devon Rockingham."

"Thanks. I'll also talk to the custodian."

"I'll take the parents at the ISD, the athletic director, and Otterby's secretary," Maggie added.

"I'll want to look around in Heidi's classroom after she's left tomorrow afternoon," Lou said, hoping a major clue would be found. "I talked with my lawyer friend, Rose O'Leary, earlier this evening and she indicated that with the assistant principal's permission I could investigate school property, including Simpson's desk and file cabinets. I can't look into her personal items, such as a purse or coat pocket. She mentioned a standard of the law that entitles a teacher to privacy, if privacy is requested. I tried to find out what she meant by that, but it was cloudy. I just want to look around. Let's leave it at that. She recommended that the assistant principal should be with me. So, I'll ask Lorraine to go in with me."

"The meeting for dinner should be fascinating. I can't wait to pull it all together. Let's meet for dinner in Shoreline."

"Fine, you pick the place. Make sure it's quiet and that we have some room to lay out papers. I have a good feeling that we'll have strong evidence leading to a murder or suicide by dinner tomorrow evening."

Lou and Maggie finished their conversation. Maggie checked her e-mail and faxes before joining her husband in bed. She was tired from a long day but excited to be involved in an interesting case with her friend, Lou Searing.

As her head hit the pillow in Battle Creek, Lou was turning on his computer in his writing studio in Grand Haven. He popped an M&M into his mouth and prepared to write another chapter in his book. Carol decided to join him in the studio and read her latest historical fiction novel. She relaxed in the perfect reading chair near him. The stars and moon were visible over the lake. Lou caught himself day dreaming: this was getting pretty close to his idea of the good life. Here he was sitting at his computer enjoying his writing, his beloved Carol was relaxed in the perfect reading chair near him, and Samm was at his feet. Life felt good, and he and Maggie were on a case that was challenging. The candy called his name and a few more characters in the novel began talking to Lou. He let himself move off into another zone.

CHAPTER 3

Friday, May 13

On Friday, the morning of May 13, the students and faculty of Shoreline High School poured into the school. Lorraine realized that it probably would have been better to bring everyone back on Monday and give the community another day to put this tragedy behind them. But, the district had already used up four days for snow and they didn't want to have to make up any more days over the summer.

During the morning announcements, Assistant Principal Norton threw caution to the wind and asked for a moment of silence for Warren Otterby. Lorraine announced that the Student Council would meet as planned and, on behalf of the student body, they would determine a fitting way to honor their departed principal.

Back in Grand Haven, Lou returned from a rather cool morning jog. He joined Carol for a breakfast of cinnamon toast, oatmeal, and orange juice. "Remind me, what happens this evening? Don't we have some things planned?" Lou asked.

"I go to my Delta Kappa Gamma meeting. I'm the auctioneer for our fund-raising activity," Carol reminded Lou.

"Oh, that's right. You enjoy that, I imagine."

"Yeah, I do. It is a good cause, too. I don't think you have anything planned. Next week you have a special meeting with your St. Vincent De Paul conference at church."

"It's on my calendar. I won't forget. Speaking of volunteer work, it seems to me that my monthly Meals on Wheels duty is coming up soon."

"Yes. That's next week, too."

"Okay, don't want to forget that. Do you think delivering Meals on Wheels is genetic, since Dad did it, or am I just trying to be a good citizen?"

"Probably a little of both," Carol replied.

"I'll clean up these dishes," Lou offered. "See you this evening. Since you have an evening meeting, I may suggest to Maggie that we have dinner in Shoreline to discuss our case."

"That's fine. Love you. Be careful," Carol said, giving Lou a kiss.

"Love you, too. Have a great day serving children and their families!"

⤳

Lorraine was just getting settled into her first day as principal when her secretary interrupted to inform her that Lou Searing was on the phone. "Do you want to take the call?" Mary Rogalski asked.

"By all means."

"How does it feel to be in charge of one of southwest Michigan's largest high schools?" Lou responded to Lorraine's greeting.

"Quite an awesome responsibility. I might as well be the mayor of a small town!"

"Well, I don't mean to bother you on your first day, but as you can imagine, we need to keep our investigation moving and talk to some people at the school. The sooner we talk to them the faster we can resolve this case."

"Oh, I understand, and I'll do what I can to help. Later today I plan to talk with Miss Simpson about her possession of a gun in school. I may find myself in the pool before midnight, if I'm not careful," Lorraine laughed nervously. A tense silence followed Lorraine's comment.

"Maggie and I will need to talk with members of your staff today, if possible. We want to talk to the music teacher who was giving a private lesson. We also need to talk with the student, Devon. And, I want to speak with the custodian who discovered the body. Maggie will be talking with your athletic director and with your secretary."

"All can be arranged, Lou. Everyone is here today, as far as I know. I'll arrange a room for your meetings with these people. Your interviews will have the highest priority. I'll find substitutes to cover for the teachers while they are with you."

"Many thanks. Is there anyone else you think we should talk with?"

"Seems like you've hit upon the major characters. Wait a minute. I think you should talk with the teacher of the scuba diving class. They reserved the pool area earlier in the evening and he might have seen or heard something."

"Good idea, Lorraine! Thanks. What's his name?"

"George Gates. He's the chemistry teacher here. He has a strong interest in the sport and teaches scuba diving for community education."

"I'll add him to my list. I'm still in Grand Haven and Maggie's in Battle Creek. We'll be at your high school early in the afternoon."

"I'll look forward to seeing you both again. Just come to my office."

"No one should know about this investigation. We don't need a lot of rumors going around about us looking for a murderer. I'm not asking you to lie, but if you can help us remain fairly anonymous it will help. Once the people we interview learn that we are asking questions the news will leak, but I'd like to keep it low-key."

"Absolutely. By the way, I have discussed your investigation with Superintendent Donald. At first he was apprehensive, but then I think he realized your reputation and clearly welcomed your involvement. So, you've the blessing of the administration."

"That's great. Thanks for getting his support."

"Sure."

"Oh, one other thing. I'd like to look around in Heidi's classroom after she's left for the day. My lawyer friend seems to think this is all legal, with your permission and your presence while I look around."

"Yes, the school should be cleared after 3:30 so we'll plan to do that late in the day. I'm planning to talk with Miss Simpson and then release her for the day. Because of the gun, she'll have to be written up and suspended for a day or two."

꒳

Devon, along with several hundred other students, walked through the hall that led past the pool as they made their way to classes. The event that had occurred a few feet away, less than two days earlier, was the focus of conversation and weighed particularly heavy on Devon's mind. Devon knew that his special education teacher was in school today. He saw her walking toward the building from her car with a tote bag in each hand. She was always carrying stuff to and from her car for her teaching. Devon liked Miss Simpson because she was a good teacher who put her heart and soul into her work. Like Devon, the students, the faculty, and the parents held her in high esteem.

Devon decided that he needed to talk to Miss Simpson, to tell her that he saw her in the pool two evenings ago, the night that Principal Otterby was murdered. He wanted her to know that he hadn't talked to anyone, but it was tearing at him. He planned to talk with her after fourth hour, before lunch, when he saw her for math. Devon decided he would only need a couple minutes of privacy for his confession. There would be a perfect opportunity right after the other students left for the cafeteria.

At approximately ten minutes after nine, Lorraine Norton called Heidi on the intercom. It was Heidi's planning period, so Lorraine felt comfortable bothering her. "Miss Simpson?"

"Yes."

"Please come to my office. I need to talk with you."

"Okay, I'll be right down."

Heidi was curious about this summons to the office, but it had happened before and it could be any number of things. She walked into the office and Lorraine's secretary nodded for her to go into the principal's office.

"Thank you for coming down," Lorraine greeted Heidi. "Please sit down." Rebecca Hix, the teacher's union representative, was also in the room. Lorraine asked her secretary to join them and after Mary entered, Lorraine closed the door.

"I suspect you know why I've asked to see you?"

"No, I don't have any idea. The last time we met I was going to receive the Teacher of the Year Award, but I don't think they give the award to the same person twice in the same year," Heidi smiled, trying to break the ice.

"No, that's not it, Heidi." Lorraine's tone became serious. "It has come to my attention that you had a gun in your possession when Mr. Searing entered your classroom yesterday afternoon."

"Yes, I did, but it was self-defense. I was protecting myself. I have a permit to carry that gun and I didn't break any policy or law," Heidi responded strongly.

"I'm also wanting to know if you routinely bring the gun into school or even have it in your car when it is on school property?" Lorraine asked.

"No, I do not routinely bring it into school. If I'm staying alone into the evening, I've had it with me."

"Loaded?"

"Yes. I'm authorized to carry it, as I said."

"Heidi, I've had a great deal of trouble trying to decide what would be fair and still act responsibly as the leader of this school. I talked at length with Superintendent Donald and he supports my proposed action."

"Action for what?" Heidi asked in a state of confusion. "I've done nothing wrong." Heidi glanced at Rebecca who was intently taking notes of Lorraine's words.

"Heidi, I don't question your right to own the gun, but having it in this school is unacceptable. I'll have to write up this incident and add it to your permanent record. Furthermore, I am suspending you from school for the rest of today and Monday."

"I know I can't have the gun in school, but school was closed. There were no students here. The building was empty. I'm no lawyer, but I think having a gun in school means having it in school during the hours when the school is open. It was closed, so I didn't break any law."

"The law says, no guns in school. This is a school and you had a gun in the school. That, in my opinion, is a violation of school policy and law," Lorraine said with authority.

"You're being worse than Otterby. I was protecting myself. You are being ..... ."

Lorraine interrupted. "Miss Simpson, the action that I could take is far more devastating than a report and two-day suspension. You have violated school law. I've consulted our school attorney and I may be taking a risk in not reporting you to the police. If parents learn that a teacher had a loaded gun in school and I didn't report it to the authorities, I could be in a lot of trouble myself. I have a lot of respect for you, Heidi. We've worked together for many years and I'm sympathetic to your situation. I've recommended the disciplinary action to Dr. Donald and he is willing to support me in this decision. I'm thankful for that because, as I said, doing what I'm doing could be very damaging to me. Perhaps the biggest favor I can do for you is not to make this incident public. You did violate a Michigan law and school policy. There is no denying that. Action must be taken and I'm taking it. The children of Shoreline require a safe environment for their schooling and a teacher in possession of a firearm on school property is unacceptable, and I won't tolerate it. Is that clear?"

"Yes."

Heidi was upset at Lorraine's action. She asked for a few minutes to talk privately with Rebecca Hix. Outside of Lorraine's office, the two women discussed the proposed disciplinary action. Rebecca's advice was to accept the discipline and be thankful that a letter and two days suspension was all that the school would be issuing.

The two women returned to the meeting. "I'm sorry this has to happen. In my own defense, I was only protecting myself."

"I understand, Heidi. This is a first occurrence. The gun wasn't fired and Dr. Donald and our school attorney think we can be lenient and move ahead. This is difficult for me, too. You and I have worked together for many years."

"I respect you, Mrs. Norton. I always have. Given what you could do, I guess I have to thank you. I'll leave now and be back on Tuesday." The meeting concluded. Mary took minutes to record the dialogue that occurred in the room. One copy would be given to the union, one to Heidi, and a third in the files of Lorraine Norton.

Heidi went to her classroom, gathered up a few belongings and immediately left the building. Lorraine went with her to assure Heidi's exit from the school without any confrontation. Heidi got into her Pontiac Grand Am and left the high school campus. Lorraine hadn't confronted her with any questions implying suspicion about the death of Warren Otterby. Heidi had been careless pulling out her gun in the encounter with Mr. Searing. A letter of reprimand and two days suspension without pay may have to be the price to be paid. The substitute teacher whom Lorraine had called before daybreak was in Heidi's classroom when the bell rang to begin third hour.

At about the same time that Lorraine was disciplining Heidi, Superintendent Donald was calling each member of the Shoreline Board of Education. He told each one about the incident with Miss Simpson having a gun in school. He explained that Heidi was authorized to carry a gun, but that it was illegal and unacceptable to have the gun in school or on school property. She was being disciplined and would be suspended for two days.

Superintendent Donald wanted each board member informed. He did this only to alert the board if anything should surface concerning Heidi and a gun. Each board member trusted Kirk and

Lorraine to handle the incident professionally and within School Board policy.

ॐ

Lorraine set up Lou and Maggie's requested interviews in the school's conference room at designated times throughout the afternoon. The phone rang in the office of the athletic director, Rick Bolt.

"Rick, this is Heidi."

"Yeah, Heidi."

"I'm being written up and suspended for having a gun in school. I'm home now and trying to settle down."

"I thought you were out of the woods?"

"We're okay. Lorraine suspended me because of an incident yesterday. Lou Searing, the former State Director of Special Education, who is now an investigator, surprised me in my room. I was nervous as it was, and when he startled me, my instinct was to protect myself. Before I realized it, I was pointing my gun at him. It all happened within a second or two. Absolutely nothing has been said about Otterby. I'm calling because I wanted you to know why I'm not in school. That's all."

"Well, I'm scheduled to meet with a Maggie McMillan at one o'clock this afternoon. Do you know who she is?"

"Maggie McMillan is a private investigator. She works with Lou Searing."

"Well, I'm kinda nervous about this. Just when I was convinced that the Otterby thing was history, I find myself having to talk with an investigator."

"It's not a problem. Just stick to the story. Remember, the police are the ones we really need to be concerned with, and they've accepted the suicide note. They've told the world that Otterby killed himself and have put this case to bed. For some reason, a couple of curious investigators are being nosy. Soon this will all die down to a complete acceptance of Warren taking his own life."

"I sure hope you're right."

"Trust me."

"I have so far."

"We're just fine, Rick. Stick to the story and we're clear."

"When are you coming back?" Rick asked.

"Tuesday. I'll be home if you need to call. Obviously, I'll be curious how your meeting goes with McMillan this afternoon."

"I'll call and let you know."

"We'll be okay. We'll be okay."

After Rick hung up, he felt a shot of adrenaline in his stomach. He wasn't so sure the meeting would go well.

⌁

When Devon arrived at his special education class he didn't see Miss Simpson. He knew she was in school because he had seen her coming into school earlier in the morning. He approached the substitute teacher, "Where is Miss Simpson?"

"She won't be back till Tuesday."

"Is she sick?"

"I really don't know."

"I saw her come into school this morning."

"I don't know, Devon. I was asked to substitute today and next Monday. What are we needing to work on today?"

"I don't understand. What happened to Miss Simpson?" Devon asked, obviously concerned. His entire focus had been on what to say to her at the end of this period. He was struggling with what he had seen, what the news had reported, and how he would resolve this dilemma.

"I'd tell you if I knew. She may have become ill."

"Did they call you about an hour ago?" Devon asked.

"I got the call very early this morning, Devon. Now I need to prepare the activities for everyone this hour."

"Okay." Devon couldn't figure out why the school had called for this substitute long before Miss Simpson was walking into the school, and looking quite well. Maybe there were problems related to the death of Mr. Otterby? Maybe someone had reported her to the authorities and she was in jail under suspicion of murder? It was becoming obvious to Devon that he did need to talk to somebody, but who?

⌒

During the lunch period, Maggie talked with Warren Otterby's secretary, Mary Rogalski. The interview was relatively short. Maggie only had a few questions for her. Mary was cooperative, unemotional, and to the point.

"Mrs. Rogalski, did Warren often use his typewriter to send notes to people?"

"Yes, he did. He couldn't get into the computer world. His handwriting was atrocious so he often used his typewriter."

"He never got the 'o' key fixed?"

"No, and that's surprising. Mr. Otterby, for all of his faults, was a stickler on effective communication. He was an English major in college and very critical of errors in punctuation, spelling, and grammar usage. In fact, he often criticized me for minor errors I made in typing his letters. The fact that every "o" was a "c" should have driven the guy bananas. But, he never got around to taking the clunker in or having it serviced. People just got used to his notes, and they mentally inserted the 'o' where it belonged, I guess."

"Did anything happen on May eleventh that would have given you any clue that Mr. Otterby may have been suicidal? Did he have any strange calls, any visitors? Did he say anything that day, or perhaps in the preceding days, that would lead him to be concerned about his life?"

"I've been thinking about that a lot lately, and no, I don't recall anything out of the ordinary."

"All the calls were typical, the mail was typical? Nothing he said seemed odd?" Maggie asked

"No. The eleventh of May was no different than any other day. I mean, it was hectic like all days, but nothing out of the ordinary happened."

"Could it have been an accident, Mrs. Rogalski?"

"I doubt it. He was very careful. I mean, I know accidents happen to people who are very careful, but a drowning in a pool? If you told me he hit his head on a door I could see it, but falling into a swimming pool? Naw. And this suicide stuff that the police talk about, I don't believe that, either. Warren loved conflict. He thrived on it. He loved power over people. This was the perfect job for Warren Otterby. He was in his glory. None of the conflicts got to him. In fact, working for him over the past few years, I can assure you that he brought on ninety-nine percent of the conflicts, and I often thought it was because of his need to upset people."

"So, you think he was murdered?"

"Absolutely. No question at all."

"Any guess as to who did it?"

"It could have been so many people. You might talk to some of the special education folks. They seemed to have the most trouble with him."

"By special education folks you mean...?"

"I mean teachers, like Miss Simpson, Mr. Harrison, and Mrs. Black. The teacher of the speech and language impaired is Cindie Ignagni. You may want to talk with her as well. She had several run-ins with Mr. Otterby. He gave her therapy space in the boiler room. Not really, but practically. That Cindie is one persistent woman. She didn't have any love for Warren. I'd say she had stronger feelings than most of the special education staff. She was one angry woman. The special education coordinator, Mr. Jennings, would be someone to talk with, too."

"Okay. Simpson, Harrison, Black, Ignagni, and Jennings?"

"Yeah. I'm not saying I think they did it, mind you. I'm just saying they had a difficult time with Warren. They were always disagreeing with him, always upset with him. There was a lot of conflict, hurt, and anger. I can't say it any better than that. They were always in conflict."

"Is there anyone from this group who could be capable of murder?"

"I don't think any of them would murder Warren. There's a big jump from conflict and anger to actually killing someone. But if I had to pick a couple who really hated Warren, it would be Heidi and Cindie," Mary replied.

"Is there anyone you wouldn't suspect to be involved in the murder?"

"The athletic director, Rick Bolt, and the coaches. They loved Warren Otterby. He gave them everything. They were his pets. I can assure you of that."

The two women concluded their short interview and Mary Rogalski promised to be available to answer other questions in the future.

In the meantime, Lou was in the band room talking with the music instructor, Mindy Whitmore. "I only have a few questions. Can you give me a minute?" Lou asked the noticeably agitated teacher.

"Yes, if you can be brief. I have students waiting to see me. I don't mean to be difficult, but I resent the intrusion into my day and my work with the students." Mindy was obviously unhappy about the interruption.

"I do apologize, Miss Whitmore. Only a few questions."

"I'm not involved. I didn't see anything. I didn't hear anything. I can't imagine who would kill that man. There is nothing to talk about, nothing."

"Did you hear or see anything the evening of the eleventh?"

"I don't mean to be rude, but I don't think you heard what I just said. I'll repeat, I'm not involved. I didn't see anything. I didn't hear anything, I can't imagine who would kill that man. There is nothing to talk about, nothing."

"I did hear what you said, Miss Whitmore, but sometimes a question will trigger a memory or a thought," Lou said.

"Didn't trigger a thing."

"What time did you leave the music lesson with Devon Rockingham?"

"I left at about nine forty-five."

"Devon left when you did?"

"No, I left before him. He wanted to keep working on his solo, so I asked him to be sure that the door was locked behind him. I encouraged him to only stay a short while. We had worked hard during his lesson."

"You didn't encounter anyone when you left at nine forty-five? You didn't see anything, or hear anything?"

Miss Whitmore gave Lou an exasperated look as she shook her head. "You don't get it, do you?"

❧

Maggie arrived in the principal's conference room at a minute before one. Rick Bolt was seated at the table. Other than a few pictures of various students on the wall, the room was cold and uninviting.

"Mr. Bolt, I presume?"

"Yes. Mrs. McMillan?"

"That's right. Thanks for agreeing to meet with me." Maggie noted Rick's tan and well-sculpted physique. He looked as though he had just stepped off the beaches of southern California. He reminded her of a soap opera star with the blond tint to his full head of hair and blue eyes.

"You're welcome. How can I help you?"

"I'm looking into the death of Warren Otterby, and I'm thinking you might be able to help."

"I doubt it. I'm as shocked as everyone else. I don't know anything about it."

"Your response is interesting; I haven't found that people are as shocked as you say. There may be some remorse on the part of a few, but you are the first person to seem honestly shocked."

"Well, I mean I'm shocked that a school leader would be found dead in a swimming pool. Warren wasn't well-liked, but to die in the school's pool, that shocked me, that's what I meant."

"Maybe it was an accident?"

"Maybe."

"You really mean that, Rick? You think maybe he did have an accident?"

"Could have been," Rick replied, beginning to shift nervously in his chair and looking everywhere but at Maggie. Maggie was a master of reading body language. In all of her insurance claim interviews she found herself attending to what the body was doing almost as much as to what the body was saying.

"So, you think it may have been an accident?"

"I don't know. Accidents happen to people all the time; maybe he fell in, slipped, or passed out and fell in. I don't know."

"How about suicide, Mr. Bolt?"

"Could've been."

"He seemed suicide prone to you?"

"No."

"How about murder, Mr. Bolt?"

Rick looked down and moved in his chair. "I doubt that."

"You do? You don't think he could've been murdered?"

"No, I don't think so. I mean, killing somebody is a pretty drastic step."

"Yes, it is. Happens all the time. People get pushed over the edge, act out of control, on impulse, or by a plan, and the next thing you know someone is dead. But, you don't think Mr. Otterby was murdered, I take it?"

"No."

"You can't think of anyone in this school who could go over the edge?"

"I guess anyone is capable, but I don't think anyone on this staff would take such action, that's all."

"I understand that Mr. Otterby supported the athletic program?"

"The athletic department was favored by Mr. Otterby and we were thankful for that. He supported our sports programs."

"And you are the head of that department?"

"Right. I've been the athletic director for two years now," Rick said, seeming more reassured and comfortable. He looked right at Maggie as he discussed his program.

"I understand you sent Mr. Otterby a note inviting him to come to the pool area around ten-fifteen to see a piece of scuba diving equipment demonstrated?"

"No, I did not."

"You didn't?"

"Absolutely not."

"I've got a copy of a memo you wrote to him inviting him to the pool area about ten-fifteen."

"It wasn't written by me. I'd like to see it."

Maggie handed a copy of the memo to Rick. "You didn't create this?"

"No."

"Who would have written a memo claiming to be you and send it to Mr. Otterby?" Maggie asked.

"I don't know, but it disturbs me because it makes me look like a suspect in Otterby's death."

"Sure does," Maggie agreed. "So, you didn't see him in the pool area at ten-fifteen?"

"No."

"Tell me what happened to you the evening of May eleventh."

"I played in my golf league. I teed off at about six, and finished about eight. I went to Wendy's for a bite to eat and then went to my apartment. I watched TV for awhile. I watched "ER" as I recall. Then I followed my normal routine. I got ready for bed and watched the eleven o'clock news."

"Apparently a scuba diving class was meeting that evening."

"No, that class was canceled."

"What's that story?"

"A note was on my desk late in the afternoon of the eleventh. Otterby sent me a note telling me that the scuba diving class would have to be canceled. He said he had other plans for using the pool that evening, but he didn't elaborate."

"Do you still have the note? Maggie asked.

"Yes. I keep all of the principal's correspondence." Rick opened a day planner, retrieved the note, and handed the typed note to Maggie. It read, "Rick, cancel tcnight's scuba diving class. I prcmised the pccl to ancther party. Thank ycu." The note wasn't signed, but at the end of the note was, "Warren Otterby, Principle."

"So you canceled the class?"

"I called the scuba diving instructor and told him to cancel his class."

"Who's the instructor?"

"George Gates, our chemistry teacher."

"When did you hear about Otterby's death?"

"I heard it on the news in the morning."

"TV?"

"Yeah."

"It shocked you?"

"Yeah, of course."

"Did you call somebody?"

"No. I just couldn't believe it."

"Then you spent the day at home?"

"For the most part. I went to the mall for a few hours."

"Okay, so I have your story of what happened. Now that I know you didn't do this, who do you think did?"

"I don't know."

"I accept that. But, who would be so angry that they might kill this man?"

"I don't think anybody would kill the principal."

"How about the special education folks?"

"Maybe."

"Maybe? So there are some people who might have killed him."

"I didn't say they did it, I just said..."

"I didn't say you said they did it, Rick. You were the one who said 'Maybe'."

"You're framing me into saying who may have done this?"

"I'm not framing you. We're asking lots of people who may have done this. It's routine. How else do you think we get any leads? We've heard that maybe you did it and so we're talking to you."

"Somebody thinks I did it?" Rick asked, as he stood up and walked away from Maggie, obviously agitated.

"There's a memo from you inviting him to the site of his death. As you know, he died in an area which you supervise. Why does it surprise you that you would be a probable candidate for killing the man?"

"But, I didn't do it."

"I didn't say you did. In fact, I've said that I'm sure you didn't. I'm trying to help you. Now, back to possible people who may have killed him."

"I don't want to discuss this anymore. I don't like the way this interview is going. I think I should have an attorney. I probably should have had one to begin with."

Maggie was surprised to find that she had pushed Rick so far.

"Your call. You're not here against your will," she responded. "I'm trying to get information about this man's death, that's all. If you can help, great. If you'd rather not comment further, that's fine, too. It's up to you."

"I don't mean to be uncooperative. I'm simply saying I don't know who may have done this. If I had a theory I'd tell you, but I don't. I've told you my story and I have no more to say."

"That's fine. Thank you for talking with me. Am I welcome to ask you questions in the future, if I need to do that?"

"Sure."

Rick left the room feeling a little off balance. He didn't think Maggie suspected him of any involvement in Otterby's death.

⌘

Devon Rockingham had a study hall hour beginning at two o'clock. Lou and Lorraine had talked about the procedure for interviewing him. They concluded that it would be more comfortable for

Devon if Lorraine talked to him first. Lou and Lorraine talked about the questions she would ask and what Lou hoped to learn from the interview. Lorraine didn't think of herself as an investigator, but she felt comfortable asking questions. After all, the process wasn't unlike getting to the bottom of conflicts that occur in the high school.

Devon came into Lorraine's office as the bell rang for the next class period. Lorraine tried to make him feel at home, "Good afternoon, Devon. We're really looking forward to your performance in the state solo and ensemble competition."

"Thanks. I hope I'll do okay."

"Oh, you most certainly will. We expect that you will be successful, very successful."

"I hope I won't let you down. Why did you ask me to come here? I don't think I did anything wrong."

"Oh, no, you didn't. I wanted to have a little time with you. There are still some questions about the death of Mr. Otterby. A couple of people who are private investigators are in school interviewing people who may have some information that might reveal what happened two nights ago."

"Why would you want to talk to me about that?" Devon asked nervously, as he quickly postured himself to not let on that he had seen the whole thing.

"Well, as these detectives are piecing the story together, they've learned that you had a music lesson with Miss Whitmore the evening of the eleventh, and that you finished around ten, or shortly thereafter. The music room is fairly close to the swimming pool area. The detectives are curious to know if you saw or heard anything?"

There was a pause. Devon dropped his head, took a deep breath before answering, "I didn't see or hear anything."

"You went to your locker and then went home?"

"Yeah."

"The normal route for you to take between your lesson room and your locker would be past the balcony door to the pool. You didn't stop and look into the pool?"

"I did stop and look in, but I didn't see anything."

"Fine, that's all the investigators are wanting to know. Since you didn't see or hear anything, and knowing that you looked into the pool area will be helpful to them."

"I'm glad I could help," Devon replied, feeling guilty that he was lying to his principal. He looked down because he was ashamed of himself.

"Let's see. What time would that have been, when you looked into the pool from the balcony door?"

"About ten-fifteen."

"Are you sure?"

"Yes. Miss Whitmore left at about a quarter to ten. I decided to stay for a half hour to practice my music. I put my bassoon away at ten after ten. I remember thinking that I was stopping a little early, but I was tired and I wanted to get home. I put my bassoon away and then walked toward my locker. I looked into the pool at about ten-fifteen."

"And you saw absolutely nothing?"

"Nothing."

"Okay, thank you for talking with me Devon."

"Sure. Could I ask you a question?"

"Of course."

"Where's Miss Simpson? She came to school this morning, but when I got to the resource room, a substitute was there."

Lorraine was taken aback by Devon's observation. She took a few seconds to gather her thoughts. "Miss Simpson needed to be away from school for a couple of days, Devon."

"So you called a substitute after she had already come to school?"

"That's right. She'll be back Tuesday, Devon."

Devon rose to go to his study hall. He was confused. Did he believe the substitute, who said she got the call before dawn, or did he believe Mrs. Norton who said the call was made after school started. He had no reason to doubt either woman. This was not making sense to him. He was sure Miss Simpson was in trouble, and it undoubtedly had to do with what he had seen the night of May 11.

⌇

Lorraine asked Mr. and Mrs. Buckley to come in around three o'clock to talk with Maggie. They were on time.

"Thanks for coming in. My colleague, Lou Searing, and I are looking into the death of Mr. Otterby," Maggie began.

"Not a tear is going to fall from my eyes, Mrs. McMillan. In fact, I've never been happier about a news event since that astronaut walked on the moon." Ed Buckley's tall, skinny frame swayed from side to side as he spoke. His wife, Darlene, sat very quietly. Maggie knew immediately that she was shy and she didn't expect more than a word or two from her. Ed was the talker, the dominant of the two.

"You didn't admire Mr. Otterby I take it?"

"There was nothing about the guy to admire!"

Darlene looked at him, and in a quiet and judgmental way said softly, "Shouldn't be sayin' that to the woman."

"No sense tryin' to paint him out to be somethin' he's not. He was useless, absolutely useless to us parents."

Maggie didn't want to officiate a couple's dispute, so she tried to steer the conversation into her control. "I've got a few questions for you and I'd appreciate some honest answers."

"Ask what you want."

"I've learned that the two of you and another parent were overheard saying that you were planning to send Mr. Otterby a bomb?"

"That's right. You know, like them... what are they called these days, ah, ah, terrorists. Yeah, that's it. We were going to send him a bomb so that he' be blown away."

Darlene was quick to add, "But we didn't kill that man, ma'am. We didn't do that. No ma'am."

"I understand. So, you and some other parents were planning to kill him, is that it?"

"That's it. He wasn't doin' anything to help our kids with disabilities. Nothing at all. And, when we got the state and federal government behind us, he just ignored all that."

"For example?"

"Each kid's got an IEP, like a contract, telling us what the school will do. Well, he wouldn't do it!"

"Wouldn't do what?"

"Says Sam will get psychological services, social work services and a special class. He's got none of that. It's illegal for Otterby not to provide that, no question about it. It's a no brainer where the law is concerned."

"You complained?"

"Yeah, to Otterby, Superintendent Donald, the ISD, the state, the federal government. They all told him to do it. He just laughed."

"Not reason enough to kill a guy, is it?"

"Over and over, no services; he takes the whole process in his own hands, hurts kids and laughs at the system. He lived in his own world. After awhile, if the system doesn't take care of the problem, the people gotta take care of the problem, and that is what we wanted to do, but the bomb was just talk."

"So, you drowned him in a swimming pool?" Maggie suggested, getting right to the point. Darlene appeared very nervous, while Ed took the opportunity to tell it like it is.

"He got what was coming to him!"

Darlene quietly spoke once again, "We didn't kill that man, ma'am. No, ma'am. We didn't do that."

"Do you know who did?" Silence. Heads bowed. More silence.

Maggie tried again, "If you didn't do it, do you know who did it?"

"Ed's right. We're glad it's done, but we didn't do it."

"I accept that, but my question was: do you know who did it?"

Silence. Maggie knew that she had gotten all she was going to get. She would contact the third parent who was rumored to have been involved in the bomb planting conversation. She thanked the couple for coming in.

While Maggie was trying to get information from Mr. and Mrs.

Buckley, Lou was talking with the scuba diving instructor. "Mr. Gates, I understand you were teaching a scuba diving class two evenings ago in the pool?"

"No. The athletic director, Mr. Bolt, told me to cancel the class."

"Cancel the class?"

"Yeah, I've got six students in the class. I called them and canceled until next week."

"Why did Bolt cancel the class?"

"He said that Otterby had plans to use the pool and he was sorry, but he had no choice."

"So, you canceled class?"

"Right. I told them to come next week."

"Did you associate this with Otterby's death when you heard he had died in the pool?"

"No, I didn't think of it till you just mentioned it. I thought he died near midnight and my class was much earlier in the evening. I didn't draw any relationship."

Lou didn't question Mr. Gates further. He felt he was getting honest answers. He thanked him for coming and went on to see Tom Hines, who was coming to work earlier than usual for the meeting.

Lou had a few extra minutes before meeting with Tom. He went to find Lorraine to ask her to accompany him to Heidi's classroom for a look around.

Inside the classroom, Lou immediately went to Heidi's desk. He found one of those sharp pointed pins that you snap receipts or messages onto. It could be a lethal weapon, but could also be found in many offices as a way to save phone messages. He looked at the messages. They were all routine, until he came to one from Harriet Haskins. "Call Haskins ASAP. We need to work on a plan. Call or send e-mail to Rtbqty435." Lou recognized the e-mail address.

Everything else seemed normal. The makeshift classroom off the auditorium was typical. Examples of the students' work were on the bulletin board, books were shelved throughout the classroom, and three computers were available for student use. From Lou's experience as an educator, he could tell that Heidi had created a good environment for learning. He felt certain that Heidi Simpson was an effective teacher. Lorraine returned to her office, while Lou went to the conference room to meet with Tom Hines.

"Thanks for coming in a little early, Mr. Hines. My partner, Mrs. McMillan, will be joining us in a minute or two."

Tom nodded as a way of acknowledging Lou's comments. Tom had a book about writing a diary with him, which he placed on the table in front of him. Maggie entered the room and Tom respectively stood up. Lou introduced them. The two shook hands and exchanged greetings.

"We're looking into the death of Warren Otterby, and we'd appreciate it if you would answer some questions," Lou said. "We know that you've already gone over all of this with Detective Mallard and we apologize for having to ask you to repeat anything, but it would help us to hear your story firsthand."

Tom nodded and said nothing.

"So, if you could tell us what happened that night, we'd appreciate it." Once again, Tom nodded.

"To start, tell us about this man Otterby." Lou wanted to start slowly, so that Hines would open up a little. "We have a pretty good sense of what was found in the pool. I'm curious about this man."

"You mean, aside from being our principal?"

"Yeah, hobbies, out of school activities, things like that."

"Well, I know of two activities. He participates in those Civil War reenactment pageants, or whatever you call them. And, he gambled. He went to Vegas, played cards a lot for money, and I hear he won big money. Rumor had it that he went to Gamblers Anonymous. Most would tell you he couldn't control the betting."

"He gambled in school with staff?"

"Not that I know of. I think he separated his habit from his job. A year ago, a rumor was going around that he would use some of his winnings to pay off student athletes, but most thought it was a rumor spread by folks who wanted to frame Otterby or to get him fired. Nothing became of it."

"Any questions, Maggie?" Lou nodded for her to take over.

"Speaking of hobbies, what do you do in your spare time, Tom?"

"Most of my time is spent with my family, I guess. I like to write when I get a moment or two to myself."

"Oh, really? Lou is a writer."

"I know. I've read his latest book. I'm not a novelist. I just like to do short stories, events in my life. You know, things like that."

"Writing is a good hobby. Well, back to our questions. Have you ever seen anyone visit Otterby here in the evening, someone who was not a school employee? Possibly someone who may have been a gambling friend, for example?"

"Yeah, once a week or so, I'd see this woman coming and going. On occasion I'd see her talking with Mr. Otterby. You see, the school is open every evening. Citizens use the library and classes are always going on, but this woman seemed to seek out Otterby on more than one occasion." Tom went on, "A special education teacher was in the school that night. I received the okay for her to work late so I wouldn't activate the security system."

"Do you think she is involved?" Maggie asked.

"She hated Mr. Otterby. She really did."

"But, I asked, do you think she's involved?"

"I didn't see her around the pool, if that's what you mean," Tom said, not wanting to implicate the woman he adored from a distance.

"One more question, Tom. Do you know the name of that lady who had been in the school talking to Otterby?"

"No. I've just seen her around from time to time," Tom said, hoping like Pinocchio that his nose was not giving him away.

Maggie and Lou asked Tom to briefly revisit the night of the murder and thanked him for talking with them. They stopped in to see if Lorraine could give them a few minutes. Lou and Maggie briefed her on what they had learned and then thanked her once again for her cooperation and help. They decided to discuss the case over dinner. As they were leaving, Devon was calling Heidi Simpson.

⌁

The phone rang twice in Heidi's apartment. "Hello."

"Miss Simpson?"

"Yes. Who is this?"

"Devon."

"Of course, Devon. What's on your mind?"

"I need to talk with you."

"I'll be back in school next Tuesday, Devon. Can it wait until then?"

"I guess it could, but I'd really like to talk to you before then."

"Are you having trouble with something at school?"

"Yeah. I have something to ask you."

"Well, I'm pretty tied up. Can it wait until next Tuesday, Devon?"

"You don't want me to tell you what I know, Miss Simpson?"

"Well, I'm interested in what you know, yes, Devon. I'm always interested in my students and in helping them."

"Was Mr. Otterby's death a suicide, Miss Simpson?"

"I believe it was, Devon. The police found a note on his desk. He couldn't take the stress. It was sad, but yes, it was a suicide."

"You think he killed himself?"

"Yes. I respect the police, and that's what they concluded."

"That isn't what I think happened, and I didn't think you'd think he killed himself either," Devon said.

"Well, I don't know why you would think anything different than what the police have concluded. I think you're troubling yourself with this, Devon. Maybe you're imagining things. That happens sometimes with the trauma of stress. Maybe you could use some counseling there at school. They have a crisis team, and you can get some help if you'd like it."

"I don't want any counseling. I was going to talk to you today after our fourth hour class, but you weren't there."

"We'll talk on Tuesday, Devon. I think you're having trouble with the principal's death and you should get some help. Thanks for calling. Oh, good luck with your solo in East Lansing. Isn't your music competition at Michigan State scheduled for a week from Monday?"

"Yeah."

Devon suddenly felt more alone and determined that he should keep what he knew to himself. Nobody would be better off if he revealed what he knew.

Heidi's curiosity was peaked. Why would Devon think Mr. Otterby didn't kill himself? "Devon, maybe you should tell me what you wanted to tell me?"

"You're right. I'm having trouble, and I need some counseling. I'll talk to a counselor on Monday."

"That sounds like a good idea to me. I'm sure you're bothered by the tragedy and you'll feel better next week. Thanks for calling."

"Sure. Bye."

"Good-bye, Devon."

Heidi put the phone on the cradle and stood by her kitchen window, deep in thought. Maybe she should have pushed Devon to tell her what was on his mind. She knew Devon to be a very mature young man. He was the kind of young man who had a good head on his shoulders. He always seemed kind, honest, ethical, moral, and a fine school citizen.

Whatever he intended to tell her, it surely didn't have anything to do with her involvement with Otterby's death two nights ago. She poured herself another cup of coffee and wondered if she should tell Rick about Devon's call.

꒜

Maggie and Lou made plans to eat at Tosi's in Stevensville. They were early for dinner and decided to begin their discussion in the bar. Lou ordered a diet Pepsi and Maggie had a Bloody Mary.

"Interesting day wouldn't you say, Lou?"

"Yeah. We got some good information I think."

"Not only did we get good information, but the word is definitely out that this case is still in open status. The police may not think so, but our poking around will inspire talk that somebody thinks there is more to this story."

"Yes, and that's good. As the word spreads, if anyone has any information, they may contact us."

"Well, what have we got?" Maggie asked, ready to get down to business.

"I think we've got a murder. I've thought that all along, and while I still don't have any proof that will stand up in court, my gut says the guy was killed," Lou felt certain.

"That makes two of us."

"We're going to have a tough time with this one, Maggie. Whoever did this, did their homework and he, she, or they have to be feeling pretty good right now. So far we have no witnesses, no weapon, and nothing in the autopsy report to help us. There are a lot of motives, but they don't seem to point to one person or group. It's going to be hard to pin this on anyone without evidence, witnesses, or a clear motive. It looks like pointing to anyone, right now, can only be based on circumstantial evidence."

"It's just the first day, Lou. We've got many more people to interview."

"I know. What did you learn from Bolt?"

"Body language told me he was nervous and not real sure of his answers. He could be hiding something. He was uncomfortable with my questions and he eventually didn't want to continue. I supported him by saying I was sure that he didn't do it because Otterby was so supportive of his program, but he didn't seem reassured. He claims he didn't send Otterby that memo."

"His name was on it!"

"Yes, but he didn't sign it, Lou. His name was typed, if you recall." Lou nodded and Maggie continued, "He also said that Otterby sent him a note late in the afternoon telling him to cancel the scuba diving class that evening because he had another use for the pool."

"That matches the story I got from George Gates, the scuba diving instructor."

"Well, this needs more attention tomorrow. Start to make a list of people and things to check out, will you?" Lou verbalized the tasks in his head, demonstrating his penchant for organization and order.

"Sure."

"By the way, what did you learn from Otterby's secretary?"

"Otterby often typed memos on that typewriter with the damaged "o" key. His handwriting was very bad and he wasn't into computers. He was an English teacher and a very strong proponent of good grammar, spelling, and punctuation."

"Okay, and finally, the parents, Mr. and Mrs. who?"

"Buckley. They blew a lot of smoke, Lou. Tomorrow we should talk with the third parent. They were upset and had wishful thoughts about planning Otterby's death. My hunch about the Parent Advisory Committee involvement is dead now. They were only dreaming about his demise. They didn't have anything to do with it. At least, that's my assessment at the moment. What did you learn? You talked with the music teacher and you were going to look around in Heidi's room?"

"Yeah, Miss Whitmore first. She was a different soul. Not very cooperative. She didn't welcome me and she made no bones about letting me know that the last thing in the world she wanted to be doing was talking to me. She may have been defensive feeling a bit guilty for leaving a student alone in a building the night Otterby died. She says she did not hear or see anything, and I believe her."

"Then you talked to Devon Rockingham?"

"No, I asked Lorraine to talk with him. I thought it best that he talk with someone who knew him, someone he trusted. I told Lorraine what I wanted to learn and she talked to Devon."

"And?"

"And he says he didn't see or hear anything either. However, he did tell Lorraine that he did look into the pool area from the balcony door window. He said that he didn't see any activity in the pool area."

"Okay, what did you find when you looked around in Heidi's classroom?"

"The only thing of interest was a phone message. She got a call from Harriet Haskins of that Mothers for Justice organization. The message said, 'We need to work on a plan.' I noticed that the e-mail address matched the one I got on my home computer. So, we know she has some knowledge of, and some communication, with the Mothers for Justice organization."

"Better add Haskins to our list. This mom's group could very well be playing some role in this. Sounds sinister, if you ask me."

Lou's beeper went off. He took it from his belt and looked at the message. A local number appeared, but it didn't mean anything to him. "Guess I'll make this call." Lou took his cell phone and dialed the number.

"*Herald Palladium*. To whom may I direct your call?"

"Not sure. My pager was called from this number. My name is Lou Searing."

"Oh, yes, Mr. Searing. Please hold for Jane Wills."

Lou covered the mouthpiece and said to Maggie, "*Herald Palladium*, a Jane Wills."

"Mr. Searing?"

"Yes."

"My name is Jane Wills. I'm a reporter with the *Herald Palladium*. You don't know me, but I'm familiar with your work. Can you give me a minute or two?"

"Sure. My partner and I are at Tosi's."

"Could I join you?"

"I guess so, but satisfy my curiosity and tell me why you called."

"Well, I don't buy the police suicide theory in the death of Warren Otterby. I have a feeling in my gut, and others do as well, that Otterby died because someone wanted him dead. I've heard that you are looking into the case with Mrs. McMillan. I wanted to talk with you about it. Maybe there is something I can do to help?"

"We could talk. When can you get here?"

"It'll take me about ten minutes."

"I don't know you, but am going to trust you. We don't want any kind of sensational headlines in the morning's paper. We've got no leads and we're far from making any conclusions. For all we know, it could have been a suicide, but we can talk as long as we have your promise to be professional in your reporting."

"That's my style, Mr. Searing. You can trust me."

"See you in ten minutes."

Lou turned to Maggie. "Hope that wasn't a mistake."

"So do I."

"Well, another mind may be helpful, and she knows the people and the community. Maybe it's a good sign that she called. Let's try to be positive."

While they waited for Jane Wills to join them, they made plans for the following day's activities. "We need to talk to the special education coordinator at the high school. I think his name was something or other Jennings. I made an association to Peter Jennings of *ABC News* when I heard the name, but I forgot the first name."

Maggie knew it. "Harlan. Harlan Jennings."

"Okay, we need to talk with him, and while I'm on special education, we should talk with the Shoreline Director of Special Education, Mr. Dunn."

"I agree," said Maggie. "We also need to talk with the teacher representative at the school. Her name, according to my notes, is Rebecca Hix. This list is getting quite long, Lou. But, I agree. They are all people we need to talk with. This story's got to come together in some way that makes sense."

A new person was about to come into their lives, as Jane Wills walked into the bar. She was a very attractive woman with light brown hair, cut short. She was dressed in a stylish suit and wore coordinating high heels. Lou thought she looked like she could have been a cover girl for *Business Week* magazine. "Mr. Searing and Mrs. McMillan, I presume." Jane Wills held out her hand in greeting.

"Yes. Miss Wills?"

"Yes. I'm pleased to meet you. I've heard of your success on past cases and I've admired your work. I enjoyed your last book, Mr. Searing. Did it happen like you wrote it?"

"Pretty much. As a writer, I need to spice it up a little for reader appeal, but what you read is a fair account of the death and the complicated series of events that occurred to solve the case."

"I also admire you, Mrs. McMillan. You are so independent,

bright, and a superb model for people with disabilities. I'm thrilled to meet you."

"Well, thanks. Can we buy you a drink?" Maggie asked.

"No thanks. I'm on my way home. I'll only be a minute or two. I wanted to meet you and to volunteer my services if you should need them as you solve this one."

"Tell us a bit about yourself," Lou welcomed. "What work do you do at the *Herald Palladium*?"

"Well, I've graduated from obits to social events, and now I'm covering some local and regional stories. This is the first mysterious death for me, Mr. Searing."

"You can call me Lou and I don't think Mrs. McMillan will mind if you call her Maggie." Maggie nodded approvingly.

"Okay, thanks. As I was saying, and as I told Lou, I don't buy the suicide theory of Duck Mallard and the police. When I heard that you two were working on the case, I knew you'd get to the bottom of it and I wanted to be there when you did. To show my appreciation I want to make myself available to you, and should I come across any information that you might find helpful, I'll let you know."

"Thanks for your compliments and your belief in us," Maggie responded. "I think we'll solve it. It may take awhile though. So far, we have no evidence, weapon, suspect, or single motive, but we're working on it."

Lou interrupted, "Since you don't buy the suicide theory, do you have a theory about how he died? Do you think there's a special education connection?"

"I've heard that. I doubt it. I really do. People are upset, but I don't see them killing a guy over their issues. My belief is that someone outside of education wanted him dead. Got nothing to back that up, but reporters and detectives have to listen to their gut. I find that when I do, my gut is often right on."

"Sounds like you've been helpful already, Jane. We thank you," said Lou.

"All theory, though. A prosecutor can't convict on theory. I don't need to tell you that. If my thoughts are helpful, fine. Here's my card, please call me at work or home or use e-mail if you think I can help."

"We'll probably do that, Jane. Thanks."

"I would be remiss if I didn't say that I'd like to come out with the story of who killed Warren Otterby before the television or radio guys or before competing newspapers do. It would be a feather in my cap to get the scoop on this one. My editor is not big on embarrassing the police force. We have to live with them all year long and the editor will be reticent to come out with a story that embarrasses them, but a story is a story, and if you could bring me along with this, I'd really appreciate it."

"You're the only media person to come along. So, you've no competition at this point," Lou said. "The important thing for us is facts and not sensationalism in your reporting. We can't control what you say, but once you use us for your gain, and it jeopardizes our work or embarrasses us, you're history."

"Well, I'd expect to be, and I'd deserve it. No, that won't happen. The only thing that will get into the *Herald Palladium* will be facts and an honest story of what happened. It will only appear when it's worthy of being told to the public."

"Glad to hear it. Well, Jane, you're welcome to join us for dinner if you'd like," Maggie said.

"Thanks, but I'm on my way. Thanks so much for agreeing to meet with me. You two are great." As Jane handed business cards to Lou and Maggie she said, "My bet is with you to solve this thing and to bring justice to this mess. I look forward to hearing from you."

During dinner, Lou and Maggie planned their work for the weekend. Maggie went over her list. "Here are the people we said we wanted to talk with: Mrs. Neff, Harriet Haskins, Harlan Jennings, and Rebecca Hix. We also want to retrace the walk Devon took from the music room to his locker." Maggie organized her thoughts as she read the list.

"We may want to wait until Monday for most of this work. I'll call Mrs. Neff and Harriet Haskins," Lou suggested.

"Good," said Maggie, who added her contribution, "I'll call

Lorraine, tell her our plan, and ask her to assist us in setting up interviews with Jennings and Hix."

With their work complete, the detectives enjoyed dinner before heading for their respective homes. The day was well-spent. And, the case was developing. A lot of information and the scattered pieces of the puzzle were all beginning to line up. It would take more time and perhaps a few lucky breaks to put it all together.

CHAPTER 4

Saturday, May 14

In Grand Haven, Lou and Carol sat down to breakfast at the Dee Lite Restaurant. They ordered a healthy bowl of bran flakes with fruit. Lou asked for some decaf coffee and Carol requested tea. The specialty at the Dee Lite is the Full-Farmer. Most of the time Lou and Maggie ordered the Half-Farmer and even that was more than they needed to get some energy to start the day. Lou and Carol usually ended breakfast with a walk along the channel. It was good exercise and gave them a chance to see the yachts heading out into Lake Michigan for fishing or sightseeing.

As they were eating, Katrina Goodheart, the Grand Haven Director of Special Education, stopped at their table.

"Good morning to the Searings! I was just on my way to the bookstore to get a copy of your book, Lou. What a coincidence seeing you."

"Good morning, Katrina. Sit down and join us. Thanks for buying the book. You are helping me pay for this meal," Lou said with a smile.

"Working on a case at the moment?" Katrina asked.

"As a matter of fact, I am. Maggie and I are looking into the death of the principal down in Shoreline."

"Oh, yes, I've been following that in the paper. Are you close to solving it?"

"Not close, but we'll get there."

"When are you going to solve the real mystery in special education, Lou?"

"The real mystery? What do you mean?"

"Well, the mystery, as I see it, is why do we have so many regulations and so much paperwork? We've hardly got any time to serve the kids. My fear is that when the kids graduate we'll have perfect files filled with evaluations, plans, and discipline reports, but we won't be making any difference in the lives of kids because of all the time spent in meetings and writing paperwork!" Carol nodded and smiled, signaling her agreement.

"You're right," Lou admitted. "We've gone too far. It's a mystery. Why does compliance seem more important than outcomes? I've been working on that mystery for a long while now. I'll get back to it when I finish with the Otterby case."

"I wish you would, Lou. We've got to get to common sense or we'll drown in paper and meetings. I'm not bitter, but I'm frustrated, I guess. I can recall the old days when we spent all of our time tutoring and teaching and working with children. Now it seems there are meetings, forms, and people from Lansing and D.C. who have us focused on being legal instead of working to teach the children."

"Good point. I'm in that generation, too, Katrina."

"Well, I'll leave you two to enjoy your breakfast. Nice to see you. Stop over to my office when you find some free time, Lou. As you know, we've got a great reputation for working with our general education colleagues. We're proud of what we are doing. I want to share an evaluation of our system."

"Sure. I'll call for an appointment in the next few days."

"You'll autograph your book at that time?"

"Be glad to."

"Nice to see you, Katrina. Drop out to the house when you want a nice evening walk on the beach," Carol offered.

"I'd love that. Thanks. You'll see me soon."

Lou and Carol finished their breakfast and enjoyed their walk along the channel. They knew that it was only a matter of days before the summer crowd would be sharing their city. When the Coast Guard Festival came around early in August, the city would be packed with vacationers having a good time.

Lou and Carol drove home to be greeted by Samm and their cats, Luba and Millie. Carol opened the beachfront door to hear the gentle sound of waves lapping upon the shore, and the rustle of leaves as the breeze gently caressed them. It was a beautiful morning. Samm anticipated her walk along the beach. Lou and Carol took turns reading sections of the newspaper.

"Want to flip a coin for taking Samm for a walk?" Carol hoped Lou might offer to relieve her of that duty.

"Oh, I'll go. It'll give me some think time," Lou volunteered.

"Okay, I'll gather up the recycle materials. Today is recycle day."

⌒⌒

Meanwhile, in Battle Creek, Maggie was sleeping in. Tom was off with his golfing buddies at Pebble Beach in California. She felt she deserved the extra rest.

When Lou and Samm got back from throwing and retrieving tosses of driftwood, Lou retreated to his studio. He planned to write and make a phone call or two to complete his part of the bargain. He decided to call Harriet Haskins in New York. He dialed and after two rings he heard a voice respond, "Hello."

"Good morning. This is Lou Searing from Grand Haven, Michigan. May I please speak with Mrs. Haskins?"

"Speaking."

"Mrs. Haskins, I'm calling because I'm looking into the death of Warren Otterby in Shoreline, Michigan."

"Never heard of him, Mr. Searing."

"I understand. Let me refresh your memory. Mr. Otterby was the principal of Shoreline High School, and one of his special education teachers was Heidi Simpson."

"Sorry, but I've never heard of either of these people. Should I have?"

"Well, you sent Mr. Otterby a letter last month explaining that you expected immediate results in terms of helping children with disabilities."

"Mr. Searing, we're a nationwide organization. I send at least fifty letters like that each month. The signature is computer-generated and only my secretary would know who gets these letters."

"Oh, really?"

"We get a constant stream of complaints from all over, and we have a series of letters that we send to try and scare people into action. Usually it works and sometimes it doesn't."

"Miss Simpson, the special education teacher, do you know her?"

"Sorry. We deal with parents almost exclusively. If this Miss Simpson is a problem to parents, we'll write to her and apply some tactics to have her come into an understanding of what the law requires."

"You wouldn't have a problem with Heidi. She seems to be very supportive of parents and children and to be following the appropriate procedures."

"So nice talking to you. Sorry I can't help. Have a good day."

"Wait. One more question, please."

"Sure."

"Do you remember sending me an e-mail message concerning my investigation into the death of Mr. Otterby?"

"Once again, we communicate with hundreds of people everyday via phone, letter, fax, and e-mail. I don't recall sending you an e-mail, Mr. Searing."

"That's strange."

"What's strange?"

"Well, a principal dies, and is probably murdered, in Shoreline, Michigan. On his desk is a letter from you telling him to shape up or there would be intervention from your organization. He died. On the teacher's desk is a phone message from you asking her to call. I come home from the first day of looking into his death and I have on my computer an e-mail from you telling me to remove myself from this case and to put my energy toward catching people who are not so evil. Now, you flatly deny knowing anything about this letter, this death, this teacher, and this e-mail to me."

"I can understand your surprise, but to repeat, I don't know you, this Miss Simpson, or any principal who died recently."

"Is your screen name Rtbqty435?"

"Yes."

"Any symbolism there? Not that's it any of my business. I'm just curious."

"No secret. The six letters are the initials of my three children and the 435 is my weight goal for this year." Lou quickly imagined with whom he was dealing, a woman who heads Mothers for Justice weighing more than 435 pounds.

"So, you seem to be in the dark about anything I've said in relation to the death of this principal in Michigan. Is that correct?"

"Absolutely. Haven't a clue."

"Thanks for talking with me."

"Good luck. Hope you solve whatever it is you're investigating."

Lou was quite surprised that this woman didn't know anything about this case. If she did, she was a good actress because she sounded convincing.

Within a few seconds of hanging up the phone, Harriet Haskins was dialing the phone number of Heidi Simpson.

"Heidi. This is Harriet Haskins."

"Yeah. What's up?"

"I just got a call from Lou Searing in Michigan."

"Former State Director of Special Education turned investigator," Heidi explained.

"Yeah, guess so. Nosy guy," Haskins said.

"He's looking into the death of Otterby."

"It sounded to me like he was placing special ed folks at the scene of the crime."

"Sure, he would. Lots of people do. Searing and his partner can look and question everyone and they'll always come up empty-handed. Kinda neat to watch them struggle only to go nowhere."

"Well, just wanted you to know that he called me. I didn't give him any information. I claimed to know nothing. We'll see what happens."

"My motto is stick to my story and everything will turn out fine."

"Okay, I'll trust you and hope you're right."

Lou called Mrs. Neff and asked her about the parent comments and the bomb threat against Otterby. "Is this true?"

"Yes, it's true, but there's nothing to it. Ed Buckley is always talking like that. He feels better when he can sound tough and get people up to taking, or at least considering to take, decisive action. But, nothing happened. Ed and most of us lean on each other. We only dream of easily getting rid of our problems. Parents didn't kill him. We've got kids to raise and we'd like to think we're a bit more intelligent than thinking we could get away with such drastic action."

"I didn't think there was any truth to the rumor, and Maggie McMillan agrees. I needed to hear it from you to give us a crutch back to reality. Thanks for talking with me, Nancy."

"Are you liking your retirement?"

"I live in Dockers and sweatshirts. I write, investigate, and spend time with Carol. 'Tis a pretty good life."

"Good. You deserve it. Continue to enjoy your time, and I hope you solve this death here in Shoreline."

"Thanks. We will."

Lou spent the rest of the weekend absorbed with his hobby. There was more to the life of Lou Searing than writing and investigating. He and Carol amassed quite a private collection of antique ear horns or trumpets that they enjoyed demonstrating. Lou got interested as a result of his own hearing loss. He had worn hearing aids for decades now. Carol used to teach children who were deaf and hard of hearing in Kansas, Ohio, Texas, and Michigan. Their combined interest in hearing aids, along with a love of antiques, made for a natural hobby. On Saturday afternoon they drove to Kalamazoo to visit with the curator of the Western Michigan University Museum who was planning a display.

CHAPTER 5

Sunday, May 15

Lou and Carol sat in their usual pew for eight o'clock mass at St. Patrick's Catholic Church in Grand Haven. Carol, a Catholic all of her life, received a parochial education, schooling in the convent and was a sister in the Ursuline Order of Paola, Kansas, for fourteen years. Lou met Carol following her decision to seek a release from her vows, and became a convert. The Catholic faith meant a lot to both of them.

Maggie on the other hand, was not one for weekly church attendance. She didn't find the church experience all that meaningful and chose to serve people through her work as her gift to her Creator. On this particular Sunday morning, Maggie was resting in the arms of Morpheus and enjoying some extra winks. Later in the morning she read the *Chicago Tribune* and the *Battle Creek Enquirer*, ate pancakes with strawberries and cream, and spent most of the day relaxing and doing practically nothing. If there was one religious practice Maggie took seriously, it was to rest on Sunday. She liked the concept and vowed to practice, to perfection, that age-old tradition of resting on the seventh day.

There was one other person who was about to find himself significantly impacted by a sermon that Sunday morning. Devon

Rockingham was seated between his mother and father in the First Methodist Church in Shoreline. The sermon was titled, "And The Truth Shall Make You Free," presented by the Reverend Dr. Philip Wheeler. Reverend Wheeler was a tall, handsome and distinguished-looking man.

A collection had been taken, the money was brought to the front of the church and the congregation stood singing the "Doxology." The congregation prepared to sit, ready to listen to a sermon by one of Shoreline's most respected Protestant ministers. Light was shining through the stained glass window high above the altar. Devon looked up to see a likeness of Jesus meeting with his disciples. Thinking suddenly of the murder, he wondered what Jesus would tell him to do with his dilemma.

"Let us pray," Dr. Wheeler began. "Oh, God, may the words of my mouth and the meditations of my heart be acceptable in thy sight, Oh, Lord, my strength and my redeemer. Amen."

The strong Methodist theology, accompanied by a few stories and some humor, kept the congregation awake.

Dr. Wheeler brought Devon to attention with a startling narration. "Let me tell you one more story where the truth made someone free. I take you to a high school in Columbus, Ohio. A young man, a fine athlete and student, came upon a drug sale. It involved his friend and the star of the school's basketball team. The young man was torn. He couldn't turn his friend in and yet what he saw was wrong. The young man struggled for a few days, knowing in his heart that he should tell someone. He feared peer ridicule. He thought of confronting his friend privately, to tell him what he witnessed. He wanted to go to his school counselor and tell him what he saw. He wanted to go to his parents and tell them what he saw. He wanted to go to the police and tell them what he saw. Instead, he went directly to Jesus Christ. He went to his church, he went up to the altar, knelt down and said to Jesus, 'I have a difficult situation and I need your help. Please guide me,' he prayed in silence. He listened. He rose to his feet and started to leave the church. At the back of his church he found a Bible on a table in the narthex. He picked it up and randomly paged through the New Testament. His eyes fell on John 8:32 and he read, 'and the truth shall make you free.'

"This young man believed at that moment that the Lord Jesus Christ had answered his prayers. He went first to his friend and told him the truth, that he had seen the drug sale. He told his friend that he was going to tell the truth, and that he was going to share what he had seen with the boy's parents and let them handle the situation. Because he had seen a law being broken, he said he would also inform the police. He told his friend that he cared for him, even loved him, and because of his love and because of his need to allow the truth to set him free, he would share the truth and he did." The minister paused a moment.

"And, my sisters and brothers in faith, you know what happened? Before the young man could talk with the parents of his friend, the friend had told his own parents and the father contacted the police to say what had happened. The drug pusher was apprehended and arrested. The two boys went into counseling for their problem, and are today, the leaders of their school's DARE program. Because the young man had the courage to follow Jesus Christ, had the strength to confront the truth, and had the desire to do what is right, he was free, free of guilt, free of worry, and free of censure from others." Dr. Wheeler paused.

"My friends in Christ. Do you find yourself burdened today? Do you have something in your life that cries out to you to satisfy in your heart? I tell you along with Jesus Christ that the truth will make you free. Let us pray. Almighty God, please guide anyone here today to allow the truth to free them so that peace, the peace you promised to all who follow you, can come over us and bring us the peace that passeth all understanding. We ask this in the name of our Lord and Savior, Jesus Christ, Amen."

Devon looked up again at the stained glass window, and there was Jesus who seemed to say, "I've answered your prayer."

Chapter 6

Monday, May 16

Lou drove directly to the office of Joe Dunn, the Director of Special Education for the Shoreline Public Schools. Joe was a veteran of special education. He was in his final year before retiring, with almost forty years devoted to serving the educational needs of children with disabilities. Joe welcomed Lou into his office, gave him a cup of coffee and asked how he could help.

"I imagine you've heard that Maggie and I are looking into the death of Warren Otterby."

"Yes, that word has gotten around, Lou."

"Wherever we go and whoever we talk to, special education seems to be a common issue. Nobody is pointing a finger at any one person, or even a group of people, but apparently Warren Otterby did not support attending to the laws, rules, and policies of serving children with disabilities. In not doing this, he's seen as less than supportive. Some think that he may have been killed by someone, or perhaps a group conspiracy involving special education people."

"Yes, a common belief, and to be perfectly honest, one I have as well. Warren was very difficult to deal with. When I say very difficult, I mean VERY difficult. The staff would meet with me regularly and try to plead their case for getting him fired or minimally to see to it that he showed some respect for the rights of the students in his school."

"Let me cut right to the chase," Lou said. "Do you think, or do you know, that there is a special education connection?"

"No, I don't know. I can't imagine that any of my staff would do this to Otterby, or to anyone for that matter. We were pretty upset with the guy, but murder, no way. We understand conflict, we understand resistance to serving people who are perceived to be different. Minorities always have to fight for what they have and we understand this. Unfortunately, Warren Otterby was a man who didn't value people who were different, and when I say different I mean in any way other than himself. So, he didn't value women, people with disabilities, Catholics and Jews, the gay community, Blacks and Hispanics, and the list goes on."

"Can't believe a guy like this could hold a responsible public position," said Lou, shaking his head in disbelief.

"I can explain that. Warren Otterby was a man who sought power. He got his power much like a poker player. His whole career was like a poker game. He used this power in a double or nothing situation a few years ago. He wanted to be principal of any school, and he was always passed over by someone more qualified. This really got to him. He befriended the superintendent of the Shoreline Schools at that time, a Stu Jansing, and the story goes that there was a bet on a golf course that got into some big dollars. Apparently, Jansing owed Otterby several thousand dollars as they approached the last two holes. Otterby knew that the high school principalship was coming open soon. He told the superintendent that he'd call off the bet and wipe the slate clean in exchange for a job recommendation.

"Stu justified hiring Otterby as principal. It was easier than explaining to his wife a multi-thousand dollar hole in their shared bank account. The superintendent remained a man of his word and Warren got the job. Eventually the superintendent regretted this appointment, in addition to his stupidity on the golf course.

"Things have a life of their own, and the School Board didn't want to pay the thousands it would take to pay Otterby off, or to take him to court. We all just plodded along, hoping something would happen. Well, something did happen, and if it was murder, someone or some group took the law into their own hands and disposed of the despicable man."

"H-m-m. Very interesting. Everything has a history, doesn't it?"

"Sure does."

"I'm certain that you know of Heidi's suspension for having a gun in school?"

"Lorraine called and discussed it with me. I supported Lorraine's action."

"Is Heidi capable of killing Otterby?"

"Oh, I suppose anyone is, but I doubt it. Let me explain that gun thing."

"Please do."

"Well, as you saw, Heidi is a beautiful woman. A few years ago she was abducted and raped. Ever since that time she has been authorized to carry a gun. She is terrified of surprises and, even to this day, is uneasy around people she doesn't know walking toward her or talking to her in a public place. She has had quite a bit of training in using the weapon. She's taken courses in effective use of the gun and practices with the police at their range west of town. So, for Heidi to have a gun in school when the school was closed to all students is no surprise. I trust that she was acting responsibly."

"That explains her quickness and behavior when I surprised her in her classroom Friday morning. She really looked like she knew what she was doing."

"Oh, yes. She is very professional. She suffered with that attack, and she won't be intimidated again."

"So, you don't think Lorraine knew of her permit?"

"I'm not sure. Lorraine is a great administrator and she's acting consistent with her good sense of doing what is right. You're going to see the exact opposite of Otterby as Lorraine takes the helm in leadership. The change will be like night and day."

"Joe, do you think the parents' group had anything to do with this?"

"No. I don't. I've been working with them. We've worked with the state and federal special education offices to get our school into compliance with the law. We're guilty, because of Otterby, of hundreds of violations. The State Board was about to withhold our state and federal money. So, no, I don't think the parents had anything to do with it."

"How about Cindie, the speech pathologist?"

"Warren put her next to the boiler room in a small closet-like setting. She was furious, but no, Cindie wouldn't kill him. In her dreams, maybe, but she wouldn't act on her feelings. Neither would the other teachers, Lou. I know it looks like we're prime candidates for taking the rap on this death, but I'll be very shocked if that's what you conclude."

"Well, okay. You don't seem to see a special education connection, do you, Joe?"

"No, and I don't think I'm saying that to protect my turf. As I know people, the issues and the system, this is not a special education matter."

"Thanks. You retiring this year?"

"June thirtieth is my last day."

"Well, I'm here to tell you, it's a great life. Hope to see you on the other side, as they say."

"Got a lot of fish waiting for me, Lou. The golf course calls my name as well."

"On my way out, let me ask you, what do you think happened to Warren Otterby?"

"I go back to that poker story, Lou. My guess is that he got in deep with someone, or something, and just as the superintendent got in over his head, Otterby needed a way out. Maybe he couldn't get out and his only escape, or so he thought, was killing himself. I don't know. But, I don't have any trouble with the suicide theory. It makes sense to me."

"We're not finding any evidence, clues, or suspects, and no clear motives pointing to any one person. We've got some stories that don't fit well, and inconsistent observations from some people. Maybe he did just drop off the diving board into whatever awaited him in the afterlife."

∽

While Lou was talking with Joe Dunn, Maggie was talking to Rebecca Hix, the head of the teacher's union. "There's a lot of talk surrounding the death of your principal," Maggie said, giving Rebecca an opening to remark.

"Whoever did it is going to get a holiday named in their honor and they should give us all a day off to honor that person's birthday!" Rebecca exclaimed. Rebecca Hix was a teacher with five years of experience. She was verbal, young, and committed to teacher rights. Many speculated that without the glasses, with her long dark hair let down, and given a bit more fashion, she'd be anything but a school marm.

"The guy was that despised, huh?" Maggie inquired.

"You betcha. In fact, most of us teachers wish you guys would just pack up your curiosity and move on out of here. Whether he killed himself, as he surely did, or whether somebody killed him, he's gone, thank God and now let's just get on with our lives."

"Well, there is this little thing called truth and justice. I guess that's why we're looking for answers."

"If he killed himself, we thank him for sparing us his cruel ways. If somebody killed him, so be it. Anyway, you didn't want to meet with me to get my joyful opinions about his death."

"I wanted to meet with you to learn whatever I could. I'll take opinions or facts. I'm trying to learn as much as I can about this man and his death."

"Well, why don't you ask and I'll answer."

"It seems that coaches liked this guy and others didn't. Have I got that right?"

"Nobody liked Otterby. There is not a member of the teaching staff, and that includes coaches, who admired, respected or possibly even liked Otterby."

"Oh, really? I thought the coaching staff liked him because he favored their programs."

"That's the side they show to the public. You talk to these coaches privately and they reveal how they despised the man. They were afraid that the Michigan High School Athletic Association would discover his illegal practices and forfeit their games, bar them from competition, give them bad reputations, and interfere with their abilities to be employed elsewhere.

"Most importantly, the coaches did not want to be embarrassed within the conference and the state. The coaches wanted to have honest, play-by-the-rules programs. But, Otterby would do such outlandish things in the name of winning that the coaches were afraid to stand up to him. Anyone who stood up to the guy didn't get any favors. A case in point is special education. Those folks challenged him, reported him, tried to embarrass him and what did it get them? Nothing. In fact, they even got less than nothing, if you can believe that."

"I'd like to ask you about Heidi Simpson."

"Great teacher. The pride of our school. Extra-mile woman. She is an example of what we in this profession hold dear. She is the epitome of teaching. She cares about the students, works in the community, serves on committees. She's got it all."

"Was she involved in the murder of Warren Otterby?"

"Not on your life. I heard she was in the building that night, working on IEP forms. See, that's the kind of teacher she is. How many teachers do you know who are so dedicated that they spend most of the night at their place of employment?"

"Well, to be honest, that's just it. To me it seems like a pretty questionable thing to do. First of all, it isn't safe; secondly, she should be able to complete all the work that needs to be done in a comfortable setting, such as home. The fact that she stayed so late in a school isn't necessarily a sign of commitment. But, that's my opinion, I guess."

"One person's commitment is another's weakness, I suppose. What else do you want to know?"

"Let me get right to the point. Do you think any teacher in this school caused Otterby to die last Wednesday night?"

"Absolutely not. Do you really think any of us teachers would risk a life in prison for him? Give us some credit for common sense, pahlease!"

Maggie could see that she wasn't going to get anything else from Rebecca. The woman wasn't about to share any information contrary to the good side of teachers, even if she knew someone was involved.

The two women said their farewells.

❧

The doorbell rang in Heidi's apartment. "Miss Simpson, I'm Detective Mallard with the Shoreline Police. May I come in?" Mallard recognized her from the police shooting range where he often saw her practicing, but he didn't know her by name nor had he ever visited with her.

Heidi was stunned and she felt a wave of nausea flow through her body. "I guess so. Why are you here?"

"Just have a few questions for you," Mallard said, noticing Heidi's stunned reaction.

"Should I have my lawyer with me?"

"It's up to you."

"Yes, I'll call him. Sit down if you like. I'll be back in a minute."

Heidi called Harold Marshburn, a young and articulate lawyer, one of Shoreline's finest attorneys. Heidi had learned to trust Harold when he assisted her with the rape crisis.

"Do you have any idea why the detective is at your home?" Harold asked.

"I imagine it has to do with the death of our principal. I had nothing to do with it, but I was in the school when he died."

"If you had nothing to do with it, tell him whatever he wants to know. I don't think I need to be there unless you want me there for support."

"Yes, I want you here. I'd feel much better having you know what he asks and what I say."

"I can be there in five minutes."

Duck Mallard knew Harold Marshburn. He respected him even though he hadn't been in Shoreline long. Harold arrived within a few minutes and the three began their discussion.

"Miss Simpson, as you know, Warren Otterby was found dead in the high school pool Wednesday night. We've learned that you were in the school that night. Is that correct?"

"Yes. I was in my classroom working on paperwork for my special education students."

"Did you have a gun with you?"

"Yes. I have permission to carry the gun. I need it for security."

Duck knew of Lorraine's discovery of the weapon and of their discipline. He decided not to press the issue.

"You stayed in the school late the night Otterby was found dead?"

"I left around eleven-fifteen."

"Did anyone know you were spending such late hours in school?"

"Yes. I told Mr. Otterby and Tom Hines."

"Why did you tell Tom Hines?"

"So that he wouldn't engage the security system. Any movement in a hallway could be detected by sensors and set off an alarm and cause all kinds of commotion."

"Yeah. We get false alarms on that system from time to time."

"Tom knows I do this once a year. It's no big deal."

"It was approved by Otterby?"

"Sure."

"You had problems with Otterby, didn't you?"

"Everyone on the staff had problems with Otterby. You can't single me out in that category."

"Yes, but you had strong emotions about him and his lack of support for special education. Isn't that right?"

114

Normally, Harold Marshburn would caution his client about offering information about these types of questions. Harold felt comfortable with the line of questions. He also sensed that Mallard was talking with Heidi as a matter of protocol and that he didn't suspect Heidi of killing Otterby.

"That's right. I didn't care for the man, and that is as soft as I can make it. I despised, hated, and found little worth in a man who treated us, and children, the way he did."

"Well, Miss Simpson, we'll need to keep you on the suspect list."

"I had nothing to do with his death, Mr. Mallard."

"Could be, but you were in the building when Otterby died, and you had a weapon in your possession. There won't be any warrant for your arrest, but it doesn't look good for you at the moment."

Heidi looked at Harold for assistance. Harold, with a straight and emotionless face, nodded toward her.

Mallard left and Harold asked Heidi to tell him her side of the story, from beginning to end. Harold took copious notes as she spoke. Before leaving, he cautioned her not to talk to anyone else without him present. Harold Marshburn was less certain of Heidi's innocence as he walked to his car. A long and difficult court battle potentially lay ahead. If Heidi was implicated in a serious crime, he'd have a difficult time proving her innocence unless some other suspects emerged soon.

৵

Heidi Simpson called Rick Bolt. "Can you talk for a minute, Rick?"

"Sure."

"I've got a question."

"Shoot."

"There's a balcony in the pool area isn't there? It seems that when we have swim meets, students can enter from a door up there. Am I right?"

"Yeah, there's a door up there."

"Is there a window in the door?"

"Yeah, but to respect the privacy of the students in swim classes we painted the small window with some type of opaque paint."

"Is the door locked?"

"Most of the time. On occasion, kids go into the balcony area when there are no swim classes. They hide out there instead of going to class."

"Are you in your office in the pool area right now?"

"Yeah."

"Go out and check to see if that paint is still covering the window in the balcony door and that it's locked."

"Why?"

"Please Rick, this is important."

"Okay, I'll be back in a minute."

Rick was gone for several seconds. He looked up at the door and was surprised to see that the paint was missing from the window. He wanted to be certain, so he went up into the balcony area. Sure enough, the paint was gone and the door was locked. He returned to the phone.

"The paint's been removed. It looks like someone used a straight-edge razor to scrape the paint off the window."

"That means it was possible that someone saw Otterby murdered," Heidi reasoned aloud.

"What's the problem?"

"One of my students called me. He said, 'Mr. Otterby didn't commit suicide last week, did he?' When I assured him that he did and that's what the police reported, he seemed to doubt me."

"You think he saw Otterby die?"

"Devon had a music lesson that night and he could've witnessed Otterby's death on his way to his locker after the lesson. The balcony door is on his way from the music room to his locker."

"Has he said anything to anyone? Have you been confronted about it?"

"The police were at my apartment a few hours ago asking questions. They heard that I was in the school late that night, that I had a gun, and that I didn't come out to make my presence known. I'm sure they're thinking that I did it. My lawyer is quite concerned and he's told me not to talk to anyone without his presence. It doesn't look good for me. I hope you don't come under the same suspicion."

"I think I already am. Detective Mallard is coming over to school to see me in a half-hour."

"Have a lawyer present, Rick."

"I don't have one, and I don't have the money to pay for one. Besides, it's a waste of money."

"A case can be brought against us and some jury could be convinced that we did this, Rick. Think about having a lawyer with you. This is going to be a tough time for us."

"Thanks for the advice, but I'll talk to this detective, tell him our story, and let the chips fall where they may."

"It's your call. Devon is going to talk with me tomorrow about whatever is bothering him. I'll let you know what I learn after I talk with him."

"Okay."

"Before I go, Rick. What happened to that window? Who took the paint off, and why, and when?"

"I don't know. I'll try to find out."

The two hung up after agreeing to touch base as the need arose.

Rick called the secretary to the principal. "Principal's office."

"Hi, Mrs. Rogalski. This is Rick in the athletic office."

"Hi, Rick. What can I do for you?"

"I just noticed that the paint on the balcony window of my pool has been scraped off. What's the story behind that? Is it a prank, something I need to send in a work order on?"

"Last Tuesday, Warren told maintenance to scrape the paint off of that small window so that he could see into the balcony as he made his rounds. Apparently some kids were sneaking into that area. With no window, they could stay hidden for a long time. Warren thought it best to get the paint off for security reasons."

Rick's heart started beating faster than normal.

"We have to have that painted over again for privacy, for the kids in swimming."

"I mentioned that when he told me what he was going to do. He laughed it off. He said something like, 'No such thing as privacy anymore. I want to see in that window and that's that.' I put him through to maintenance and inside of a half hour, that window was clean."

"That happened last Wednesday?"

"Wednesday morning, late morning."

"I'll talk to Lorraine about painting it again. I'll be responsible for the kids who get into my pool area without permission, but I want that window covered. These kids don't need gawkers while they are in the swimming classes."

"I'm sure Lorraine will agree."

"Okay, thanks."

Rick called Heidi right back. "Warren told maintenance to scrape the paint off the window, and they did it late Wednesday morning."

"What was that all about?"

"He decided he wanted to see in the balcony area as he took his walks through the school. He said that kids were getting in and were out of view. So, that window was clear of paint the night Otterby died."

"And, Devon Rockingham probably did see what happened last Wednesday night. If Devon thinks I'm involved, I'm in big trouble."

Rick added, "They found a note to Otterby. They said it was from me, inviting him to the pool around 10:15 p.m."

"Oh, my God! I feel like I'm going to throw up," Heidi trembled anxiously. "Searing and McMillan are investigating and they're good. We're in big trouble, Rick."

"We're bright people. We just need to put our heads together and figure a way out of this mess. They have no evidence, nothing but circumstantial evidence. Even if Devon thinks you're involved, he isn't going to tell on his teacher and potentially cause her to spend a life in prison. Kids don't tell on others. Haven't you been this kid's salvation?"

"Well, he won't graduate without my support in special education, if that is what you mean."

"Yeah, he won't put himself through a public trial and attention when he'll be hurting the very woman who helped him. He's probably also got a crush on you, as beautiful as you are. Again, he won't do that to you. I say you can relax. The kid will be on our side. Right?"

"Well, you do make sense. I did help him quite a lot. I think he does respect me and like me. You're right, all he wants to do is go to college and be a musician. He wouldn't want all the attention, the media, the comments from kids in school. I think you're right. He won't say anything to hurt us."

ॐ

"On my way to my locker I looked in the window of the pool balcony, and there was Miss Simpson holding a gun and pointing it at Mr. Otterby, who was up on the diving board taking one step at a time until he was forced to jump in. His hands and feet were tied. Two guys were beside the swimming pool and they jumped in, but they didn't help him up. They just cut the ropes and got out of the pool. Then the three of them left the pool area and Mr. Otterby drowned." Devon was in third hour World History. He was rehearsing what he would say if he chose to inform the police. "I tried to talk to Miss Simpson, but she didn't seem to want to know what I had seen. She thought I needed counseling. But, I know what I saw, and what I saw was a man being murdered."

"Devon," the history teacher, Laughton Lancour, interrupted his train of thought. "Would you please provide your analysis regarding the beginning of the first world war and how it was different, or the same, as the beginning of the second world war?"

"Sorry. I wasn't paying attention. I've got a lot on my mind. Let me see. Ah, World War I began when one nation bombed another in Europe. World War II began when a man shot at another man in Hawaii."

A couple of students raised their hands. Mr. Lancour called on one who correctly explained the relationship between the two world wars. Devon was embarrassed, because he really knew the answer to the question. He simply blew it.

Mr. Lancour sensed that Devon was not himself. He attributed it to his upcoming solo and ensemble competition at MSU on Monday. It was the only event in this young man's life that could cause him to be acting so oddly. The Devon Mr. Lancour knew would never totally confuse the facts behind the two major wars.

When the class was over, and the students were leaving the classroom, Mr. Lancour stopped Devon and told him he'd like to talk with him after school for a few minutes. "Am I doing something wrong?"

"No, I'm concerned that you may be slipping in my class and I thought we could talk about that."

"I've got plans after school, but I'll stop by."

"Thanks, Devon."

⸎

Early in the afternoon, Heidi made plans for Rick to meet with her at her apartment. She believed they needed to reassess the situation and plan for the future.

Lou and Maggie were in the high school and wanted to trace the route Devon would have taken from his music lesson to his locker. After getting directions from the principal's secretary, Lou walked and Maggie drove her motorized chair to the elevator where they went to the second floor and on to the music room. "Okay, if Devon left here about ten after ten, he would've come out this door and taken a direct route to his locker. He'd turn and go in this direction and it would take him right past the balcony to the swimming pool," Lou concluded. Maggie followed Lou on the route Devon most likely had taken the night Otterby was killed.

They approached the door to the pool. It was locked, but they noticed the window in the door. Maggie couldn't see through the window from her wheelchair. Lou looked at the painted window and said, "Devon couldn't have witnessed anything through this paint. It's probably painted to give privacy to the kids in the pool area."

"H-m-m, I don't see how Devon could have seen anything that night. He could have heard something though, but he told Mrs. Norton that he didn't see or hear anything, and I understand the kid is very trustworthy," Maggie remarked.

Rick had repainted the window just a few hours before Lou and Maggie's pass through the hall. He couldn't wait for permission, or for maintenance to get a work order. He wanted it done quickly.

Lou told Maggie that he wanted to see if he could talk to George Gates one more time. Maggie said she'd go on to the conference room and meet him there.

Lou found George alone in his classroom. It was about two o'clock. "Mr. Gates. I'm Lou Searing. You will recall talking with me a day or two ago about canceling your scuba diving class the night Warren Otterby was killed."

"Oh, yes. Pleased to see you again."

"Thank you. I realized in looking over my notes that I didn't ask you about your demonstration of the scuba diving equipment to Mr. Otterby. You told me your class was canceled and that you called your six students, but apparently you were also in the pool area shortly after ten to demonstrate this new equipment along with Mr. Bolt. Correct?"

"No."

"No? I thought that's what you said."

"I said that Mr. Bolt told me to cancel the class because Mr. Otterby had other plans for use of the pool. I did go to the pool and try out the new equipment. But, I did not demonstrate it to Mr. Otterby."

"I stand corrected. Please tell me about your time in the pool area that night."

"What do you want to know?"

"All the facts, including the amount of time you were there, who was present, what you did, and what was said by people present. You know, your side of the story."

"I was experimenting with the new equipment around nine-fifteen."

"Alone in a pool. Seems that you would know better than that, Mr. Gates."

"I wasn't alone. I was with another teacher."

"Who was that?"

"Heidi Simpson."

"You and Heidi were in the pool area about nine-fifteen, so you could test out the new equipment. Okay, go ahead."

"I put on the scuba gear and fell into the pool. I retrieved a few things from the bottom. I got out, and the two of us talked for about two to three minutes." Heidi left, I removed the equipment, dried off, returned the scuba equipment to the storage area and left."

"What time was it when you left?"

"About twenty, or quarter to ten I'd say."

"Did you see anybody around the pool area, in the locker room, or outside? Anybody who you would call suspicious?"

"Tom Hines, the custodian, knew I was using the pool to test the equipment. I told him I'd be out by 9:30 or 10:00 p.m. But, I wouldn't be suspicious of Tom."

"Were the lights on in the pool area when you left?"

"I guess they were. It wasn't dark, if that's what you mean."

"Was any group using the pool when you arrived for this demonstration?"

"No. I already said, I canceled our class."

"Thank you, Mr. Gates."

⸙

Lou and Maggie had some time together, so they decided to talk with Harlan Jennings, the high school special education coordinator. The three met in the principal's conference room. This room was becoming home away from home for Lou and Maggie.

Maggie began, "Mr. Jennings, thanks for meeting with us. I think you know why we are here today?"

"Everybody's talking about it. We all know that you guys are investigating this death. We've got mixed emotions."

"Really?" said Maggie in a surprised manner.

"Yeah, seems like a clear case of suicide. We don't know what it is that causes you two to keep looking at this as a murder."

Lou thought for a second before continuing, "Harlan, our dilemma is that we can't determine the principle cause of death."

"The principle cause of death, Mr. Searing, is suicide," responded Harlan.

"You really believe that a man who seems to love power and control, who had a virtual laboratory to practice this obsession, would jump into the swimming pool of his kingdom and kill himself?"

"Well, I see what you're saying, but he left a note."

"Are you sure that Warren Otterby typed and set that note on his desk?" Lou asked.

"Well, I'm basically a trusting guy. That's what the police said, so I assume that's what happened."

"That's the theory of one group of investigators. We're not so trusting. What's important to us are facts. If the facts lead to the conclusion that this man took his own life, then we know that the cause of his death was his own mental condition. However, if the facts lead to a conclusion other than suicide, then we'll have a whole new outlook on what happened in the school pool last May eleventh."

"Yes, I guess you would."

Lou surprised himself with this discourse. If nothing else, it served to be a lesson for Harlan that he shouldn't believe everything he hears.

Maggie came to the rescue, "Mr. Jennings, we have some questions for you."

"I'll help if I can."

"Did you ever overhear the special education staff talking about killing Warren Otterby?"

"All the time."

"All the time?" Lou said, acting a bit surprised. Such honesty was refreshing.

"Who said what, when, and why? Can you be specific?" asked Maggie.

"All of us, all the time, because we didn't believe he cared about us or our kids."

"Go on."

"Well, the talk was purely out of frustration. At least I don't think anyone was seriously intent on murder..."

"Examples, please."

"Well, you know, in discussion someone might say, 'I'd like to kill him' or someone would say, 'Who'd be willing to put money into a kitty for a contract on Otterby?' You know, stuff like that. It was always innocent; just expressions of frustration. Nobody in special education killed that man."

Lou asked, "You remember the early part of our discussion?"

"What early part of the discussion?"

"The point I was making about investigators needing to find facts. We can't always believe what seems obvious. It looks like you're learning this lesson."

"What do you mean? I don't get it."

"Well, you constantly heard people talking about killing a man, but instead of taking it for the truth you ignored it. You're doing the same thing we're doing in this investigation. We heard something speculated as fact, but we don't agree that it's really what happened. We have much in common, Mr. Jennings."

Harlan wasn't sure he got Lou's message, but he didn't challenge it. He went on, "Yeah, I guess so. Anyway, to be honest with you, yes, I heard comments about wanting Otterby killed, but they were just wishful thinking. They came out of frustration with the lack of attention we were getting to serve the needs of the students we care about."

"Would it surprise you if someone in special education were found guilty of killing Warren Otterby?"

Lou and Maggie noticed a telling pause. After a few seconds Harlan said, "Well, in this day and age, I'm not shocked about anything I see or hear. I'm kind of dumbfounded. There's so much crime, hatred, and crazy stuff happening in society. If I heard that one of our staff killed the guy, I'd probably say, 'So, what else is new?'"

"I guess we should stop being philosophical and ask you specific and concrete questions, but we're in a quandary too. We have no witness, no weapon, no clear motive, and as Lou said, no principle cause of death."

"Well, guess I'm not much help. I know the special education staff. Yes, we were frustrated, angry, mad, upset, scared, and furious with Warren Otterby. There is no conspiracy that I'm aware of. I never heard anyone make any statement that would give me the impression that they acted alone or with anyone else in a murder plot to kill Warren Otterby."

"Thanks, Harlan. You've been helpful. We appreciate your talking with us," Maggie shook his hand appreciatively.

ॐ

Devon stopped in to see Mr. Lancour when school was over for the day. "You wanted to talk with me?"

"Oh yes, come on in and sit down, Devon."

"You think I'm slipping a bit?"

"Yes, I think so and I'm concerned for you. You are such a fine student, Devon, but lately you don't seem to be yourself. I'm not trying to be nosy, but I'm wondering if something is bothering you, and, if it is, maybe you need to talk to your counselor, your parents, or your minister."

"I'm okay. I've got a solo and ensemble competition coming up next Monday at MSU. Maybe that's it."

"I don't think so. You've been going to competitions all of your academic life, but you haven't acted this way before."

"What do you mean, 'acted this way?'" Devon asked defensively.

"Well, for example, today I asked you for your analysis of the beginnings of the two world wars. Remember?"

"Yeah, I answered, it didn't I?"

"No, you got the stories all mixed up, and it was at that point that I knew I needed to talk with you. The Devon I know would never make such a blunder."

"Well, I've got a lot on my mind lately. It's more than the music festival this weekend."

"Do you want to talk about it?"

"No, I can't. I mean, I could, but I don't want to. I'm troubled by something I saw, that's all. I'll get over it. I'm okay."

"Again, I'm not trying to be nosy, but it seems to me that you need to share what's bothering you, and the sooner you do it the better you'll feel. Trust me on this one, Devon. If thoughts are troubling, there are people who can help you, and I'll be glad to point you to these people. A counselor, doctor, or Reverend Wheeler are all qualified. If they had your trust, they would get you the help you need."

"I'll think about it. Thanks."

"You're a talented young man with a very bright future. If you need some help, admit it, talk it out, and you'll feel better. I promise you."

ᒐ

Before heading home to Grand Haven and Battle Creek respectively, Lou and Maggie met one last time in the principal's conference area to collaborate and to plan their next steps.

"I really didn't reach an 'Ah ha' moment today. It wasn't a waste of time, but I don't feel I'm any closer to solving this thing at this hour than I was driving down here this morning," Lou sounded slightly depressed about the progress of the case.

"I agree. There are a few inconsistencies in stories and a few other mysteries still hanging. Why would Devon say he looked in the window but didn't see anything, and not mention that the window was painted? Gates said he had to cancel his class because Bolt had another group using the pool, but there was no other group using the pool. Gates, however, did go to the pool to try out the equipment around nine, and Heidi Simpson was with him. Mothers for Justice leader Haskins says she never heard of you, yet she sent you e-mail. So, we have lots of funny loose ends, but nothing to call the police on."

Lou asked the most logical question, 'Where do we go from here? It doesn't seem like we have anyone to talk to. We still have no witness, no weapon, no helpful autopsy information, no clear motive. All we seem to have is a strong belief that the man did not take his life. Who did, and why?"

"Well, I suggest we sleep on it," Maggie responded wearily. "Maybe we need a rest and a period for our thoughts to settle. Something will come to us now that we've opened a few doors. According to Jennings, the word is definitely out that we're looking into this death. Someone with information will reach out to us, or lead us to some new evidence."

"I agree. I'm ready for a long stroll on the beach. It's warm and the moon and stars will be out tonight. I think I'll get Carol and Samm to join me in a nice, long walk along the sandy beach."

"I think I'll switch gears awhile and do some more work on another case I'm looking into on the side."

"What's that?"

"Oh, it's another insurance claim case. I can't seem to leave those alone. It's hard to believe that people would steal thousands of dollars from a company outright. It's even more shocking to realize that they think they have the intelligence, and the ingenuity to pull it off. The case I'm working on involves a guy who is claiming that his car was stolen and he wants the insurance money for it. A junk car dealer in a nearby community is ready to testify that the guy brought the car in for salvage money. I mean, the guy thinks I can't figure that one out, and for his stupidity he's going to get free room and board in some jail cell for awhile. People never cease to amaze me!"

"Well, I can only handle one case at a time," replied Lou. "And, this one has me stymied. In the past when I get to this point I usually conclude that maybe I'm wrong, maybe the logical explanation is the right one, but I'm so sure that this guy would not take his life. He had no reason to. A guy like that doesn't admit to a weakness and he doesn't do it in front of an entire community. It would go against his grain to not show dominance and control, even up to the end. He didn't kill himself, but who killed him? Heidi? Gates? Bolt? Haskins? A conspiracy? Did Otterby have a non-school enemy who is using the school, and people in the school, to take the hit for his or her murder? On the other hand, maybe he did slip and fall. Maybe it was an accident. My mind needs a rest."

They headed to the parking lot together. Maggie used her remote control device to open her van. The doors opened, and the lift came down to the asphalt. She drove onto the lift, flicked the switch and moved up and into her van smoothly. The door closed, and she wheeled up to the steering device where a set of controls awaited her commands. The specially designed van allowed her to be mobile and to be independent.

Lou followed Maggie's van out of the parking lot. Maggie turned left to go to Battle Creek, and Lou turned right to head for Grand Haven where Carol, Samm, Luba, Millie, and the sounds of waves and warmth of the sand awaited.

჻

Devon Rockingham's girlfriend was Wendy Miller. Devon's family and teachers felt she was a perfect match for Devon. She was in the National Honor Society. She was first chair clarinet, and she was popular. She was elected to the homecoming court last October. Wendy was a good listener, and with Devon she did a lot of that. Devon was verbal in terms of what he was experiencing in life, his dreams, his frustrations, and the ups and downs of being a senior with a learning disability.

They had been to a movie and had stopped at Burger King afterwards. "I've got to share something with you, Wendy," said Devon. "Something's been on my mind for too long and I've got to let it out, and get some advice. I trust you, so I'm going to ask you to listen. Okay?"

"Sure. What's on your mind?"

"Well, you're the only one to know that I witnessed the murder of Mr. Otterby."

"You did, Dev? Oh, my God! What happened?" Wendy asked, shaking her head in a state of disbelief.

"I was walking to my locker from my music lesson, and I noticed that the paint was off the swimming pool balcony window. I looked in and there was Mr. Otterby up on the diving board. He was taking one step at a time. It looked like his hands were tied behind his back and his feet were tied. The woman pointing a gun at him and talking to him was Miss Simpson."

"Your teacher, Miss Simpson?" Wendy asked, astonished.

"I think so. If it wasn't her, it was her twin sister."

"Did she see you looking at her?"

"No"

"Then what happened?"

"He just got to the end, jumped in, and went down. He struggled to get loose and then went limp."

"Oh, gee, Dev. That must have been terrible to watch!"

"I didn't know whether to try and stop it or call 911. My mind got one message and then another. Finally, I just decided not to get involved. You know? I didn't want all the attention. I didn't want to turn in Miss Simpson."

"But murder, Dev! She killed our principal." Wendy was careful not to judge Devon's behavior, but she was surprised. Why didn't he act in some way other than to keep this crime to himself? Wendy didn't agree with Devon's choice, but she was pleased that he had confided in her.

"Yeah, maybe I should have. But, I didn't."

"Dev, you were in a terribly stressful situation."

"There's more that leads me to think Miss Simpson did it. On Friday, I saw her come into school, just like she always did, with her tote bags and stuff. When I went to my class at eleven, a substitute was there. I got a different story from the substitute and Mrs. Norton. I think she's in trouble, and she's not in school because she killed Mr. Otterby. If she is, it isn't because I said anything. You're the first person I've told."

"What are you going to do now, Dev?"

"I don't know. I wanted to tell you what I saw. I trust you, and I thought you might give me some good advice."

"Well, for one thing you're withholding information from the police, and that's probably illegal. I think you need to think about that. I also think you should tell an adult. You could talk to Dr. Wheeler about this, or tell your parents or the police."

"So far, I'm keeping it to myself and hoping it'll just go away."

"It won't go away, Dev. You know that."

⚘

As Lou was driving to Grand Haven, one thought kept coming back to him. A comment he had made to Maggie in the restaurant, "Did Otterby have a non-school enemy?" Lou knew, as an experienced investigator, that it is often the non-obvious that can lead to a break. He recalled his conversation with Tom Hines, who spoke of Otterby's gambling. Lou also recalled that it was a golf bet that had gotten him a recommendation for the principal job. Lou vowed to himself to see if he could learn anything more about Otterby's gambling habits.

⚘

At eight o'clock Rick pulled into one of the visitor slots in front of Heidi Simpson's apartment. When her door opened he was welcomed by Heidi and Nancy Neff. He didn't recognize Nancy, but Heidi introduced them. She noted that Nancy was a parent of a student with a significant hearing loss at Shoreline High. Greetings were warm yet serious.

Heidi served soft drinks, pretzels, and potato chips before beginning. "Thanks for coming together. We've got a problem, and we need to work together. I am very certain that all is going to be just fine, but we need to talk.

"From what I've been able to detect, Rick and I may be serious suspects in the murder of Warren Otterby. Me, because I was in the school, I carry a gun, and to be honest, I hated the man. Rick, because Warren died in his pool, and because somebody must have placed a memo on Warren's desk from Rick inviting him to the pool area about the same time he was killed. So, my guess is, even though the police have publicly suspected the death to be a suicide, they are continuing to investigate, and Searing and McMillan are building a case against us. They may even be shadowing us and know that we are meeting right now."

Rick added, "In addition, Heidi was actually in the pool area that evening. She was with George Gates when he tested the scuba diving equipment. He knew she was staying late in the school. He asked her to join him in the pool area for safety reasons. We don't know if the police know this, but Heidi was at the scene of the crime before it happened."

"That's right, Rick. It doesn't look good for me."

"Why is Nancy here this evening?" Rick asked.

"Oh, I guess I should've explained that. Nancy is a good friend of Lou Searing. I thought Nancy might be able to talk with Lou and get his support. I didn't get off to a very good start with him, and I doubt I could convince him to pull for us."

Nancy spoke for the first time. "I think Lou would be willing to go to bat for you. He's been a strong supporter of special education, teachers, parents and children."

"Great," said Heidi. "There's also a possibility that Devon Rockingham may have seen something that night. The small window in the pool balcony door had been scraped free of paint, and he might have seen something. I don't know with whom he has talked. He may have seen me in the pool area with Gates and tied that to Otterby's death. When we talked on the phone, I didn't encourage him to tell me what he saw. I told him we'd talk tomorrow, when I'm back in school."

Nancy agreed to call Lou the next day to see if she could convince him to put his investigative skills on the side of Heidi and Rick.

⌇

Lou and Carol carried a blanket and picnic basket as they strolled down the beach. They sat on a large piece of driftwood near the shore to enjoy sandwiches and fruit for dinner. The lake's surface was as smooth as glass. Boats were floating along the horizon. Seagulls were practicing takeoffs and landings while looking for a dinner of their own.

Samm ran back and forth, retrieving sticks that Carol and Lou tossed for her along the shore. The tourists hadn't descended on Grand Haven yet, and the beach was peaceful and private. The Searings enjoyed this rare luxury.

Lou put his arm around Carol and the two faced west to watch the sun sink into Lake Michigan. The pastels of the sunset were beautiful. Lou imagined that the sky was a painter's canvas and an invisible artist wielded combinations of yellow, orange, blue, and pink oils with his brush. The show of nature entertained them, and they were thankful for the presence of mind to take time for enjoying the beauty that was always about them.

Once the sun was down, Lou made a small fire from sticks and driftwood that Samm helped him collect. Carol took out some graham crackers, Hershey candy bars, and marshmallows, and they enjoyed a beach treat of S'Mores. The crackle and warmth from the small fire, the aroma of the burning wood, and the light from the sunset reflecting off the surrounding beach had the effect of lulling Lou away from the Otterby case.

"What a wonderful way to spend an evening with the woman you love," Lou broke the silence to whisper in Carol's ear.

"We're pretty lucky to have all of this beauty at our back door," offered Carol.

"We sure are. And, I might add, pretty lucky to have each other to share the beauty."

"I thank God every day, Lou. I really do."

They spent the rest of the evening watching the fire go from flames, to embers, to ashes. It became chilly and the dew began to gather on the driftwood. Samm stirred and sleepily urged the couple back to the warmth of their home. As they made their way back to the house, thousands of stars and the bright moon in the western sky beamed down on them.

CHAPTER 7

Tuesday, May 17

On Tuesday, Heidi was back in school. Her students seemed glad to see her. Devon entered the class last. She was eager to speak to him, but Devon seemed to have changed his mind about telling her what he had seen. Wendy was right, he decided. If he was going to share what he knew with an adult, he should do it with somebody who wasn't a suspect in the death of Otterby. He decided not to tell her what he had seen almost a week ago.

When class was over Miss Simpson asked Devon to stay for a few minutes. "I've got to go. I'm meeting some friends for lunch."

"Sure, Devon, but last Friday you seemed quite anxious to talk with me about the death of Mr. Otterby."

"I know, but now I don't think I want to talk about it."

"Did you want to tell me because you needed to get something off your chest, or was there some other reason?"

There was a quiet pause. Devon didn't look at her, and if there ever was a moment when he might have changed his mind it was that minute. Devon picked up his backpack, flung it over his shoulder and said, "Mr. Otterby didn't kill himself. I saw you holding a gun at him and you seemed to be telling him to walk off the end of the diving board."

"Oh, no, Devon, I would never do anything like that. You're con-fused."

"Maybe I am. The woman looked just like you, Miss Simpson. The woman standing there was you."

"No, Devon, it wasn't me. I wasn't in the pool area that night. You've made a big mistake thinking that it was me."

Devon simply shrugged his shoulders as if to say, "I don't know."

"Have you told anyone, Devon?" Heidi asked, full of apprehen-sion about what she was hearing.

"I told Wendy, but no one else. I think it's only right to tell the police what I saw. I don't want you to get hurt, though."

"I certainly understand your need to do what you think is right, but I was not in the pool area last Wednesday night when Mr. Otterby took his own life. If you can trust me, and I hope you can, I'm telling you the truth."

Devon looked at her in a very sympathetic way. He wanted to believe her, but he knew what he saw and he was quite certain that Miss Simpson forced the principal to his death.

Devon walked out of Miss Simpson's classroom wishing that he had not told her that he saw her kill Mr. Otterby. He knew that from this moment on, he would view Miss Simpson differently. He could never look at her again without being confused about what he saw and her claim of innocence. He also realized that if Miss Simpson killed Mr. Otterby, she could do the same to him, the only one who knew what happened and who would be in a position to tell the authorities or someone who would convince him to do so.

Devon had a flashback to his minister and last Sunday's sermon telling him that the truth would make him free. He wasn't free, but he wasn't being hassled by police, the media, and the kids in school. He seemed to be caught between wanting to be honest by getting the truth out and getting on with his life uninterrupted. Should he continue to slap justice in the face?

Heidi Simpson was in agony. In addition to Lou's and Maggie's suspicions, there was a witness thinking he saw her with a gun forc-ing Otterby into the pool.

❦

Maggie planned a trip to Muskegon for her work on an insurance investigation. She was going through Grand Haven, so she called Lou to see if they might meet and discuss any new ideas.

Lou had been up for several hours. He was settled into his studio for a long and uninterrupted session of writing. The ringing telephone startled him out of focused concentration.

"Hi, Lou, want to meet for a few minutes this afternoon? I'm coming through on my way to Muskegon, and I thought we could think this Otterby thing through a little more."

"Sure, what time will you be here?"

"I'd say shortly after noon."

"How about meeting me at Charlie Marlins? It's right off U.S. 31 and easy to find. The dining room looks out onto the bayou and the boats are all around. You'll love it."

"Sounds great. Say, one o'clock?"

"Good. I'll bring all the information I have to date, and you do the same."

"See you in a few hours."

Lou called Charlie Marlins and made a reservation for two by a window for one o'clock. He looked forward to talking with Maggie and enjoying the view.

❦

Heidi called Rick Bolt to report what she had heard from Devon. After giving him the bad news, Rick put another nail in the coffin.

"Heidi, all of this happening to us because of an unpainted window six inches square. If Devon talks, we're in court fighting for our good names."

"I'm just as scared as you are," Heidi replied, reaching the depths of despair. In all of her life, the future never looked as dim as it did at this minute.

It became obvious to Rick that circumstances made them prime suspects. He said, "This doesn't look good for us. We're good friends and that would lead people to think we killed Otterby. I'm suspect because of the note that Otterby got and the fact that the murder took place in my pool. You're suspect because he hated special education, and had no love for you as a person. You were in the school, with a gun, and now, if that all weren't enough, one of your students tells you that he saw you kill the principal."

"You're right, it doesn't look good, and quite frankly, Rick, I'm scared, real scared."

"On the positive side, I'm hoping that Lou and Maggie will come over to our side and help us."

"I agree. Did you talk with Detective Mallard yet?"

"He's due here in about fifteen minutes. I'm hoping I can be cleared at that time."

"Well, please call and let me know what happens. We're in this together, if only to save our lives, our careers, and our mental health."

୬

Lou and Maggie were seated comfortably in Charlie Marlins on the Grand River. They informed the waitress, obviously a college student beginning her summer job at the restaurant, that they were there for a working lunch. They ordered chicken salad sandwiches, water, and Diet Cokes. They instructed the waitress that they wished to be left alone and not interrupted. The waitress understood, brought them their food and drinks and left them to their work.

Before leaving them, the waitress offered assistance by pulling another table over to give them some working space for the heavy folders of paper that were beginning to spread across their eating space. The restaurant was almost empty, since the lunch crowd was about gone, and there wouldn't be any more heavy traffic for a few hours.

Lou thanked the waitress and made a mental note to up the generous tip he already planned for her. He always liked to reward ingenuity or the ability of a waiter or waitress to see a situation and to serve the client better.

While Lou and Maggie were having lunch, Devon was having a meeting with his music teacher.

"I think you'll be just fine Monday. You've worked hard and you've a marvelous reputation going into this event. Don't let the event being on a Monday throw you off. The music building at MSU wasn't available on a Saturday in May."

"I was curious why the event was on Monday. I feel that I've peaked. I'm sure there's room for improvement, but I'm getting a bit tired of these pieces. Discipline, discipline, discipline. That seems to be my nickname, doesn't it?"

"It's the mark of a fine musician, and you are certainly that. I want to go over the plans for Monday, even though it is a few days away. You should begin to internalize the plan, and then you won't have to be thinking the slightest bit about it. Nothing should detract your concentration from the pieces you'll perform." Mindy Whitmore spoke in a serious tone of voice.

"The Trailways bus will take all the musicians and chaperons to MSU. We'll leave the school parking lot at seven-thirty. To be honest, I'd rather you were transported by your parents, instead of the bus. I know you'd like to be with your friends, gossiping and listening to rock music on your headsets. But, that's not the kind of preparation I have in mind for the most important competition you'll face before your recitals at Julliard."

"Aw, it won't be bad. Everybody will be nervous going to the competition."

"I've had a chance to preview the schedule, and you'll perform your solo at one-ten. I suggest no lunch. You should eat something around eleven but that's it. You can eat afterwards, but nothing from about eleven-fifteen on. I expect you in the warm-up room one-half hour before your performance. That will give us enough time to get ready. I don't want a lot of running around in downtown East Lansing, either. You can take a walk around campus, but I want your mind on the pieces you'll perform."

"I know all of this. We've been doing this for years now, Miss Whitmore."

"Discipline, Devon, discipline. It's important to be disciplined. You'll be hearing this from coaches and managers for the rest of your life, so you might as well get used to it at a young age. Do you have any questions?"

"What time is the ensemble event?"

"Oh yes, I'm more concerned about your solo and I tend to forget the quartet. Let me see, you are scheduled for two o'clock. You won't have much time between your pieces. You'll feel more relaxed and at ease for the ensemble. Any more questions?"

"No, but my parents aren't going. Dad had to be out of town on business, and Mom thinks she is coming down with a bad cold. I hope I don't get it."

"You'll be okay. We'll talk again before Monday."

⌣⌐

Duck Mallard met with Rick Bolt in the office of the athletic director. After a few pleasantries were exchanged about sports in general and the early move by the Tigers in the baseball season, Mallard got down to business. "Got a few questions for you, Mr. Bolt."

"Sure. How can I help you?"

"I need to know about the plans that were made to use the pool last Wednesday night."

"Wednesday night is reserved for a scuba diving class. The class is taught by George Gates, the chemistry teacher here at Shoreline. Mr. Otterby sent me a note about mid-afternoon and told me to cancel the scuba diving class. Apparently he promised the pool to another group. I called George and told him to cancel the class. He said he would."

"I've learned that George did come in, and he tried out the new equipment. Further I've learned that he asked Heidi to be there with him, as a safety precaution."

"Yes, I've heard that too. That has nothing to do with my responsibility for this pool and the scheduling of groups, et cetera."

"I realize that. I was pointing out that apparently two members of the staff were in this area between nine and ten o'clock. Where were you that evening?"

"I played golf in my league late that afternoon and early in the evening. I went home afterwards and went to bed."

"Can anyone vouch for your whereabouts that night?"

"Not for when Otterby was allegedly killed, or committed suicide. I was home alone and no one saw me."

"You live alone?"

"Yeah."

"Any neighbors hear you come in or did you have the TV on loud or anything?"

"I keep to myself. I doubt anyone saw me come in. I have a corner apartment by the parking area, and I don't often see a neighbor. I'm quiet about TV and music noise because I want my neighbors to treat me to the same courtesy. I doubt anyone would know when I arrived or if they hear me once I'm inside."

"I'd like to talk about the note you sent to Otterby about..."

Rick interrupted, "I didn't send or give him any note."

"The note requesting him to come to a demonstration of the diving equipment?"

"I did not write any such note, Detective Mallard. I'm being framed."

"Did you type it at school, or at home, on a computer or typewriter?"

"You're pretty good with those 'have you stopped beating your wife' questions, Detective. I repeat, I did not write and deliver any note to Mr. Otterby. You won't find any fingerprints on the note and you won't..."

"But we did, Mr. Bolt."

"You did what?"

"We found your prints on the memo. It's going to take a good lawyer to convince a jury that the note didn't come from you."

"I don't care what it takes, I did not write that note."

"Your relationship with Miss Simpson, could I ask about that?"

"A good friend."

"Good enough to want to help her get rid of a thorn in her side?"

"I resent that, and this interview is over. I probably should have asked my lawyer to be here with me, but I thought that might imply some guilt. I didn't want that because I'm not guilty of anything. I also know that I don't have to answer any questions put to me by a police officer and as of this minute I'm exercising my rights. Finished."

"I understand, Mr. Bolt. These kinds of things can be stressful. I'm just trying to do my job, and that means getting to the bottom of this man's death. Thank you for your time."

Rick showed the detective to the door and sat heavily in his chair. He could feel the rapid beat of his heart. For once he was thankful that he was in excellent physical condition. He thought it best to take a brisk walk to help him relax and take the edge off his fear.

⌁

Lou and Maggie finished their lunches. Lou ordered a single dip of chocolate ice cream to spoon while thinking. Maggie had a lot of paper spread out on the tables. Lou had most of what he had written memorized by now.

"Something's got to pop, Lou. Somehow I think that if I look at this stuff long enough it will."

"As I said to that man, Harlan, the other day, if we could only determine the principle cause of death, we'd be far ahead."

"That's it Lou! That's it. You hit it! Oh, I wish I could get out of this chair and give you a kiss!"

"What did I say to elicit such a reaction?"

"You said, 'The principle cause of death.'"

"Yeah, I did. And that wins a prize?"

"It sure does. The word is a homophone, sounds the same with two different spellings and meanings. When you want to express the title of the head of a school, the word is spelled with the last two letters being A and L, pal."

"Right. Most people know that. Get to the point, please."

"Well, when you made that statement I was looking down at the suicide note from Warren Otterby. In that note he says, 'I've given my career to Shoreline schools as a teacher, and as Principle,' and he spells principal the wrong way: P-R-I-N-C-I-P-L-E. When his secretary was interviewed, my notes reflect that she said that he was a stickler on grammar, spelling, and punctuation. The principal of a school would never spell PRINCIPAL, P-R-I-N-C-I-P-L-E."

"I agree with that. Not to dampen your enthusiasm, but perhaps it was a nervous mistake. After all, the man was supposed to be in a state of mind to kill himself. What difference would a misspelled word mean when you are about to die?"

"I know what you're saying, but a principal doesn't misspell his title, ever!" Maggie said with enthusiasm.

Lou looked up at Maggie, as he was startled by a recollection. "I think I found the next puzzle piece."

"Meaning?"

"Well, you recall meeting with Heidi. We were talking about the IEP meeting?"

"Yeah, I remember. I asked who went to that meeting?"

"Precisely. For some reason you asked her to write down the various participants. Do you still have that note?"

"Oh, sure. I have everything. Here it is."

"How did she spell principal?"

"Oh, my God, Lou. Look at that: P-R-I-N-C-I-P-L-E."

Lou then reminded Maggie of the note from Warren to Rick. "Was the word 'principal' used in the note that Otterby supposedly sent to Rick canceling the scuba diving class?"

Maggie retrieved the note from her files. "Here it is. Oh, my gosh, another misspelling!"

"Bingo. Still a lot of circumstantial evidence, but at least it's our first clue for explaining something other than suicide. Warren may not have written that suicide note, nor the memo to Rick. This along with Heidi's misspelling in her writing to you suggest it's very possible that Heidi typed the notes purportedly from Otterby."

"It sure is. We finally have a suspect. And, we have a clue to back us up!"

Before Maggie left for Muskegon, Lou suggested that some attention be given to looking into Warren Otterby's private life. "I don't mean to take the wind out of our sails right after discovering a good possible link to Warren's death, but I think we need to delve into Otterby's personal life," Lou said.

"You think the murderer could be someone outside the school community?"

"I don't know. I'll admit that a few things are falling into place. Heidi and Rick are fairly obvious suspects, but I'll feel better if we rule out a few other possible motives."

"For instance?" Maggie asked.

"Maybe Otterby angered someone with his gambling. He's gotten up to some high stakes according to one story we've heard. Maybe he pushed drugs on the side and got himself into trouble in the drug scene. Maybe he was hitting on some woman and ran into a jealous husband. Maybe he threatened somebody for some reason and he took the hit before he could act. I don't know, Maggie. I only know that we're not doing a thorough job if we don't look beyond the school."

"You won't get any resistance from me, Lou. What do you suggest?"

"I think we should talk to his sister in Dallas. I think we should ask around to find out who his friends were, and I think we should look into phone logs, mail, address books, stuff like that. There's no question that we're looking for conflict in his life, and if we find any, we'll need to rule it out as reason for his death."

"You want to pursue that and tell me if there's anything you want me to do?" Maggie asked.

"Sure. The sister lives in Dallas and so does mine. I haven't seen her in several months. I'll go down there and see if they were a close brother and sister. If they were, my guess is that she'll have some tips about Warren's personal life."

꒳

Laughton Lancour was right on time for his appointment with Reverend Philip Wheeler. The two sat in the minister's office at the First Methodist Church. The room was decorated heavily in leather. The chairs were covered with a dark blue and very comfortable grained leather. The minister's desk was clean and tidy. In the book cases, religious writings were plentiful. The office was cozy, a good place for counseling.

Laughton began, "Thank you for meeting with me on short notice."

"Not a problem, Laughton. My door is always open to any of God's children, and especially to the members of my flock. You and Lucie are important members of the congregation."

"Thank you, Dr. Wheeler."

"What brings you here today, Laughton?"

"Well, I know you'll think I'm sticking my nose where it doesn't belong, but I have an intuitive feeling that you should hear about something that's been on my mind."

"It's important to act on those intuitive feelings. Thankfully, I'm in the office today. I was supposed to speak at a conference in Cleveland this afternoon, but I woke this morning with quite a headache and didn't feel up to the trip. The planning committee was very understanding and a standby speaker was asked to substitute. Maybe this was supposed to happen?"

"I don't know about that, but I'm here because I'm concerned about Devon Rockingham."

"Mature and talented young man."

"Yes, he is. He's an extraordinary example of dedication. He's dedicated to his family, his music, his church, and his academics."

"What's the problem with Devon?"

"Well, he isn't himself. He seems to be bothered by something. I've been working with young people for almost thirty years and I'm getting so that I can be fairly accurate in predicting when my students are troubled, getting into drugs, in love, or facing some serious dilemma. Understanding the moods of the young is almost as challenging as keeping up with the history content of my courses."

"I take it young Rockingham is expressing himself in such a way that you are concerned that something is bothering him."

"Yes, and I usually don't go running to each student's minister, priest, or rabbi, but I care so much for this young man. Since we both go to the same church, and I value your skill in working with youth and their families, I had this intuitive feeling that if I share my concern with you, you will know what to do and Devon will be the better for your intervention."

"Thanks for your confidence. Do you have any clue about what may be bothering him?"

"He said he was troubled by something he saw."

"Do you know what he saw?"

"No, he said he didn't want to talk about it, and I didn't pry. I suggested that he share what was on his mind with an adult he respected. I got the feeling that while he thought it was good advice, he probably would continue to carry the burden around with him."

"Have you talked to his parents?"

"No, I didn't want to violate any confidence with Devon. My inclination was to share my concern with you. I'm interested in your advice before I proceed."

"I think maybe a conference with his parents, Mary and Ron, would be a good idea. But first, I think I'll ask to speak to Devon myself. I'll tell Devon about your concern and that you didn't want to violate his confidence. I'll see if I can get him to talk about his problem. If it seems appropriate, I'll approach Mary and Ron. I'm happy to help this young man, if he's open to my help."

"Thank you, Dr. Wheeler."

"That's what I'm here for, Laughton. Thanks for caring enough about Devon to stop in and share your concerns. I'll call him soon. We'll see if we can't get to the bottom of what's bothering him."

The two parted company and Laughton felt much better for sharing his concern with his spiritual leader. He knew Dr. Wheeler could handle the situation appropriately. He was fairly certain that Devon wouldn't be upset with him for taking this proactive step.

On the way to his car in the church parking lot, Dr. Wheeler brought up the subject of a serious car accident involving one of the elders from the church. Wheeler was on his way to Shoreline Hospital. His talk with Devon could wait a few hours.

$$\backsim$$

Lou returned home after his lunch with Maggie. He got comfortable in front of his computer and re-entered the world of his novel. The phone rang. Nancy Neff was on the other end of the line.

"Hope I'm not bothering you, Lou?"

"Not at all. What's on your mind?"

"I'm calling to ask you to help me and a couple of my friends."

"Will help if I can."

"Well, we'd like to hire you and Mrs. McMillan to work for us in investigating the death of Mr. Otterby."

There was a silent pause while Lou collected his thoughts. "I know most private investigators work under a contractual relationship, but I've always gotten involved for the satisfaction of solving a crime. My commission comes from book sales and that's enough. I've never been hired before."

"There's always a first time, Lou. Will you help us?"

"Who is 'us,' Nancy?"

"It started out being Heidi Simpson, but more and more of us are feeling like we are being framed in a conspiracy."

"Explain."

"Well, Rick Bolt is a suspect now. The police detective told him that one of his fingerprints was found on the note that Otterby received from someone asking him to be in the pool area at ten-fifteen. I could be a suspect because of threatening comments about wanting to kill Otterby. The Mothers for Justice organization is also potentially involved because of threatening correspondence sent to Otterby before his death. The two in the most trouble are Heidi and Rick. All of us know of your respect for special educators and your support in our commitment to children. We want you to help us find the real killer, if Otterby was killed. We can't pay you thousands of dollars, but we'll work out something to make it worth your while."

"I'm going to have to think about this, Nancy. Normally I want to be free of bias when I investigate. Things don't look good for Heidi, I'll tell you that right now. If circumstantial evidence were enough to warrant the arrest of a person, I'd be pretty close to talking to the prosecutor about having her arrested for Otterby's murder."

"Oh God, Lou. No. That would be a terrible injustice."

"The only thing lacking is a witness, Nancy. Think about it. She was in the school with a gun, she hated the man, and she's a friend of Rick's who could cancel that class to make the pool accessible for the murder. She's already lied to me, so I have to question her honesty. If we had a witness who saw her with Otterby around ten-fifteen, she'd be in jail without the possibility of bail. Quite frankly, Heidi is near the top of my list of suspects, Nancy."

"I'm very sorry to learn that you're thinking Heidi did this, Lou. I can't give you that piece of evidence to clear her, but I know in my heart she's innocent. I guess I can only hope you will think about helping us."

"I appreciate your respect for my work, but I want to be free of any bias on this case. I'll be as fair as I can be, and I'll seek all leads. If I'm able to find Heidi innocent, based on the facts, great. If she's a suspect, based on the facts, that will have to be the conclusion. You can tell your friends that I'll be fair. If they wish to give me any information that I would find helpful, I'd appreciate that."

"They'll be disappointed, Lou. But we respect you, and if this is the way you wish to proceed, we have no choice but to honor your decision."

"Thank you. By the way, Heidi and Rick need very good lawyers.

As I said, it doesn't look good for either of them, especially Heidi. I'll work with Mr. Marshburn, if he would like my assistance, but I won't get into a client-investigator relationship. It simply isn't my style."

"I understand. Thanks, Lou. I look forward to our celebration when Heidi and Rick are no longer suspects and the guilty party is apprehended. That'll be a happy day."

♪

Jane Wills was meeting with her editor at four o'clock. She asked for an appointment to discuss an idea for a feature story that could be award-producing for herself and for the *Herald Palladium*. Jane's editor was Patricia Babcock, a young, up and coming newspaper woman destined for a job with the *Chicago Tribune* or some other large city newspaper. She was always open to new ideas. She had produced award winning articles in her earlier years with various small town newspapers.

"You've got an idea for a story?" Pat asked.

"I've got an idea, yes. I wanted your best thinking because I've admired you and your choices for features over the years," Jane urged, realizing that a little flattery might get her somewhere.

"What's on your mind?" Pat seemed interested but impatient.

"There's a student at Shoreline High School. He's a senior. His name is Devon Rockingham. Most who know the music world in this town predict a great deal of success for him in the years ahead. He plays the bassoon in a way that makes the instrument come alive and take on a life of its own. This kid dreams of being an international musician. He's very good with this lanky tube of an instrument. He's an artist—put the sound of his bassoon with other instruments and the resulting sound is innovative and very moving."

"You sound like his agent, Jane."

"Well, I do think he's got a very bright future."

"So, what's your story suggestion?"

"Next Monday at MSU, Devon is competing in his last high

school solo and ensemble competition before attending the Julliard School of Music in New York City."

"Jane, I don't mean to be rude; but, what's your story idea?"

"I'm sorry. My idea is to do 'A Day in the Life of Shoreline's Music Phenom, Devon Rockingham'."

"Great idea. Go with it!" Pat exclaimed. "You have my full support. Take a photographer, use our intern from Western Michigan University and cover his day from waking up in the morning to his celebrated arrival back in Shoreline. I'll see that it gets full attention here and we'll run it as the lead article in the local section of the Tuesday edition."

"Oh, that's great. Thank you, Miss Babcock."

With the approval of her editor, Jane Wills began to plan her story on Devon Rockingham. It would be a marvelous human interest piece and one that would be fun to follow up on as his career blossomed.

CHAPTER 8

Wednesday, May 18

Lou and Carol awoke to a rainy day. Looking out at the "Big M," as Lou often referred to big, blue Lake Michigan, he saw that the lake was calm, as droplets of water crashed against its crust. The rain changed the color of the beach from a light tan to a light brown. Samm seemed lazier than usual, sensing that she would not be allowed to romp along the beach today.

Belgian waffles were satisfying in contrast to the cool and wet morning. Carol gave Lou a kiss and then left to go to work with her families. Lou retired to his writing studio. He turned on his e-mail to see if he had any overnight mail. His cup of decaf coffee beside him produced a steady stream of steam swirling above the rim. Some mail had arrived. The first item was a letter from his sister in Dallas. There was another message from Rbqty435. He opened the letter from Mothers for Justice and read, "I can see that you are not content to let the dead dog lie. You still seem to want to try to find a murderer when there really isn't one. I hope you're considering what your constant investigating is doing to the lives of people. Instead of accepting what the police concluded, thanks to you and your partner, people are beginning to doubt and to accuse others. A lot of nasty rumors are going around and many people are getting hurt. If this is your idea of fun, it's sick. For the sake of a lot of innocent people, I ask you to end your foolish prying and prodding into people's lives. Please stop this worthless use of your time and allow innocent people to get their lives back."

Lou made a copy of the letter. He clicked on the "reply" icon and typed, "Got your message. There's nothing more honorable than seeking the truth. Once we, or the judicial system, determine the truth, people can adjust to what really happened and then true peace can come over people. As much as you want me to cease, I'm compelled to continue. We're close to winding this up and soon all will know how Warren Otterby died. Thanks for writing. Lou Searing."

Once his message was sent, Lou clicked on the message from his sister in Dallas. Gayle was reporting a beautiful late spring day, family activities involving her husband, son and daughter, and plans for the weekend. Lou always enjoyed hearing from Gayle. Now that their parents had passed on, he realized that Gayle, along with his brother, Bob, were his family roots. The three were close as siblings, but the realization that together they were all that remained to continue longstanding family traditions made their bond much stronger.

While reading his sister's mail the computer voice came on, "You've got mail." Lou finished his reply to his sister and retrieved the new mail. As expected, it was another message from Rtbqty435. Again, as predicted, it was a threat, "I can see you're not planning to take my advice. I caution you to watch out, you'll encounter people who will not appreciate your work."

Lou wondered if he should respond or simply leave it lie. He chose to let it be. He closed his e-mail account and chased some M&Ms with decaf coffee. He opened into his recent novel and concentrated on the next scene in the murder mystery. Samm was at his feet. Lou glanced out of the bay windows and saw that breaks were occurring in the clouds off to the west. The sun might appear before noon.

⤳

"**M**aggie?" asked a female voice.

"Yes, this is Maggie McMillan. Who's calling?"

"This is Jane Wills from the *Herald Palladium*. I'm checking in to see if you and Mr. Searing are getting any closer to solving this murder?"

"Not really, Jane. We still lack any evidence that would convince a prosecuting attorney to authorize the arrest of anyone. We still have our suspicions, and we believe that Otterby was murdered. Unfortunately we're not much closer than when we talked with you a few evenings ago."

"I know you two will get to the bottom of this. I hope you'll bring me into the final stages of the investigation so that I can break the story."

"Sure, Jane. We'll do that."

"Good. I've got the go-ahead from my editor to do a story on Devon Rockingham."

"Related to the death of Otterby?"

"Oh, no. As you know, he's performing at MSU on Monday at the state solo and ensemble competition. I'm doing, 'A Day in the Life of Devon Rockingham,' story. I'll have an intern with me, and a photographer. We'll follow him throughout the day. The Tuesday edition will have a pictorial and a long article about this exceptional young man."

"Well, I'll look forward to reading it, Jane."

"Thanks. Your first reaction a moment ago was that I'd do an essay on Devon regarding the death of Warren Otterby. Is he involved?"

"Oh, no. He had a music lesson in the school and was in the general area of the pool when Otterby died. Lou asked Mrs. Norton, Assistant Principal, to talk with him about what he might have seen or heard. He told her that he didn't hear or see anything that evening. Neither Lou nor I have talked with him. We thought he'd be more comfortable talking with someone he knew and trusted."

"So, it's possible that Devon did see or hear something that night?"

"He says he didn't see or hear anything. At this point we have no reason to doubt him. But, when you said you were doing a story about him, and since he's familiar to me as someone who was in the building that night, I jumped to a wrong conclusion, that's all."

"I see."

"Good luck with your story, and we'll let you know when we get a break in this investigation."

"Thanks, Maggie. Have a good day. I've got to call Devon's music teacher now, and his parents, to get the go-ahead to shadow him on Monday."

꒰ꕥ꒱

Reverend Wheeler was driving north to Traverse City for a conference of Methodist ministers when he realized that he had not called Devon, as he had told Laughton Lancour he would. He made a mental note to call the Rockinghams that evening. It was important, because the Reverend was a man of his word. He also knew that young people have a lot of emotions and are tormented by a host of things. Given Devon's maturity, he suspected that whatever was on Devon's mind would pass. He assumed that when he talked to Devon, he'd conclude that the problem was minor.

Dr. Wheeler pulled into his driveway at eight-twenty. He was tired from the trip to Traverse City where he had given a speech. He greeted Mrs. Wheeler, looked through his mail and went through his phone messages before heading to the hospital to visit a few members of his church. When he finally stopped to catch his breath, he realized it was ten-thirty. He remembered that he was going to call Devon Rockingham, but decided it could wait until Thursday.

CHAPTER 9

Thursday, May 19

The word in the teachers' lounge was that the investigation into the death of Warren Otterby was escalating. The two people looking into the death—the older man, bald with hearing aids, wearing Dockers and sweatshirts, and the woman in the motorized wheelchair—had been in school on more than one occasion. The police detective was also seen and rumored to have been talking with Heidi and Rick. Rumors were evident and opinions were everywhere.

Staff, students, and parents were getting used to Lorraine Norton as their new principal. Everyone appreciated her as a breath of fresh air. She provided healthy leadership at the high school.

Lorraine asked Mary, her secretary, to call Lou in Grand Haven. Lou, walking through the door from a jog with Samm, heard the phone ringing. "Hello," Lou answered, panting from a long and vigorous run.

"Lou?"

"Yes."

"Are you okay? Sounds like you're having a heart attack."

"Oh no, just exercising so I hopefully won't have one. Is this Lorraine?"

"Yes. Calling to get an update on your investigation."

"Sure. Seems like weeks since we've talked."

"Yes, it does. Well, what's happening? The buzz around the faculty is that the authorities are very suspicious of people in the school being involved. Are the folks right?"

"That's a fair conclusion. We're working on it. We're talking, thinking, hypothesizing, and planning our next steps."

"Good, I'm glad to hear it."

"Lorraine, while you're on the line, let me ask if anything has happened around the school that may in any way relate to this case. I should have been checking in every day. Do you have anything for me?"

"The only thing I can think of is the window painting."

"The window painting? What's that about?"

"Well, you recall that Devon told me that he looked through the balcony door window the night of Warren's death, but that he didn't see anything. I learned from my secretary that last Monday Rick Bolt called and asked about the paint being scraped from the window. She told him that Warren had maintenance scrape the paint off so that he could see into the balcony area. That happened late in the morning on the day of the death. Rick explained that the window needed to be painted so that students would have privacy in the pool area. He didn't go through me or maintenance. He didn't put through a work order request. He painted the window himself."

"Yes, the last afternoon that Maggie and I were in your school we took the route that Devon took the night of the murder and the window was painted. I was wondering if Devon was using his imagination."

"Oh, it was clear from late morning Wednesday until Rick painted it recently. My guess is that Devon did look through a clear pane of glass and that he did see something going on, but he's choosing to keep it to himself. Do you think he saw something, Lou?" Lorraine asked.

"Hard to tell. Maybe I should talk to this young man."

"Yes, I think you should, Lou."

"Is he in school today?"

"Yes. I saw him come in this morning."

"I can be down there by noon. Would you arrange for me to talk to Devon at about one o'clock?"

"Sure. Do you want anyone else there with you?"

"I'd like both his mother and father there, if possible."

"I'll call Mrs. Rockingham and see if she can come."

"Okay, I'll be there around noon. My presence will get folks talking again, but I can't hide from the truth and the truth is that we need to keep working on this case."

"See you soon, Lou."

☙

Lou called Maggie to brief her on what he had learned. He told her of the threatening e-mail exchange. He told her Lorraine's painted window story and that he was planning to go to Shoreline to interview Devon Rockingham around one o'clock. "Do you want to be there with me?"

"Yes, I'd like to be there, but I think the fewer people the better. So, maybe it's best that you go alone."

"I disagree. I think Devon might relate to you, since both of you have a disability. I see this as a critical interview. Devon is the only person involved that neither one of us has talked with. We always seem to play off each other's questions. I've asked Lorraine to invite his mother and father. I think it's time for all of us to have an open and frank discussion about that night at Shoreline High School."

"I agree. I'll be there about one o'clock. Is that what you said?"

"Right. One o'clock."

While Lou was talking to Maggie, Lorraine was talking with Mary Rockingham. "Mrs. Rockingham?"

"Yes."

"This is Lorraine Norton, Devon's principal."

"Oh, yes. I've been meaning to call you."

"You have?"

"Yes. Devon doesn't seem himself lately. He seems down, depressed, overly concerned about something. At first I thought it was the state music festival, but that doesn't make sense. He's grown up with competition, and he actually enjoys it. So, I wanted to call you to see if you were hearing anything of concern from his teachers."

"Well, yes, as a matter of fact, I am. A few of the faculty are concerned, but we were attributing it to the music competition at MSU."

"Was that the reason you called?" Mary asked.

"Yes and no. I don't know if Devon has said anything to you or not, but he was having a music lesson at school on the night that Mr. Otterby died. He would have come by the pool balcony area on his way to his locker when Mr. Otterby was in the pool area. He told me he didn't see or hear anything."

"That's what he told me, too. He did tell me that he was in the general area. For awhile I thought his personality change could be related to the trauma around a tragic death. The violence these days is terrible. Murder in schools seems to be happening regularly. It is terrible! We see violence on TV, in the movies, and it's in the media every day."

"I tend to agree. Anyway, there are a couple of investigators who are looking into the death of Warren Otterby. Their names are Lou Searing, the retired State Director of Special Education, and his partner Maggie McMillan, from Battle Creek."

"I've heard of Mr. Searing. I used to be active in the Learning Disabilities Association of Michigan when Devon was younger. He was director at that time in the State Department and was helpful to us as I recall. He is an investigator now?"

"He got his private investigator license a few years ago, and now he writes mysteries and investigates selected cases. Anyway, he and Maggie have been interviewing people in the school and community for the past week. They haven't uncovered any major clues, at least they haven't shared any findings with me."

"Maybe Mr. Otterby did take his own life after all?"

"He could have. He very well could have. Anyway, Lou and Maggie want to talk with Devon about that night. Lou asked that you and Mr. Rockingham be invited to the interview. Can you or your husband be here around one o'clock?"

"I can, but Ron can't. He's in Chicago for the regional meeting of his sales representatives."

"I'm pleased that you can make it. We'll be meeting in my conference room. I look forward to seeing you."

"Thank you for inviting me. Ron and I sure would like to get to the underlying cause of Devon's changed personality. Obviously, I hope it isn't this man's death that's bothering Devon, but I want to know what's going on so that we can get him the help he needs."

"I understand. I'll see you shortly."

Lorraine had asked Devon to come to her office between classes. When she saw him she explained that Mr. Searing wanted to talk to him about the night that Mr. Otterby died. She informed him that Mrs. McMillan would be present and so would his mother.

Outwardly Devon expressed no emotion about the interview with several adults. Inwardly he was quite upset. He knew he would be forced to admit the truth, the truth that Dr. Wheeler had said would set him free. He was torn as he tried to decide if this was the time to get it all out. Devon thought of his beautiful teacher. Because of him, she could spend her life in prison. Miss Simpson had taught him so much, and was the one person, along with his mother, who helped him to compensate for his learning disability. Yet, Miss Simpson, he was quite certain, killed Mr. Otterby and that was not right. Thinking about the dilemma caused Devon to feel light-headed and ill.

Devon walked from the principal's office to Miss Simpson's fourth-hour class. He sat down and got out some schoolwork, "You look like you lost your best friend, Devon," Heidi said.

"I've got a lot on my mind. The solo and ensemble competition is coming up."

"I know and it will be a special day for you. You'll get the highest rating once again, I'm sure."

"I've got to get past an interview first."

"An interview for a job?"

"No. At one o'clock I'm being interviewed by a couple of detectives or private investigators. They asked my mom to be there too."

"What's that about, Devon?"

"I guess they want to talk to me about the night Mr. Otterby died."

"That has to be very stressful for you, Devon."

"I'm not going to tell them anything. I didn't see anything. I didn't hear anything."

"But didn't you tell me that when you looked through the window you saw someone you thought was me forcing Mr. Otterby into the pool?"

"Yeah, but I don't want all of the attention on me. I don't think I'll tell them what I told you."

"Well, I hope the meeting goes well. What were we going to work on today?"

"I need some help understanding these theories of governmental leadership."

"Let's look at it and get you straightened out."

"Thanks. If it weren't for you, I'd never have gotten through high school. I'm a lucky guy to have you for a teacher. Probably never said thanks, but thanks. You're a great teacher."

"Well, thank you, Devon. That's very nice of you to say that to me."

༄

Heidi walked into the principal's office. She was greeted by Lorraine's secretary, Mary. "What can I do for you, Heidi?"

"Could I see Mrs. Norton? I only need a minute."

"I'll see." She picked up the phone and told Lorraine that Heidi wished a minute with her. Lorraine approved the request. "You may go in."

"Thank you."

Heidi walked into Lorraine's office. "Good morning, Heidi."

"Good morning, Mrs. Norton. Thank you for seeing me on a moment's notice."

"I always try to be available to Shoreline's finest teaching staff."

"I know, and before my question I want to say how pleased we teachers are that you are our principal. Finally, we have a leader who respects teachers, children, and is treating all of us with dignity. We are very thankful you are our principal. I know that's the feeling that pervades this school."

"Thank you, Heidi. You're kind to say those nice things."

"Well, what I've said is true. We were denied an effective principal for so long, you stand out as a wonderful, compassionate leader."

"Thanks. What brings you here, Heidi?"

"I talked with Devon in my fourth-hour class. I told him he looked like he'd lost his best friend. He told me he was concerned about an interview he is apparently having at one o'clock with Mr. Searing, Mrs. McMillan, and his mother."

"Yes, I've set up the meeting. I sensed that Devon was concerned."

"I'd like to ask permission to be with him at this interview."

"I don't know. The interview is at the request of Mr. Searing. He should be the one to decide who is present."

"I understand. I think Devon and I have a good relationship, and I have a sense that he would be more at ease if I were there. The situation has to be very nerve-wracking. Here's this young boy with two detectives and his mother. It seems like he should have somebody in the room from his school family."

"Your request makes sense. I'll contact Mr. Searing to see if he'd approve. It's really his call, but I see your point and will suggest that you be in the interview."

"Thanks, Mrs. Norton."

"I'll get back to you once I learn his decision."

Lorraine tried to call Lou but realized that he would be enroute to Shoreline. She didn't have his car phone number. Her request would have to be made when he arrived.

160

⮞

Miss Whitmore was talking with Devon before his music class. "Have you heard that the *Herald Palladium* wants to do a story about you this weekend?"

"Mom said something about it, yeah."

"I received a phone call from Jane Wills, a writer with the paper. At first I wasn't very happy about it, but on second thought, I think the media coverage would be good for you, and it also gives you some experience dealing with reporters. You're destined to do great things, and I think it's time for you to begin to adjust to this media coverage now."

"What am I supposed to do?"

"Well, as I understand it, the reporter will interview you before, during, and following the festival. They are calling it, 'A Day in the Life of Devon Rockingham.' It's a feature story. Their photographer will be taking photos of you too."

"I don't like all the attention."

"It may be a bit distracting, but it's a part of the entertainment business that's necessary. I don't think it'll be disturbing. I told Miss Wills that I don't want you being distracted for a least two hours before your solo performance. I expect her to honor my request. They'll take pictures, and talk with you. It should be very positive."

Devon was beginning to feel the stress. He didn't mind the public eye for his music, but if everyone knew what he knew, he'd be in the public eye as an informant to a murder in his school. He was about to be interviewed by detectives, interviewed by a reporter, photographed and followed around MSU and then featured in the newspaper the next day.

⮞

Lou arrived at the high school about twelve-thirty. Walking toward Lorraine's office, she greeted him at the door. "Heidi Simpson came in to see me about an hour ago. She asked if she could sit in during the one o'clock interview. Apparently Devon told her he was being interviewed and that his mom would be there, too."

"I don't think that would be a good idea. Initially, I wanted a private talk with the boy. This is getting to look like a community gathering."

"Well, I told her this was your meeting and you'd make the decision."

"On the other hand, it would be interesting to watch Heidi's response to Devon's answers. We might get some body language information by having her present. I'll mention it to Maggie and see what she thinks. Is she here, yet?"

"She's in the conference room."

"I'll see what she thinks."

Lou and Maggie conferred on the request. "If Heidi killed Otterby, she could be wanting to be in the interview to see what is on our minds and what we've learned," Maggie hypothesized.

"I agree. If she's there then there are many witnesses to what she says or does. If she is not there, she would ask Devon what happened, and that might put pressure on him to tell her. If she is present, she'll know Devon's version of what happened. It might ultimately be less stressful for Devon because he seems to trust her a lot."

"On the down side," Maggie added, "Devon might answer differently if she's present. Maybe he did witness the murder and saw his teacher involved. He may not want to admit the truth with her there."

"Got a good point there, Maggie. Well, what does your gut say about this one?"

"My gut says that we should allow her to be in the meeting. While you talk with Devon I'll keep my eyes glued on Heidi. I'll look for her silent signals."

"Okay, she's in."

Lou informed Lorraine of their decision and she went to the phone and called Heidi.

162

Devon was first to arrive for the interview. Lorraine introduced him to Lou and Maggie. He sat down next to Lou. Mary Rockingham and Heidi Simpson arrived at the same time. Lorraine introduced Mary Rockingham to Lou and Maggie. Heidi had already met everyone in the room. Lou asked Lorraine to sit in because of her previous interview with Devon several days earlier.

The square room had a rectangular table and soft chairs. There were paintings on the wall by students at the Shoreline Middle School. Lorraine believed in displaying work from Shoreline students in her conference room. Sharing material between schools was good for public relations. She rotated the art each month.

Coffee was offered by Mrs. Rogalski, but no one seemed interested.

Lou began, "I want to thank you all for coming this afternoon. As you know, Mrs. McMillan and I, along with the police, are investigating the death of Mr. Otterby. We've conducted numerous interviews and have gone over materials obtained in the course of the investigation.

"Mrs. Norton has talked with Devon already about what he may have seen or heard the night of his music lesson which took place down the hall from the pool balcony. Devon, you told Mrs. Norton that you didn't see or hear anything. You looked through the window, but you didn't see anything and you thought this was around ten-fifteen. Have I summarized the events correctly, Devon and Lorraine?"

Both nodded affirmatively. Devon was looking down at the floor. He did not establish any eye contact and seemed to withdraw since introductions were made. Heidi was seated across the table from Devon. She kept her eyes fixed on him.

"We're not here to challenge your observations or your responses to Mrs. Norton, Devon. We have some questions we'd like you to answer for us."

Again looking down Devon mumbled a reply, "Okay."

"Let's go back to that night. You finished your lesson. Mrs. Whitmore had left about a half hour earlier. You continued to practice and then at about 10:10 p.m. you put your instrument away. You left the music room and walked down the hall toward your locker. Am I right so far?"

Devon nodded.

"I take it you noticed that the paint was scraped off of the pool balcony door window. Did you look in?"

Again Devon nodded, and Maggie saw Heidi take a deep breath. Heidi rubbed her hands together as if washing them with air.

"Were the lights on, Devon?"

"There was a light above the diving board."

"Yes, I believe that's the security light. That was the only light on when you looked in?" Lou asked.

Devon nodded.

"Did you notice the water?"

"What do you mean?"

"I mean was the water still?"

"I don't recall."

"So, when you looked into the pool area you don't recall if the pool surface was motionless and glasslike or if there were ripples or disrupted water?" asked Lou.

"I guess it was clear."

"How long did you look through the window, Devon?"

"I'd say about two minutes."

"And in that two minutes you didn't see anyone. Is that correct?"

Devon continued to look down. His hands seemed to be holding the arms of his chair much like a child anticipating a shot of novocaine from the dentist. "That's right. I didn't see anyone." Heidi took another deep breath and then closed her eyes as if in prayer.

"Is it also true that during those two minutes you didn't hear anything, either?"

"I didn't hear anything."

"Devon, I'm going to ask you to be sure about the amount of time you were looking through the window. Time is often difficult to judge. I'm going to ask you to go back to that night. Try to think of yourself coming up to the window. See yourself look in. Beginning

164

now, imagine yourself looking into the window and you tell me when you pulled away and headed for your locker." Lou glanced at his watch.

There was silence as Devon role-played his experience of a week ago. The room was very quiet and motionless, except for Heidi who continued to rub her hands together.

"Okay, I've pulled away," Devon said.

Lou looked at his watch, "That was about a minute and a half. So, unless you correct me, Devon, you were looking in the window for about a minute and a half."

Devon nodded.

"Devon, did you have any purpose for looking in that window that night?"

"No, it's always painted. I noticed that it was clear so I looked in."

"But, you weren't looking for anything or for anybody. You simply looked in because there was a window and you were curious. Is that a true statement?"

"Yes."

"After looking into the pool area, did you see anything that disturbed you?"

Silence. Devon looked up for the first time. He looked directly at Lou and said, "Matthew, chapter 26, verse 52."

"I take it you're referring to some scriptural passage?" Lou asked.

"You asked me what I was thinking after I looked into the pool area. I saw nothing and heard nothing. I was thinking of Matthew 26:52."

"Not being a Biblical scholar, could you refresh my memory of what that passage says?"

Silence. A few seconds later Devon said, "You asked what I was thinking when I left the pool area and that is what I was thinking."

"Actually, my question was, 'After you looked into the pool area, did what you see disturb you?'" Lou repeated.

Silence. Ten seconds later Devon repeated his reference to the Bible, "Matthew 26:52."

Lou decided it would be best not to pursue an interpretation, as

Devon seemed stressed by the interview. He didn't want the boy to feel he was on trial, and he realized the awkwardness of Heidi's presence in the room.

Devon's mother interrupted. "Devon is a biblical scholar in addition to his other talents. As a young boy he used to compete in church Bible scripture contests, and he always did quite well."

"I'm sure he did," Lou said. "Okay, I take it the answer to my question is that what you saw in the pool area did not disturb you, but something triggered your thoughts to Matthew 26:52."

Devon nodded. Heidi squirmed a bit in her chair but said nothing. Mary Rockingham seemed proud of her son's scripture quote, even though she had no idea what it meant.

Lou continued, "You got to your locker and then went on home. Is that correct?"

"Yes."

"Maggie, do you have any questions?"

"No, I don't think so. Thanks for being cooperative, Devon. I wish you the best at MSU's music festival."

"You're welcome and thank you. May I leave now?"

"Yes. Thank you, Devon," Lou said appreciatively.

The room emptied without much being said. Lorraine thanked Mary Rockingham for coming. Heidi walked out and went to her classroom. Lorraine hung around to see if Lou and Maggie needed anything.

"We need a Bible, that's what we need!" said Maggie.

"I've got one in my desk. I'll be back."

Lorraine returned and handed the Bible to Lou. "If you two don't need me any longer I'll leave you to your sleuthing. Kind of a strange meeting if you ask me," said Lorraine.

"Yes, it was, but it was probably our best interview. We've got some good information," said Maggie.

"Oh, really," Lorraine responded. "I never would have guessed that, but that's why I'm a principal and not a private investigator."

"If you don't mind, Lou and I will discuss this in your conference room."

"Absolutely. The room is yours till four o'clock."

Lorraine walked out and closed the door behind her. Lou sat down and Maggie pulled her wheelchair up to the table.

"Devon saw the murder," Lou insisted.

"There's no question about it. And, the way he told us was masterful. What a brilliant kid. He was incredible."

"It was awesome."

"Kudos to you, Lou. A great job of questioning. You pitched up the ball and he, like Mark McGwire, hit it over the center field fence."

"In retrospect, I wish we had the entire interview on video. You're right, it was remarkable. Let's see if our perceptions match. First of all, the most telling item was the length of time he looked through the window."

"Definitely. First he said two minutes, which is a long time. Then when you asked him to act it out, it was more like a minute and a half. Still, a long time."

"Especially a long time if there was nothing to see. Normally a person looking through a window would only look for a few seconds, only a glance if there was nothing to see. Remember, he was tired, he wanted to get home, there was nothing to see but an empty pool area with a security light shining on the water. Devon continued to look into the pool area for what must have seemed to be an eternity."

"I agree."

"And then the part about the Bible. Do you have that verse yet?" Lou urged.

"I'm almost there. Here it is—Matthew, chapters 22, 24, 25 and 26 and let's see... verse 52 says, oh, my God, Lou listen to this: 'Jesus then said, Put your sword back, for all who draw the sword will die by the sword.'"

"Devon is referencing the confrontation he witnessed. The sword refers to the weapon used and his premonition that whoever has the weapon will die because of it," Lou concluded. "Is that how you read it?"

"I guess so. It definitely tells of conflict and the use of a weapon."

"But, he told us that he saw nothing and heard nothing. How do you explain that?" Lou asked.

"I think it has to do with saving face, and Devon not wanting to implicate his teacher or to get involved in any way. He told Lorraine that he didn't see or hear anything. He probably told Heidi that he didn't see or hear anything. With us, he needed to keep his story consistent, so he told us he didn't see or hear anything. By communicating this Biblical scripture to us, he answered our question indirectly."

"Yeah, when you asked, 'Were you bothered by what you saw?' Devon quoted scripture instead of answering your question. That kid is incredible!" Maggie exclaimed.

"We still don't know what he saw, or whom he saw."

"Right, but we now know that he saw conflict. We're on our way. This, plus Heidi's misspelling of 'principal' and her feeling a need to be in the meeting is also telling," Maggie added.

"There's one major problem with Devon's comments. If we go on to conclude that Heidi is the murderer, or involved in killing Otterby, Devon hasn't specifically implicated her. He told several people that he neither saw nor heard anything that night. A jury or a judge would be confused by his cover-up. He's skilled at giving us indirect information, but it won't help the prosecutor's case when this goes to court."

"Good point."

"We'll cross that bridge when we get to it. What did you think about Heidi's reactions to what happened here today?" Lou asked.

"I didn't get a lot. She seemed nervous. She rubbed her hands often, and she took a couple of deep breaths. She even closed her eyes once or twice, as if in prayer. I don't have anything new to add to this mix."

"I agree. I glanced at her a couple of times, and her behavior seemed normal."

"Well, I think this was a major development for us today. I realize we're interpreting Devon's actions and interpreting them to support our theory. We could be off base, but I don't think so. Devon may want to tell us exactly what he saw. We'll have to give him a good opportunity to talk with us. I wonder what he would say if I had a private meeting with him?" Maggie questioned.

"We'll try to arrange a meeting soon. I'm off to Dallas and a meeting with Otterby's sister. Hopefully, I'll learn something significant. I'll keep you posted and you tell me if anything happens up here."

"We're only a phone call away."

༈

Lou arrived at the Dallas-Fort Worth International Airport late in the afternoon. The airport seemed like a city unto itself. His sister, Gayle Brink, greeted him with a hug and a warm smile. Gayle was anxious to hear about Carol and Lou's grandchildren: Ben, Nicholas, and Hannah. "Nana," Lou began, using the nickname Carol uses with her grandchildren, "usually gets out the brag book, but she asked me to bring it to you so you can see our wonderful grandchildren."

"Cute children. You're fortunate grandparents, Lou. You two need to count your blessings every day, if you're not doing so already!"

"You're right. We, or at least I, seem to take all of our good fortune for granted."

Lou's bag floated up to them on the conveyor belt. Lou pulled it off and checked to see that the name tag read "Lou Searing." It did and the two began the long trip out of the airport and toward Dallas. The brother and sister traded news of family members and the interesting and newsworthy events in the lives of both families.

At the Brink home, a spacious, southern colonial home in north Dallas with large white pillars out front and a swimming pool in the back, Lou took a few minutes to unwind from the flight. He and Gayle continued to get caught up on each other's lives. There wasn't much new information to share because they, along with Bob, remained in communication almost daily by e-mail. Nonetheless, both felt comfort in being together.

Lou made a call to Lucy Sayles, Warren Otterby's sister. He'd made arrangements to visit with her before he left Grand Haven. Lucy was home and ready to talk.

Gayle's husband, Dick, called to suggest dinner at the country club. Lou wasn't one to turn down that kind of invitation. He expected his visit with Mrs. Sayles to take an hour at most. He'd planned to be back at the Brink home and ready for dinner around eight-thirty.

Lucy greeted Lou when he arrived. She invited him into her home and offered coffee. "Thank you for agreeing to see me," Lou started. "I'm sorry I didn't get to speak with you when you were up in Shoreline handling Warren's funeral arrangements. Your brother's death has me stymied. I'm hoping you can give me some information or a clue as to why he met such a tragic death."

"I'm so thankful that you're working on this, Mr. Searing. I feel certain Warren didn't commit suicide."

"Please call me Lou. Yes, I agree. I don't think he took his life. If he was killed, it looks as if people in his school may be involved, but I want to look into his personal life to see if any leads surface there. I'm here to learn about your brother."

Lucy was overweight like her brother had been. She wore a muumuu to cover her huge body. It looked comfortable for the warm, hot Dallas afternoon. Lucy's hair was long, combed straight back, and halfway down her back. She wore glasses that sat on the end of her nose. Lou thought of a female Ben Franklin as he talked with her.

"I'm not sure there is much I can share with you, Mr. Searing. Warren was a private person and once we went our separate ways after high school, well college really, we weren't very close."

"I'm sure that what you have to share will be new to me since I've only heard of him as a school principal. I haven't learned anything of his hobbies, interests, or habits."

Lucy took a deep breath before beginning. "He was, shall we say, a loner. I guess he always was. For some reason, Warren didn't have many friends. He didn't draw people to him. He wasn't mean. He didn't bully others. It was just that people were never attracted to him. Maybe it was his weight. I don't know. He never had a girl-friend, not even a close friend who came over to the house. He inter-acted with classmates, mind you, but he never had a close relation-ship with anyone that I knew about. And, I might add, with some regret, that seems to be the case up to the time of his death."

"He never married?"

"Gosh, no. He did date a girl—I wouldn't even call her a girl-friend—for a month or two in college, but she didn't last. I always found Warren likeable; he was my brother, after all. No, he never married."

"Hobbies?"

"You know, he did like sports. He loved sports. In fact, that was the one positive in his life. As a boy, he collected photos of sports fig-ures. He went to games and always watched sports on TV. He and our father would watch the Gillette Friday Night Fights. I remember him always betting on games. Nothing big, mind you, but nickel and dime bets with other kids at school. I remember him saying, 'Won a quarter from Nick Willis today. I bet him the Tigers would win by four and they did, seven to two.' In fact, that was always something we could count on from Warren, a report on his bets."

"Might this have gotten to be a problem in his adult years?" Lou asked. "Was he a compulsive gambler?"

"Oh, I doubt it. It was difficult for Warren to part with his money. He never wanted to throw it away or take a chance on losing any of it. Gambling big-time would really be out of character."

"His lifestyle, talk to me about that."

"His weight always bothered him. He tried to diet, but nothing seemed to work. It basically didn't work because he didn't exercise or eat right. I can't criticize. Warren and I used to think our weight was genetic. Our parents were big people, and for awhile we used that as a crutch. He couldn't control his weight, but he sure could control people and ironically, that's probably why he didn't have any friends. Kind of a vicious circle."

"Interesting. I'm not a psychologist either, but seems like you have an interesting theory. Did he travel or have hobbies?"

"He didn't travel much. He did come down here about once a year to visit with my husband me. He'd stay no more than a day or two. And, he did like to go to Las Vegas. He liked the shows. He liked the climate. But, other than a couple of trips to Vegas and a yearly trip here, I don't recall his saying much about travel."

"Did he play sports?" Lou asked.

"He was too big. He would have liked to, I'm sure, but people who weigh as much as we do are only good for sumo wrestling and I'm not trying to be funny. I think he played cards, chess, and the like, but no, Warren was much too big for most sports."

"Do you know of anyone he despised? Did he ever speak of having a conflict with anyone? Did he owe anybody any money? Did he have a drug problem? Was he a pusher of drugs? Did he smuggle cigarettes, booze, drugs? I know these things are probably outrageous for you to think about your brother doing, but most families have secrets and black sheep."

"I understand why you must ask. The answer is, I simply don't know. All of those things would surprise me, but I must admit that he could have gotten involved in such things. Warren would go to great lengths to have a friend, to make some people like him. I don't know. He was always a law-abiding citizen, so it would shock me if he was doing something illegal."

"Have you got any pictures of Warren that I could see?"

"Certainly. I can show you the family albums. I might get a little emotional going through them so soon after Warren died and all, but I'll get a few albums and share them with you."

Lucy took four albums from a desk drawer in her living room. She sat down next to Lou and went from page to page identifying every person in each photo. At this rate, Lou thought he would miss dinner with his family.

"A wonderful family, Lucy. What I'm looking for is any picture that might have Warren in it with a friend, acquaintance, you know, people in his life outside of school."

"Okay, sure, this must be a little boring for a stranger. Let me see if I can find what you're looking for."

"Who is that?" asked Lou focusing on a group shot of Warren and several young people.

"That was taken on a cruise ship a year ago. He went on a cruise and had a lot of fun, as I recall. He purchased this photo and sent it to me. I don't know any of the people, but it's a good picture of Warren, isn't it?"

"Yes, it is. Could I take this back with me, Lucy? I'll mail it back."

"Of course. Do you see something that might be helpful?"

"Not sure, but it shows Warren with a lot of people who are not school people and it might be helpful down the line. That's all. Can you tell me more about this cruise?"

"He called one night saying that he had a chance to go on a cruise, up to Alaska I think, and that he was planning to go."

"He didn't say with whom he was going? Friends, principals, alumni group, anything like that?"

"Oh, yes, he said it was an alumni cruise through Western Michigan University. Sorry, I forgot. He did say that."

"This was a year or two ago?"

"Last summer. It was June of last summer, almost a year ago."

Lucy offered Lou another cup of coffee and a chocolate chip cookie. "I'll take a cookie, chocolate chip cookies are my favorite. Thanks. Maybe a warm-up for my coffee. Thanks." Lou looked at his watch; he didn't want to miss his dinner date. Guiltily, Lou reminded himself that he was in Dallas to investigate the death of Warren Otterby and not to eat fancy meals.

Lucy brought big cookies with gigantic chunks of chocolate in them. Lou thought he had died and gone to heaven. While Lou and Lucy munched on cookies and sipped hot coffee, Lou continued his questioning. "Was Warren active in church?"

"No. We were raised Catholic but he had some serious disagreements with our priest as a teenager. It frustrated him so he left the church. In fact, he's never been back in a church since then, that I know of anyway."

"What was the nature of the disagreement?"

"I don't know. I just took it as another problem with Warren's need to be in control, and as you may know, the only one in control of a Catholic church is the priest. I assumed the two had a power struggle over something and that the priest won. Warren couldn't take loss. He quit."

"Does he have any strong political affiliation?"

"I wouldn't say strong. I think he leaned more toward Republican than Democrat. He didn't like government intervention and the Republicans seem to do less of that in education than the Democrats. But, I don't recall him ever working in a campaign or wearing a button to support a candidate or putting a bumper sticker on his car to support someone."

"Did he like being principal, Lucy?"

"Oh, yes. He loved it. Maybe it was the control he loved, because he had that control over his school. He was like the priest. He could control what happened in his school. He could do what he wanted, when he wanted. He was in his glory, Lou. I think he realized that some people didn't like the way he ran his school, but he often said that leadership is a lonely business, and for the good of all, he needed to run a tight ship."

"Did he ever say how he felt about minorities and special education students?"

"Well, yes. He didn't think they should get any more attention than anyone else. He didn't like special treatment, special classes, special rights. It could go back to his younger days again, Mr. Searing. He didn't get any special attention for his problems, for his weight and his lack of friends. Since he didn't get any special help for his problems, or his perceived problems, he didn't think others should have any special help."

"But the state and federal laws disagree with him."

Lucy shook her head sadly, "I'm not saying Warren was right, or that I was proud of his attitude or how he ran his school, but being a principal and being in charge of a school allowed him to be a king in his kingdom. In Warren's kingdom, people did what Warren decided should be done. It may have been his downfall, but that was Warren."

"These cookies are great, Lucy. Make them yourself?"

"That's a Texas State Fair winner you're eating," said Lucy with pride.

"Delicious. Simply delicious!"

"All I did was add extra butter and more chocolate chips. People like the chocolate and the moist texture of the cookie. I gave 'em what they wanted. There is a big contrast in the Otterby family. I gave 'em what they wanted and Warren gave 'em what he wanted. I guess that sums it up."

"Yes, and on that note, I'll be on my way. I have a family-get-together in about a half-hour. My sister lives in north Dallas and we're going out to dinner."

"Enjoy your stay here in Texas, Lou. You call if you think I can help with anything else. I hope you solve this."

"We will. You've been helpful. Thanks. I'll get this picture back to you in the near future."

Lou pulled away and headed toward Gayle's home and dinner. The photo intrigued him. He couldn't put his finger on it, but in his gut he felt that there might be some connection between Warren's death and this cruise. He didn't mention it to Lucy, but he saw Heidi Simpson in the photo.

Once at Gayle's, and before heading for dinner, Lou called Maggie. "I've just finished a long conversation with Otterby's sister. It was a good interview and I'll give you all the details when I arrive tomorrow around noon. I'd like you to call Heidi and indicate that we'd like a meeting with her and her lawyer tomorrow at, say three-thirty."

"Be glad to, Lou. At her apartment?"

"Sure, that's good."

"I'll make the arrangements. If I have any problems, I'll call you on your pager. Will you be reachable in the next several hours?"

"I'm always reachable. I'll be at dinner, but I'll have my cell phone and beeper. Give me a call if you need to. Otherwise I'll be at Heidi's apartment tomorrow at three-thirty."

"Can you satisfy my curiosity a bit before we meet tomorrow?"

"Yeah. Warren's sister gave me a photo of a group of people on a cruise. It looks like Heidi Simpson was on that cruise. The group was an alumni gathering from Western Michigan University. I need to confirm if she was on that cruise. I'm sure there will be other things to talk about as well, but that's my primary motivation for wanting a meeting with her."

"Okay, I'll get right on it."

As the three arrived at the fashionable Gleneagles Country Club, Dick said to Lou, "Wish you were going to be around long enough to play eighteen."

"That sure would be great. I came down here for an interview and got lucky with a chance to see you and Gayle. I've got to get home to solve this murder. It's foremost on my mind. But, this course looks like fun to play. The fairways are beautiful and the greens look smooth."

The three entered the dining room at eight-thirty. Gayle and Dick ordered drinks and Lou chose decaf coffee. The family toasted to better golf and happy days ahead. The conversation turned naturally to Lou and his purpose for being in Dallas.

"So tell me more about this murder," said Dick.

"A principal was found dead in his high school pool in Shoreline, Michigan. The police initially thought it was a suicide because a note was left on his desk. Maggie and I have uncovered a lot of circumstantial evidence that points directly to school people; a special education teacher and an athletic director, to be more exact. They claim they're being framed, and maybe they are. A student in the school may have seen something. Maggie and I think he did, but he hasn't been specific about what or whom he saw. I'm down here to visit with the dead principal's sister who lives in Richardson. If there's a non-school involvement in his death, I've got to learn about other sides of the man's life."

"And did you?" Dick asked.

"It wasn't a waste of time by any means. Did I find a major clue to solve the mystery? No, I don't think so, but I did come upon one picture that might help me a bit. It is a group photo of a WMU alumni group taking an Alaskan cruise. The photo has the principal in it, along with several other people. One of the people looks to be the suspect who is a special education teacher, Heidi Simpson."

Gayle looked very surprised, "Heidi Simpson? A beautiful woman, short blond hair, perfect skin, Miss America candidate type?"

"Yes, she's quite attractive. You know her?" Lou asked.

"No, but I'm fairly certain my good friend in Ohio knew her when she was at Western Michigan University. My friend was an education major and a Heidi Simpson was on the homecoming court. I think Sherry was a junior and this Heidi was a senior. I'll bet it's the same woman. She has to be."

"Which friend is this?" Lou asked.

"Sherry Hucklebee. You probably knew her by her maiden name, Sherry Ball."

"Oh yeah, I remember her. A very good friend of yours, as I recall."

"Puts it mildly, she's my best friend."

"Does Sherry still know Heidi? Do they keep in touch?"

"I don't know. I doubt it. Do you want to call her and see what she knows?"

"Sure." Lou pulled out his cellular phone. While the salads were being served, Lou handed the phone to Gayle to dial.

It was an hour later in Elyria, Ohio, a suburb on the west side of Cleveland. Sherry answered the phone, happy to hear from her best friend in Dallas. The two talked for a moment before Gayle indicated the reason for the call and reminded Sherry of her brother, Lou. With the purpose of the call and introductions made, Lou took the phone, greeted Sherry and got right to the point of his call. "What can you tell me about Heidi Simpson?"

"She's a beautiful, articulate, and committed woman who cares about kids."

"Any skeletons in the closet that you know of?"

"Gambling."

"Gambling? In what way?"

"She hangs around with a shady crowd. With her beauty and popularity, you'd think she could pick and choose her friends and they'd be good folks, but that isn't Heidi. I don't know if you heard, but she was abducted and raped a few years ago."

"I heard that."

"Well, that devastated her. She's very cautious around strangers and carries a gun. But, I guess we all have some vice whether it be smoking, drinking, poor money decisions or whatever."

"So, Heidi's vice is gambling?" Lou repeated.

"She couldn't stay away from a bet. Her bets ranged from a dollar on Monday night football to thousands of dollars on a card game, sporting event, or a horse race."

"Did she get help for this problem? You know, professional help, support groups, Gambler's Anonymous, anything like that?"

"After the rape she did. I don't see her much anymore. We communicate once a year by sending each other a Christmas card. I think she's been trying to get help with the problem, and maybe she's got it licked by now. I really can't say."

"Did she take a cruise last year?"

"That was in her Christmas letter. She went with an alumni group from Western. I remember that because I took that inside passage cruise several years ago and enjoyed it. I mentioned it to Gayle hoping she and Dick would like to go. I commented about Heidi to Gayle only because it was a sad story. Here is this incredibly beautiful woman. She's a gifted teacher, and yet, she's in the grip of this compulsion to gamble. The stories she'd tell me when we were at WMU were scary, but also very interesting to me. After all, I was a naive girl from a rural community."

"In what way do you mean scary?"

"She received threats when she didn't pay her debts. The folks she dealt with expected payoffs and sometimes the threats and retaliation were incredible."

"What kind of retaliation?"

"Death for one. Significant injury—you know, broken bones, accidents, stuff like that. If you were going to bet with the crowd that she found herself embroiled in, you paid, and if you didn't have the resources, you found them. I gave her money once. I never saw it again and I never loaned her any after that, but she convinced me that she needed it to escape harm."

"Fifty bucks?"

"Don't I wish! I'm embarrassed to tell you what I lost, but no, it wasn't a nickel and a dime loan, Lou."

"Well, thanks. Gayle and Dick have finished their salads and are well into their land and sea. You've been helpful, Sherry. Thanks. I'll give you back to Gayle for a 'Good-bye.'" Lou handed the phone to Gayle and began eating his tossed salad.

"Boy, this is a small world story. Every time I turn around, I find more reason to suspect Heidi. Now I find out that she may have a gambling problem, and I also know that Otterby, the dead principal, had a similar problem. The two are linked in more than one regard."

"Well, enjoy your lobster and steak," Gayle said. "Try to let your investigation work go for an hour or so."

"This is very good lobster," Lou said, with a smile on his face and a fashionable bib around his neck. "The last lobster I had was in Bar Harbor, Maine, last summer, right in the heart of lobster country."

"Well, this one could have been out in a Maine bay this morning. Our chef has them flown in daily so you are getting the real thing," Dick said with pride in his country club. The rib-eye steak was equally good. Dick, Gayle, and Lou passed on dessert.

While Lou was enjoying his dinner with Gayle and Dick at the Gleneagles Country Club, Maggie was arriving home. She skillfully exited her accessible van and entered her universal design home. Maggie's home was a marvel of convenience. While designed for someone in a wheelchair, its features—wide hallways and door-ways, spacious bathrooms, and lowered countertops were a wel-come convenience for any able-bodied person. Maggie offered to have her home shown as part of the Battle Creek Home Tour and the organizers immediately accepted her offer. The home is literally a home of the future for people with and without disabilities.

In her office, Maggie found her phone message light blinking.

After turning on her computer and accessing America Online, she heard that she had some mail. She glanced below the fax machine and found a couple of pages waiting. She immediately looked them over, hoping to get the transcript from Detective Mallard. She was disappointed because the fax material was a recipe from a friend in California who, on a Christmas card, had offered to send Maggie the recipe for Chain Saw Chocolate Delight, a frozen chocolate and brownie treat that was delicious. As much as she enjoyed receiving the recipe, she was disappointed not to get the information she expected from the Shoreline police.

Maggie pushed the "play" button on her answering machine and listened to the first of three messages.

"Maggie, this is Daniel Mallard. We have the transcript you requested. We're going to have to reopen the case. This stuff gives us new evidence, and I think we need to pull back on the suicide theory. Give me a call when you get in, even if it's late this evening. My number is 555-6668."

Maggie was curious. Before even listening to the second and third messages, she dialed the number. Mallard's answering machine said to leave a message. He'd be paged and would call as soon as he could. He did.

"Hello."

"Maggie? This is Dan Mallard."

"Thanks for calling. I got your message about the transcript from the typewriter ribbon."

"Yeah, the lab technicians got it lifted and it's revealing."

"You didn't fax it to me."

"No, I wanted to talk with you first."

"What's on your mind?"

"Well, what he'd written were notes to Heidi Simpson and to Rick Bolt. They appear to be two separate short memos. To Heidi he writes, 'I'm sorry about all of the problems I've created for you and the special education folks. I've seen the errors of my ways and am looking forward to making significant changes for the better. This school has a bright future in special education and with your leadership and my support we'll turn things around. Sincerely, Warren Otterby, Principal.'"

"They don't sound like the last words of someone about to die," offered Maggie.

"I agree. That's what I mean about having to rethink our conclusions on this case."

"What did he say to Rick?"

"To Rick he writes, 'I'm sorry to be a threat to you and your coaching staff. I should never have acted in such an immature way. I'm sorry for trying to win at all costs and for jeopardizing our good standing with the Michigan High School Athletic Association. Please forgive my behavior. You will see a changed man. Sincerely, Warren Otterby, Principal.'"

"Once again, not the final words of a man about to die."

"Definitely not. However, I wish to point out that if Warren didn't type the note, which we believed to be the suicide note, he may not have typed these two notes either."

"I realize that. Did those two notes get delivered?"

"Well, that's another piece of the story. We confiscated some of Warren's possessions when we did our search of his office and found the suicide note. We took his briefcase, but didn't do more than take a cursory look inside. Late this afternoon we found both of those notes in his briefcase with his personal initials by his typed name. Both were dated the day he died. I forgot to mention that to you. So, I imagine they weren't delivered."

"But, as you say, those could have also been planted in his briefcase after his death."

"Yeah, they could have."

"Well, that's an interesting development. Thanks for sharing. Are you aggressively going back into this case?"

"Yeah. We're not going to go public with the news just yet. I'd like to know what you and Lou have uncovered. Hopefully we can work together to see this thing through."

"So, you're now willing to admit that the goose may not be dead?"

"My face is red, the goose is not dead," Dan Mallard said sheepishly.

"We don't think so, either. I'll call Lou and brief him. I'm sure he'll welcome the three of us working together. In anticipation of that, can we meet tomorrow?"

"Absolutely."

"Okay, we'll need to meet late in the afternoon. Lou is in Dallas and arrives in Grand Rapids around noon tomorrow. We have a scheduled meeting with Heidi at her apartment after school. We could meet with you around four-thirty."

"Great."

"Can you fax those transcripts, now that we've talked about them?"

"Oh sure. I'll do that right now."

"I'll send 'em on to Lou, and you can be assured that these are for our eyes only."

"Good. Thanks for calling back."

"Thanks for sharing. The plot thickens. We'll put our heads together tomorrow and perhaps some direction will become obvious."

"Have a good evening, Maggie. My best to Lou."

࿇

As the sun set over the 18th green, Dick requested his car from valet parking. Dick tipped the young man once the car was under the canopy. They drove home to sit in front of the big screen TV and watch Michael Jordan guide the Windy City's pride and joy by helping the Bulls to yet another playoff win.

That evening Lou called Carol to see how she was doing in Grand Haven. She reported that she, Samm, Luba, and Millie were relaxing at home. The evening had been peaceful. She had a friend stop in for a visit and they had taken a stroll along the beach. Lou told her about his pleasant evening with Gayle and Dick. He also reported that his interview with the principal's sister was worth the trip and that he expected to be landing in Grand Rapids by late morning. The couple wished each other a good night and warm thoughts of their reunion the next day.

⤳

Maggie called Lou in Dallas as the Bulls' game was going into overtime. "Am I interrupting anything, Lou?"

"Only overtime in the Bulls' game. I'll keep an eye on it. What have you got for me?"

"First of all, we're all set to meet with Heidi tomorrow afternoon at her apartment. Her lawyer will be there too. I want to tell you about something that I initiated on my own. I'm not trying to go around you, Lou, but I had an idea and decided to act on it."

"You've got my curiosity," Lou said.

"Well, we know that according to the police, Warren typed his suicide letter and the police confirmed that the ribbon on the typewriter did reflect that message. I was curious if any other typing had occurred on that ribbon before or after the suicide note. I called Detective Mallard and asked if I could have access to the ribbon. He agreed and added his own comment on our work by asking, 'Are you and Lou still chasing that dead goose?' I told him, 'We'll chase the dead goose until we're absolutely certain the goose is dead,'" Maggie laughed.

"Of course he countered saying, 'Well, you folks need to have something to do to bring some meaning to your lives.' Then he admitted that there could be a connection to the teaching staff, especially Heidi Simpson and Rick Bolt. Lou, they're keeping the case open pending significant evidence. Their official position is still suicide.

"I told him we were surprised that his staff didn't confiscate the note to Otterby from Bolt, inviting him to the pool at 10:10 or the letter from the Mothers for Justice lady. He said he didn't know of these. They reviewed everything on Otterby's desk and felt that those weren't there the night of the murder. I told him they were there the next day at noon. He wanted to see them, and of course, I promised to share them, especially since he was going to be helpful with the typewriter ribbon. He told me I could stop by his office and see any of the evidence.

"So, I did. I discovered that there were other messages typed on Otterby's typewriter before the suicide note. The lab technicians were going to give me a transcript of what was typed. I asked them to call me when they completed their analysis."

"Great stroke of work, Maggie. We could get another great clue with that. Ah, you're a terrific investigator. We're due for some good news."

"Well, Mallard called this evening and there are two messages typed before the alleged suicide note, and neither message seems to be from a man about to commit suicide. Do you have a fax machine where you are?"

"Yeah. I'm sure they have one. Just a minute." Lou asked Gayle for their fax machine number. She gave it to him and he passed it on to Maggie.

"I'll fax you the two messages. Remember the "o" key is damaged and the "o" looks like a "c."

"H-m-m, very interesting. So, Mallard is coming around to this not being a suicide?"

"Yup, reopening the case. He wants to work with us."

"This continues to be quite a drama, doesn't it?"

"It sure doesn't look good for Rick or Heidi, does it?"

"No, I'm afraid it doesn't. If Devon is eventually willing to say that the woman in that pool was Heidi Simpson, my guess is the prosecutor will issue a warrant for her arrest, and it will be quite a fight in court."

"Well, I'll let you get back to Michael Jordan and your relatives."

"Thanks for the call. I'll drive right from Grand Rapids to be at Heidi's apartment by three-thirty, and then we'll meet with Mallard. Correct?"

"That's right. Have a safe flight, Lou. See you tomorrow."

184

᠀

The Brink's fax machine sounded the familiar one ring and then slowly and methodically spit out two pages of material from Maggie. It was the transcript she had been promised from detective Mallard. Handwritten on the fax was a message from Maggie: "Hi, Lou. For your eyes only. Maggie."

᠀

Reverend Wheeler was checking his phone messages at eleven o'clock when it dawned on him that once again he had forgotten to contact Devon Rockingham, as he had promised Mr. Lancour he'd do a couple of days ago. Once again, it was too late. He'd call in the morning before Devon would leave for school. That would be a good time. He'd call Laughton Lancour as well and apologize for his tardiness in reaching the boy. This wasn't like him, but there was too much going on to get all the sheep in his flock taken care of. Dr. Wheeler no longer felt there was any need to call Devon, but that wasn't the point. He told Laughton he would do it, so he would have to live up to his reputation and be a man of his word.

CHAPTER 10

Friday, May 20

The citizens of Shoreline had something to talk about. Subscribers to the *Herald Palladium* read the lead article in their morning paper, "New Information in Principal's Death — Otterby May Have Been Murdered." The article began, "The *Herald Palladium* has learned that new information has surfaced in the death of Shoreline High School Principal, Warren Otterby. After a series of interviews, following the police announcement last week of a probable suicide, current talk is of a possible conspiracy to murder the principal. Added to this new twist in the investigation is a persistent rumor that the murder was witnessed. Unnamed sources indicate that the possible eye witness was a student who may have seen the murder through a window in the balcony door. There have been no warrants for arrests, but it appears that the once believed theory of suicide has given way to a possible homicide."

The article was not attributed to a staff writer. With Lou in Texas and Maggie in Battle Creek, neither saw the paper. It wasn't until Lorraine called Maggie around 10:00 a.m. that the details in the article were revealed. Maggie quickly reached Lou with the news.

Detective Mallard was furious with the leak and quick to suspect that Searing and McMillan were responsible. The article was an embarrassment to the Shoreline Police and, Duck Mallard thought, much too premature. He called the editor of the *Herald Palladium* to see who was responsible. He was told that the source of the information was reliable and that the paper would stand by its story. The editor did say that the source of the information was not Searing nor McMillan and claimed never to have heard of them.

Lou called Jane Wills because he suspected that she had convinced her editor to run the article based on something that she had learned. "Good morning, Jane. This is Lou Searing calling from O'Hare airport in Chicago."

"Calling about the article in the paper this morning, aren't you, Lou?"

"Yeah. I'm curious about what the newspaper knows and why they feel it is strong enough to publish."

"I'm glad you called. I've been feeling a bit embarrassed about this. I thought that you'd suspect me of having something to do with it."

"I'm not suggesting that the information is false or ill-timed, but I'm curious to know who is feeding the editor the information. I didn't realize anyone knew of our theories and information. I was taken aback to have the readers of the paper know what Maggie and I know, that's all."

"I understand. I know nothing about the article. That may sound strange, Lou, but it's the truth. I feel like somebody has been in my sandbox on this issue. I've been asking staff, and so far I'm getting nowhere. I'll keep probing and let you know if I learn who is giving us info and who is on the receiving end. The broadcast media had nothing on this story, so whoever is feeding the paper isn't going to radio or TV."

The newspaper's announcement was the first strong indication to the murderers that suicide was no longer believed to be the principle cause of death.

꒰ꞈ꒱

Devon Rockingham was now at the center of the drama. This was exactly where he didn't want to be. He trusted Dr. Wheeler's advice that the truth would make him free, and so far he only felt trapped. Most of the people in the school—students, faculty, and administration—suspected that Devon was the "witness" to the crime. He had told his girlfriend Wendy, hinted to Miss Simpson that he suspected she was involved, and he had suggested to Searing and McMillan and others in the room that he saw conflict and a weapon used via his biblical reference. So, in a sense he was telling the truth, but he had not come forward in a formal way to tell the world what he had seen a week ago Wednesday night.

People of the community were talking. Most felt certain that Devon had witnessed the murder. Rumors were spreading that it was probably Heidi Simpson and Rick Bolt who committed the crime. Heidi and Rick found themselves living inside a fishbowl with everyone looking in at them. In class, in the hall, and sitting at staff meetings there was a sense of questioning in the eyes of everyone they encountered.

Lorraine asked Heidi and Rick to come to her office. She empathized with what they were going through, having herself become aware of the rumors throughout the school and community. Heidi took advantage of the meeting and Lorraine's compassion to ask if she could use some of her sick leave days to be away from school. She told Lorraine that her doctor had advised her that stress and the accusations were beginning to affect her health.

Lorraine said, "Under the circumstances, I think a few sick leave days would be most appropriate. How about you, Rick? How are you doing?"

"The thing is on my mind a lot and it might be less stressful to be away from school, but to me, being away might indicate that I participated in his death. I didn't, and I'll keep coming to school and hope that time will heal."

"I understand what Rick is saying," Heidi said. "He has to do what's best for him. For me, I'm going to, with your support, take a few sick days. I think people are pretty well-convinced that I did this, and if Devon comes out and convincingly puts me at the scene of the crime, I'm in for a long trial that may put me in prison. I'll tell you where I am so that you'll be able to reach me. I'd like to visit my parents and explain all of this to them. They live in Minnesota. They need to be prepared for what might happen to me in the future."

"I respect your decisions," Lorraine said. "I'll call for a substitute who'll take your class on Monday."

"I have a meeting with Mr. Searing and Mrs. McMillan later this afternoon," Heidi said. "After meeting with them, I'll pack up and head for Minnesota. Let me give you my parents' address and phone number now and then I'll have that out of the way."

The two teachers shook hands with Lorraine. Rick and Heidi returned to their classes, feeling very good about Mrs. Norton's support.

Devon's parents, under their doctor's suggestion, asked Lorraine for permission for Devon to remain at home for several days until the situation was settled. The trauma was unhealthy for him, and he had this important music competition coming up at MSU.

Mrs. Norton was sympathetic and helpful. She arranged for a homebound teacher to be the link between teachers and Devon while he stayed at home and worked on his schoolwork and practiced for the competition from his father's office.

The murderers were very concerned that the news of their perfect crime may have been witnessed by a student in the high school. Prior to the murder, the pool area had been thoroughly studied. Each door and window was identified and tested for privacy. As of one o'clock on Wednesday, May 11, all windows were covered and all doors were locked. The balcony window, it was perceived, did not need a final check because it was painted. The slip was not noticing that the balcony window had been scraped between the 6:00 p.m. check and the murder. Having the kid witness the murder meant that he could talk, if he hadn't already. If the student did see the murder and talked, the murderers would have little hope of winning in a trial by jury. The only thing that could assure freedom, as opposed to life in prison, was to silence the student. It would take another attempt at the perfect murder for this to happen.

꒜

Lou and Maggie arrived at Heidi's apartment about the same time. Heidi's attorney, Harold Marshburn, had been with Heidi for several minutes before the scheduled meeting. He wanted to meet with her and brief her on what to say, what not to say, and to try and limit her remarks to simply answering the investigators' questions as clearly and as briefly as possible.

Heidi welcomed Lou and Maggie into her apartment and ushered them into her living room. They shook hands with Mr. Marshburn and took their seats. The living room was decorated with a lot of glass and modern furniture. The carpeting was white, so white that Lou decided not to take coffee or tea if it was offered. He didn't want to be responsible for spilling a drop on the carpet. To offset the white carpeting, Heidi had a black leather sofa and black-upholstered chairs.

Heidi offered drinks, but all declined. Lou began the discussion. "Thanks for meeting with us this afternoon." He looked directly into the eyes of each listener. "We thought it best to clear the air, so to speak, on some of the things under investigation. I want to personally explain to you, Heidi, that my decision not to offer my services to you and Mr. Bolt has nothing to do with my belief of your innocence or guilt. Rather, it has to do with our wanting to be free of any bias as we do our work."

"Oh, I understand, that. We just thought that with your being so supportive of special education, students, and teachers, we could count on you to be on our side."

"You can count on us being on the side of justice. If you're innocent, we'd be relieved, thankful and would share in your relief. If you're involved in this murder, we..."

"Mr. Searing, I did not kill Warren Otterby. I killed him many times in my imagination—I won't deny that. He was evil. Do you understand? But, I did not kill him!" Heidi demonstrated her emotion with a shrill tone of voice and obvious agitation.

Attorney Marshburn responded, "You'll try to understand that my client is under a lot of stress given the false accusations that are being made about her. This teacher's career is in jeopardy."

"We're aware of the stress and the frustration that you're under, Heidi. We want to get this thing settled as much as you do. Our meeting here today is a step in that direction."

Harold interjected, "We accept your unwillingness to investigate this case on our behalf. Now, you had some questions for my client?"

"Yes. Heidi, I've found a photograph of a group of alumni from Western Michigan University and it looks like you are in the picture. Could you verify that?" Lou asked, handing the photo to Heidi and her lawyer.

Heidi did not immediately respond. She looked at her attorney to get a go-ahead signal. Harold nodded and Heidi spoke. "Yes, I did go on a cruise last summer to Alaska. And, yes this man is Warren Otterby."

"Was it difficult for you to share this cruise with a man whom you have described as 'evil'?"

"Yes and no. Yes in a sense that I can't forgive him for the way he acts as a principal and the way he treats the teachers and students. No, in the sense that we're both addicted to gambling. You probably didn't know that about me, but it's a problem in my life, and I admit it. I don't do drugs and I don't have a host of other vices, but I do have a problem with gambling. Warren was a gambler too. I don't know if you know that, either. So, on this cruise I was able to see this side of him and he became an opponent. In the casino, he was a new personality, someone who took risks, big risks. I didn't like him or respect him, but we were on equal footing, so to speak. We both gambled, knew the ins and outs of the activity, and we did a lot of gambling on that cruise."

Lou continued the questioning without admitting that he knew both were gamblers, "Did he pay off his debts?"

"The price to not pay off a debt is sometimes high."

"Could one pay with his life?" asked Maggie.

Once again there was silence. Harold suggested that Heidi not answer the question. Maggie made note of her refusal.

"What can you tell us about Warren Otterby and his gambling here in Shoreline?"

Heidi pondered the question and seemed confused, "I'm not sure I understand your question, Mrs. McMillan."

"Do you know if he gambled here, in town? You know that he did on the cruise. If he gambled in town, did you gamble with him? Who did he gamble with? What kind of gambling did he do? Horses? Cards? Sports?"

"Oh, I see." Once again she looked to Harold for direction. He nodded, indicating it was all right to proceed.

"Yes, I knew of Warren Otterby, the gambler. Yes, I gambled against him, mostly sports. He had several people he gambled with. I know a few, but certainly not all. On the cruise he talked about the three you mentioned: horses, cards, and sports."

"Let me ask again. Did he pay his losses?"

"Let me respond again, the price not to pay is high."

"Meaning?"

"Meaning in the gambling business, you pay. You find someway to pay. School kids can say they had their fingers crossed or they were just kidding, but in our circles, you pay."

"Maybe Warren Otterby didn't pay, Miss Simpson. Maybe his price for not paying was drowning in the high school swimming pool. Is that possible, Miss Simpson?"

Heidi nodded, "It's possible."

"Do you pay your losses?" Maggie asked.

Once again Heidi looked to Harold for guidance. Once again he nodded for her to proceed. "My record for paying my debts is pretty good."

"Pretty good means you don't always pay?"

"Let's just say I use discretion. Like Kenny Rogers sings, 'You gotta know when to hold 'em and know when to fold 'em.' I say, you've gotta know to whom you need to immediately pay, and how much, and when and to whom you can pay on an installment plan."

"An installment plan?"

"Yeah, like a loan you pay back a little at a time."

"Did Warren pay or not pay on the installment plan?"

"It depends on who he was in debt to."

"Was he in debt to you, Miss Simpson?" asked Lou.

Harold reached over and touched Heidi on the arm. She looked at him and he shook his head.

"I can't answer that. Sorry." Maggie took note of this refusal.

"Let me come right out and ask you, do you have any idea who killed Warren Otterby?"

Once again Heidi looked to Harold for direction. Harold shook his head negatively. Heidi simply said, "I can't answer that."

"You can't think of anybody who might have done this to him, nobody at all?"

She repeated, "I'd like to help you, but I can't. Unless maybe Phyllis Weaver." Harold looked like he regretted her comment, but he let her continue to answer the questions.

"Who is Phyllis Weaver?"

"She lives in Kalamazoo. She's a sick lady."

"Is Phyllis an installment plan type of gambler?" Maggie asked.

"Not on your life."

"Did Warren know Phyllis?"

"I don't know."

"Describe Phyllis Weaver."

"She looks like a model. She's quite a beautiful woman actually. She has short blond hair, medium height, and a figure most women would die for."

"Does she live in Kalamazoo? Is her name and address in the phone book?" Lou asked.

"Yes to both questions."

"What makes you think that maybe Phyllis Weaver killed Otterby?" Lou continued.

"She's got no patience for no-pays. Absolutely none. I owed her one grand a year ago and I knew that if I didn't pay in twenty-four hours in cash, I was going to meet some fate. I feared for my life. I found the money and relaxed, but if you owe Phyllis and you can't come up with the money, you won't sleep well that night."

"You may not get through the night?" Lou asked.

"May not."

"So, if Otterby owed Phyllis Weaver some money and he couldn't come up with it, he could die in his swimming pool?" Maggie asked.

Once again, the indication from the attorney was to let that question go unanswered. Heidi did. Maggie noted the lack of response.

"Let me wind this up by saying what the two of you already know. It doesn't look good for you, Heidi. We want to solve this thing and if you can give us any information that helps us do that, we'd welcome it. The circumstantial evidence is quite high and it has you in the pool area that night. There's probably enough circumstantial evidence to convince the prosecuting attorney to have you arrested. I've seen weaker cases go to the judge."

"I've taken a couple of sick days at school," Heidi said. "I'll be going to Minnesota as soon as I can pack. Mr. Marshburn has my address and phone number if you need to reach me. I expect to be back in time to see Devon perform at MSU on Monday afternoon."

"Thanks for talking with us today."

"Sure. Listen, I don't need to get on the wrong side of Phyllis. I didn't say she did it. The last thing I need is for her to know that I'm pointing a finger at her. You asked who I think did this. I said I didn't know, but it could have been Phyllis, just as it could have been the Pillsbury doughboy. I've got enough over my head without having a sick woman after me for thinking she may have killed somebody."

༜

Lou and Maggie drove to the police station to talk with Detective Mallard. "Got a whole new look at this case," Duck said. "Don't like to admit it, but I guess I should've taken you up on your offer to help last week."

"We understand," Lou responded. "We respect your work, and realize that professionals don't tend to like having strangers interfering. What's past is past. How can we work together now? I think we're pretty close to having this thing figured out."

"I'll tell you this, we're about to present our case to the prosecuting attorney. We've asked the student, Devon Rockingham, for an interview in an hour. The family lawyer informed me that while the Rockingham family didn't want to be seen as uncooperative, they would only allow Devon to be questioned if we had a subpoena. I requested one and the prosecuting attorney has issued one. He and his mother are coming down here, and I'm hopeful we can get a good description of what he saw that night. If he saw Heidi Simpson, we're going for a warrant for her arrest."

"I see. Since Maggie has shared with you what we know, I assume you have some additional information?"

"No, nothing other than a description by Devon, and I expect him to implicate Miss Simpson. This is what we've got based on your findings and ours. I'm quite certain Heidi Simpson is the murderer. She was in the pool area that evening, she stayed in the school late hoping not to be discovered. She had a gun with her. She lied to you about using the phone, which tells me you can't trust her alibis, and it also feeds her covering up the possibility she did it. She disliked, or to be stronger, hated Otterby, and even referred to him as evil. For me, this adds up to a good reason for killing the guy. If Devon puts her in the pool area with Otterby, we're going for an arrest."

"Does the name Phyllis Weaver of Kalamazoo mean anything to you?" Lou asked.

"Oh, sure. Why do you bring up her name?" Duck asked raising his eyebrows and cocking his head to one side.

"We've learned that she's rather street smart in the world of gamblers. She expects payment and threatens those who don't follow their loss with the cash."

"That's her reputation."

"We've learned that Warren had a gambling problem. A possible scenario is that he may have owed Phyllis some money. He didn't pay and she had him put to sleep, so to speak."

"That's possible, I guess. We know that Heidi has a gambling problem. We didn't know Warren was into gambling," Mallard admitted. "Actually this feeds my case against Heidi. If Warren weren't paying Heidi, that's one more reason to suspect Heidi."

Maggie broke in, "Whoever murdered the man had to know his school, the calendar of events, his whereabouts, and how to access his office and use the typewriter for the suicide note. I can see where this Weaver woman may have a reason to kill Otterby, but she wouldn't, it seems to me, commit the act in the school. She'd blow up his car, or run him down coming home from work, or entice him to a remote area and put him away."

"Unless," Lou said, "You wanted to make it look like someone in school killed him."

"Of course, but she'd need an informant."

"Precisely. That might have been Tom Hines."

"The custodian?"

"Tom Hines gets a copy of the calendar of events at the school. He would have known about the upcoming Curriculum Advisory Committee meeting. He has the keys to all rooms, including the pool. He knows the staff and school issues, and all the inner hostilities. Custodians are often the most knowledgeable people in a school. He would know when Otterby's office was unoccupied, and have access to it without suspicion. Maybe Tom Hines is the murderer? After all, he found the body. He was alone."

"You've got a point there, Lou," Duck Mallard said. "To me, so much hinges on what Devon saw. The talk we have with him in a few minutes is key."

"Have you got a picture of Phyllis Weaver to show Devon?" Lou asked.

"Yeah. I'll have one of my officers bring it to us. I'd like the two of you in on the interview. You've talked with him before, and he gave you that biblical reference. He's familiar with you and he trusts you.

This time Heidi won't be listening, and I'm hoping he'll tell us exactly what he saw."

⁓

Devon was getting ready to go with his mother to the police department. "Guess it's time to tell the police what I saw that night, Mom."

"I think it would be the right thing to do."

"I don't want to get involved and be responsible for Miss Simpson getting hurt, and I don't want all this stuff coming up in court."

"I know, Dev. It won't be easy, but you'll be working with people who are skilled in these areas. Just try to relax and tell the detective what you saw. Leave the future to the future, all will be well."

The police conference room was institutional looking, with a table, several chairs, a window, and some audio and video taping equipment in a corner. A pitcher of water and some plastic cups were on the table. Devon was nervous as he waited for Detective Mallard to enter the room. As the room filled, everyone took a place around the table: Devon, his mother, the Rockingham family attorney, Sid Anthony, Lou, Maggie and Detective Mallard.

Mallard began, "Thanks for coming in this afternoon, Devon. As you know, we're investigating the death of Warren Otterby. We're hoping you'll tell us exactly what you saw that night in the high school pool. We'll do what we can to protect your anonymity. Devon, we'd like you to tell us what you saw that night. We'll ask questions as you describe the scene."

Head bowed, hands clasped together, as if in prayer, Devon waited a few seconds and then quietly began. "I noticed that the paint had been scraped off the window, and some light was coming through. I stopped and looked in. I saw Mr. Otterby on the diving board. He would take a step at a time toward the end of the board. A woman was on the pool deck beside the diving board. She held a handgun up and pointed it at Mr. Otterby. Two men were in swimming suits and were near the deep end by the diving board. They seemed to have knives in their hands. There was some talking going on before Mr. Otterby would take each step, but I couldn't hear what was being said. Anyway, Mr. Otterby got to the end of the board. He jumped in and sank to the bottom. It looked like he was trying to break free from rope around his wrists and ankles. After he stopped moving, the two men jumped in. I thought they were going to save him, but they cut the ropes and got out of the pool. The three of them left.

"I was upset by what I saw, but I didn't know whether to try and stop it or not. I went into the bathroom because I thought I might get sick. I took some deep breaths and felt a little better. Then I went to my locker, got my stuff, and went home. I decided not to tell anyone because I didn't want a lot of attention on me."

"That's understandable. Do you know who you saw in the pool area?"

"The woman holding the gun looked like Miss Simpson. That's another reason why I didn't want to tell anyone. She's a wonderful teacher who's helped me a lot in school. I didn't want to be the one to get her in trouble."

"You saw her face, Devon?"

"No. It was her hair and clothes. It was her, that's all. From the side and from where I was looking, it looked like her."

"Do you remember what she was wearing?"

"No."

"I mean was she in a dress? Slacks? Shorts? A swimming suit?"

"I think she was wearing slacks and a blouse. She wasn't wearing shorts or a swimming suit. She looked like she would look if it were a school day."

"What was her body style? Thin? Overweight?"

"She looked like Miss Simpson. The best way I can describe her is to put Miss Simpson down by the pool and you'd say that the woman was Miss Simpson."

"But you didn't see her face. You didn't hear her talk?"

"No."

"It could've been somebody else? Somebody who looked like Miss Simpson?"

"I guess so."

"Did you recognize the two men?"

"No."

"You never saw them before?"

"No."

"What were they wearing?"

"Swimming suits."

"Can you describe them? Fat, muscular, thin?"

"They were average guys. They were white, medium height, not fat, not muscular. Just two regular looking guys."

"I'm going to show you a picture of someone from the front and side and you tell me if this person could have been in the pool that night." Mallard showed him the photo of Phyllis Weaver.

"I don't think so. I didn't see the face close enough to say."

Mallard turned to Lou and Maggie. "Do you two have any questions?"

Maggie jumped in, "Devon, when we talked with you, you told us how long you looked in the window and then you gave us a line of scripture. It seemed to represent what you were thinking when you looked into the pool that night."

"Yeah."

"Why didn't you tell us what you saw, like you're telling us now?"

"For one thing, Miss Simpson was there. I didn't want to tell you she was there, or that I thought she was there killing the principal. But, I wanted to tell you that I was seeing conflict and that a weapon was being used. The best way for me to do that was to talk about a similar scene, and a reference to the Bible was my way of doing that."

"We got that, Devon. You did a great job of communicating that."

"Thanks. The second reason is that Mrs. Norton was in the room, and I'd already told her that I didn't see or hear anything, and I didn't want to admit that I'd lied to her. I think she likes and respects me, and I didn't want to have to admit that I'd not been honest with her."

"Sure. Devon did you see anybody from the time you witnessed the murder until you left the school parking lot?"

"Yeah. I saw a custodian."

"Did you two talk?"

"No. I passed him on my way out of the building, on my way to the parking lot."

"Anything abnormal about that?"

"No. He was just standing by the door."

"He didn't say anything?"

"I think he said, "Good night or good-bye. That's all.""

"Anybody else?"

"No."

"Did you see any strange cars, any people who normally wouldn't be in the school area at that time of night?"

"It all seemed normal to me."

Lou took over. "You're at home now, is that right?"

"Yeah. I have a tutor who helps me with my school work, and I'm practicing for the competition at MSU."

"Where's your performance, Devon?"

"I'll be giving a solo at about one o'clock in the music building on the MSU campus. An hour later I'll play in a quartet, in the same building."

"Nervous?"

"Yeah, a lot of pressure on me, but I like it."

"Your parents will be going with you?"

Mary Rockingham responded, even though the question wasn't directed to her, "Devon's father has a very important business meeting in Chicago. I'll be there. I haven't missed one competition since Devon was a little boy. I'll be there."

"We have no more questions, Detective Mallard," Lou said.

Mallard thanked Devon and his mother for coming in. All rose for farewells. After Devon, Mary, and their attorney had gone, the three conversed.

"More circumstantial evidence, Duck," Lou began. "We keep getting more for a jury to doubt. The witness testified that he could not positively identify the suspect. He says he didn't see her face, only a profile, body type, and hair color, length, and style."

"Yeah," Mallard countered, "I was hoping he'd be able to positively identify a suspect, but he didn't."

"Do you think he still may be holding back?" Maggie asked. "Do you think he knows it was Miss Simpson but he still doesn't want to be the one to turn in his teacher? This way he can be honest and say he saw the murder but can't be the one to pin the murder on his teacher."

"Could be. The kid's very intelligent," Lou remarked. "He knows what he's doing. He was able to design and plan how to discreetly let us know what he saw. Most kids wouldn't be able to keep that kind of secret. He seems to be playing with us, cooperating, but not giving us all we need to move forward."

"The kid does seem very bright, and sure, he could be toying with us," Mallard responded. "All of his moves are well thought out and planned. I've a sense that he's telling us the truth. Remember that he was about 30 yards away, and the only light was the security light above the diving board. She was facing the west end of the pool and the view from the door would be to the side. So, when he says he didn't get a good look at her face, he was probably telling the truth. If she turned to the right, to go to the locker room, he would have a facial view. If she turned to the left, he wouldn't. I forgot to ask him that."

"I assume that this Phyllis Weaver has short blond hair?" Maggie asked.

"She did when these mug shots were taken, and let's see, these were snapped six months ago."

"What was she arrested for six months ago?"

"DUI is her usual offense."

"Can't control herself, simple as that. She can't control her booze, her actions when under the influence, her gambling. She always seems to be under the power of one of her addictions. She could've killed Otterby out of some sort of revenge, but I'll tell you the one compelling reason I have *not* to suspect her. She's about as bright as a brick wall. Beautiful, yes, but she would have no capability for planning a murder. I can't imagine her being able to plan a meal with a refrigerator full of food, let alone a complex murder involving two accomplices and a plot that has us wallowing in confusion. Phyllis could have been standing there with a gun, but if she was, she was merely a pawn on the chess board of murder."

"One more thing before we go," Maggie said. "What do you make of the newspaper story, Duck?"

"That has me confused, too. I thought you two were behind it. Then I thought Jane Wills was behind it. I found out that I was wrong on both counts. Usually the editor is open with me and shares what he knows, but for some reason he isn't cooperative. He swears by his source and won't reveal it. The information shared is consistent with where we are, so it's not far-fetched reporting. It's just that we don't know who's feeding them information. I'm a little leery of the motivation, too. Why would the informant tell the newspaper what we know? What would be the motivation for doing so? Strange. Lots of strange things going on with this case."

Lou was anxious to get up to Grand Haven. He was missing Carol, Samm, Luba, and Millie. He told Maggie he'd be in touch. All three promised to continue sharing information. Duck Mallard thanked Lou and Maggie for meeting with him. They seemed to be pulling together.

ॐ

Lou did a lot of thinking while driving. During his hour plus drive up U.S. 31 to Grand Haven, Tom Hines kept coming to mind. He was the only person who, like Heidi and Rick, seemed to be a suspect. Lou made a mental list of the reasons why Hines could be a key figure. He was in the building when the murder occurred, he discovered the body, he had keys to the entire school, he had a schedule of evening activities in the school, he knew of Warren's gambling problem, he had access to Warren's office and typewriter without suspicion, and he knew Heidi would be in the building. Lou's intuitive hunch told him that Tom Hines was involved. But as Tevy'e would say in *Fiddler on the Roof*, "On the other hand..." On the other hand, why would Tom Hines want Warren Otterby dead? That one didn't come easily. If the murder was related to gambling, why did Tom inform Lou that Otterby was a gambler? He wouldn't want to willingly help the investigator solve the crime if he was involved. It all came down to the question: why would Tom Hines want Otterby dead and why would he willingly assist whoever else wanted Otterby dead? Was it money? Status? There had to have been some motivation for Hines to get involved. It seemed to Lou that Hines was too much involved on the periphery to not have played some part in this murder.

Lou picked up his car phone and dialed Maggie's car phone number. He was cognizant of the fact that their call could be intercepted, but he didn't think there would be any harm in that. Maggie answered the phone.

Lou could hear the background noise in the phone. "Maggie, this is Lou."

"Yeah, Lou. Must be pretty important for you to call on your car phone. As Scotch as you are, you'd usually wait till you were home."

"I've got an idea and I need you to help. Are you near Kalamazoo right now?"

"Just passing Westnedge Avenue going east on I-94."

"Please call me when you get home. We both should arrive about the same time. It isn't critical that you call as soon as you get in your door, but call me this evening for sure. I've got a theory or two I want to discuss."

"Will do, Lou. I've been thinking as I drive along, too. I'll be curious to see if great minds are on the same wavelength."

Thoughts continued to strike Lou as he drove. Lou felt that certain ideas came to him as gifts. He never knew when they would appear, but they often did. He'd noticed that when he acted on them, they usually sprang into something that would take a case in a new direction, or strongly reinforce a previous theory. Such was the case now.

⌁

Lou was glad to be home. He gave Carol a big hug, petted Samm and although the cats, Luba and Millie, seemed unconcerned about his arrival, he'd like to think he was missed. Carol announced that she'd prepared a picnic and suggested a walk on the beach, including a stop at their favorite large piece of driftwood for the meal. "Sounds great. It's good to be back home. I had a nice time in Dallas with Gayle and Dick. I also picked up some good information on the Otterby case."

"I'll want to hear all about it," said Carol, always curious about what interested Lou. Lou and Carol, along with a picnic basket and Samm, walked onto the warm sand toward a perfect evening on the shore of Lake Michigan. Always on the case, Lou packed his cell phone in his pants pocket. He told Carol that they'd probably be interrupted by a call from Maggie. She understood how close they were to solving the case.

About a half-hour into their walk along the shore, as cool water bathed their feet and ankles, Lou's phone beckoned him.

"Thanks for calling back, Maggie. I think I have a direction for us to go. If it leads to a dead end, so be it. At least we'll have pursued the possibility."

"What's your intuition telling you, Lou? I'm anxious to hear it."

"I'd like you to do a few things for us and we'll see where it leads."

"My wish is your command. Give me my marching orders."

"I'd like you to pinpoint on a Kalamazoo map, the home or apartment of Phyllis Weaver. Then, I want you to find the closest place where she could purchase a wig. Next, I'd like you to speak with the owner or manager of that store and see if he or she has any sales records over the past two weeks. See if you can find Phyllis Weaver associated with the purchase of a hair piece. Or, if the manager has no credit card record, show the photo of Weaver to the manager and see if he or she recognizes Weaver as a customer in the past two weeks."

"You're thinking that Weaver would look like Heidi if she had a similar hairpiece. Your theory is that Devon saw Phyllis looking to be Heidi that night?"

"That's one theory, Maggie. What I think may have happened is this: the murderers are not Heidi and Rick. The first plan, which was to be the perfect crime, had the police believing in the suicide. That would've made things very simple and they almost got away with it.

"However, that plan didn't work out because of our work. The second plan was to frame Heidi and Rick. Someone, and I suspect Hines, fed information to the murderers about a wonderful opportunity the night of May 11. Heidi, with a gun, would be staying late in the school. If by any chance somebody saw something, if Phyllis looked like Heidi, that would add more fuel to the fire for incriminating Heidi. I'm thinking that we're now looking at their backup plan. If I'm right, I now fear for Devon because they've no doubt heard the rumor that Devon saw the murder. They don't know the specifics of Devon's testimony. For all they know, he could pick someone out of a lineup. Therefore, in order to remove all evidence, Devon has to be out of the picture. Are you with me?"

"It all makes sense. But, who killed Otterby and why, Lou?"

"I'm quite sure that it relates to the gambling. My guess is that he didn't pay up and that he paid the price of that dilemma. My guess is that Tom Hines knows, and if he told the truth, he'd be able to explain the entire story."

Maggie promised to look into the hairpiece. The two finished their conversation, and Lou's mind came back to enjoying his time with Carol.

As the sun began to set into Lake Michigan, Lou and Carol were finishing some fruit. Their favorite beach dessert was S'Mores, but Carol thought a switch to a healthier food choice would be good, so she prepared a container of cantaloupe pieces. While Lou and Carol shared their experiences of the last few days, Samm found a young boy, staying at one of the cottages along the lake, to throw her sticks.

The walk and picnic on the shore of Lake Michigan was a wonderful way to end the day. Carol called for Samm and she obediently came to her. With an empty picnic basket, the three walked up the beach to the Searing home. A cool late spring breeze washing them with clean, fresh air made a good night's sleep certain.

Before Heidi Simpson left for the airport to fly to Minnesota, she called Devon. "Hi, Devon. This is Miss Simpson. I'm calling to wish you good luck in your competition next Monday at MSU."

"Thanks. Guess I'm as ready as I'll ever be."

"We're very proud of you. I hope you know that. I'm planning to go to MSU to offer support to you. I can remember when I was in high school. I participated in speech contests and in my senior year, one of my teachers came to the competition. The oratory festival was at Western Michigan University in Kalamazoo. I looked out into the audience before I began and I noticed this teacher. It made me feel very good. I decided at that point that when I became a teacher I'd support my students as I was supported."

"You don't need to do that. It's a long trip for a four-minute performance."

"I know, but I'm so proud of you that I want to represent all of the special education teachers and celebrate your successful competition. I know you'll be with your friends, but if you could break away for a few minutes and share an ice cream cone, it would make me happy. That would be my way of saying 'congratulations' and a way to let you know how proud we all are of you."

"Thanks. I think the bus leaves at three-thirty and my ensemble performance is at two o'clock, so there's some time for that. Thanks."

"I'll see you there and following your last performance, we can make plans for that ice cream cone."

"Sure. I'd like that. Thanks."

Even though Devon was instrumental to her trouble, Heidi still respected his ability and his personality. She tried to look past the accusations and see a fine young man who deserved her support during this important music festival.

CHAPTER 11

Saturday, May 21

Lou was awakened at three in the morning. He was in a deep sleep. Because of his hearing loss, he didn't hear the phone. Carol sprang up, concerned that bad news could be on the other end of the line. Momentarily she prayed for a wrong number.

"Carol, this is Maggie. I'm sorry to awaken you, but I've got news for Lou on the Otterby case."

"Oh sure, Maggie. I'm so thankful this wasn't a bad news call. They usually are bad news when they come in the middle of the night."

"Sorry. But Lou always says to call whenever I have something that I think he would want to know. That's the case now, or I would have waited to call at a more reasonable hour."

"Not a problem. I'll wake him. The fresh air on the beach last night put him into a deep sleep."

Carol finally got Lou to become conscious. "It's Maggie, with some news about your murder case."

Lou took several seconds to figure out who he was, where he was, and what was happening. "Good morning, Maggie."

"Lou, got some news for you on the Otterby case."

"What's that?"

"Tom Hines was found dead, floating in the Shoreline High School pool about an hour ago. I just got a call from Duck Mallard."

"H-m-m. Well, that's an interesting turn of events. Payback time."

"What's that supposed to mean?"

"'I think this was his punishment for the paint scraped off the window. He could also have been the informant to the *Herald Palladium*, I'm not sure. After all, I'm hardly awake. Dying the same way, in the same pool within ten days of Otterby's death tells me that there's a connection here."

"I wonder where Heidi and Rick were last evening?" Maggie asked.

"Heidi should be in Minnesota. She said she was packing and leaving after we left. Remember?"

"That's right. It wouldn't make any sense for them to be involved in a murder of Tom Hines, would it?"

Lou thought for a second, "Not really, unless Tom was a part of their plan to kill Otterby and they're getting back at him for botching up that window."

"I guess there's no question that Tom Hines was involved with the murderer. We just don't know which set of people he was teaming with," Maggie said. "Well, I'm heading for Shoreline. I want to be involved as soon as possible. Mallard is already investigating, and with his spirit of cooperation I want to be on-site learning what he learns."

"Good. I'll get dressed and head down there myself. The person I want to talk with is Mrs. Hines. If anybody knows anything at this point, it would be her. See you in Shoreline before the sun rises."

Carol stood next to Lou as the conversation unfolded. She knew Lou would be leaving soon. "I'll make you some breakfast. Better make some caffeinated coffee to help you stay awake for the drive."

"Might be a good idea, but I don't want the heart to start skipping beats. You know how sensitive I am to caffeine."

"Oh, one cup shouldn't do any harm. As long as you don't take a pound of M&Ms along, one cup won't be a problem," Carol said with a smile.

Lou showered, got into a fresh pair of Dockers and put on a sweatshirt. This time he chose his sweatshirt from Bar Harbor, Maine. He went downstairs to find Carol preparing some raisin bran and a slice of toast with grape jelly. She also prepared a thermos filled with coffee.

Lou ate his breakfast at three-twenty. Samm paced around, sensing that something wasn't normal. "I'll be back as soon as I can, probably late in the afternoon."

"Don't forget that we have a dinner and pontoon boat ride at the Retsen's this evening. We're to be there at five-thirty."

"Oh, that's right. That'll be fun, a pontoon boat ride on Spring Lake followed by one of those gourmet meals prepared by Jerry and Rosemary. Looking forward to it. If by chance I'm going to be late, I'll call.

Lou was out the door, into his car and heading south to Shoreline. He'd have lots of time to think about this new development. He knew that the murderers would only have done this if they thought they would pull off a perfect crime. Lou said a silent prayer for Devon Rockingham. Tom Hines was probably paying a price for the paint coming off the window, or at least for its not being detected before the murder of Warren Otterby. He didn't want Devon to pay a price for innocently looking into a window on his way to his locker.

⟡

As Lou and Maggie were pulling into Shoreline, Heidi was leaving for the airport. Lou and Maggie had agreed to meet at McDonald's on the eastern part of town. They wanted to discuss this latest development and figure out what they planned to do next.

Maggie was waiting when Lou pulled into the golden arches. "Short night my friend?" Maggie knew the answer to her own question.

"Yeah, but with a cup of caffeine and some adrenaline flowing into the blood stream, I'm ready to go. Any more information?"

"I got here early so I went right to the police station in hopes of seeing Duck Mallard. He was there and willing to share what he knew."

"Give me the details. Let me get some orange juice and a pancake and sausage. Do you want anything? A refill for your coffee?"

"I'm fine, Lou."

Lou ordered and returned to the table with a cup of orange juice. "She'll bring my order over in a couple of minutes. Okay, what did Mallard say?"

"They got a call around one-thirty. It was from Mrs. Hines. Tom didn't come home. She said that he always comes right home, or tells his wife if he isn't coming right home. At around one-thirty she became concerned and called the police. They went to the school and found a few doors open, the security system was not on, so they knew something was strange. They combed the building and found him floating in the pool."

"The medical examiner pronounced him dead?"

"Drowning. The autopsy will be later this morning, but no signs of force, no body marks at the pool. It seems to be a similar death to Otterby's."

"Did Mallard interview anyone?"

"No. He wanted to talk with Tom's wife, but she was very emotional, as you can imagine. He had two kids, both boys in their early teens. She wasn't in any condition to be interviewed. Mallard said we'd talk with her this morning, once her doctor determines that she can handle talking about it. Mallard just threw up his hands and said, 'Got no witness, got no weapon, got no suspects, got no motive!'"

"I was quick to tell him that he did have a motive and that was to silence Hines or to punish him. I told Mallard, 'As far as I'm concerned, he either knew too much or he got what someone thought was coming to him because of that window being undetected when Otterby was killed.' Mallard agreed."

"So, the police have done nothing but look for evidence at the scene and removed the body for autopsy and tried to talk to Mrs. Hines. Is that right?"

"Yeah. While I was there, Jane Wills stopped in and took down some notes. She missed the deadline for the presses. She pointed out that the broadcast media had a heads up in terms of being able to put on bulletins or stories when they happened. She could only counter with in-depth interviews, and efforts to help solve the thing."

"Did Mallard call school folks?"

"He called Superintendent Donald and Mrs. Norton. They were very sorry to hear of the death of Hines. He was a good man and he will be missed. They were thankful that today is Saturday and they'd have a couple of days to plan what to do before school opened on Monday."

"Did Mallard give you any indication of what they were going to do today?"

"They want to talk to Mrs. Hines. Duck did make a point of saying that they needed to talk to Heidi and Rick. He said, 'If those two can't account for their whereabouts with witnesses last night between 10 p.m. and 2 a.m., I'm going to the prosecutor to seek arrest warrants. I guess he figures that the two are guilty, or at least they need to be off the streets. He also concluded that Devon Rockingham is in danger. He's thinking that if Simpson and Bolt are apprehended, it would lessen the likelihood of another murder occurring."

"My gut says we need to touch base with MSU," Lou said thinking seriously. "My guess is the next scenario for criminal action will be at the solo and ensemble event on Monday."

⊰⊱

Lou called the Michigan State University Police. He asked to speak with a detective on the force. He was put in touch with Detective Michela Robinson.

"Detective Robinson. How can I help you?"

"Detective Robinson, this is Lou Searing calling from Shoreline, Michigan."

"Good morning. Nice town, quite a summer place as I recall."

"Yes, it is. Unfortunately the natives have to share the beach and attractions with the tourists, but they bring money with them and that helps the economy."

"What can I help you with, Mr. Searing?"

"The reason for my call is to ask your cooperation on a case I'm working on at the moment."

"I take it we're going to practice some preventive medicine. Am I right?"

"I hope so."

"What've you got?"

"Monday, on your campus, is a statewide music festival for high school band students."

"Yup, looking at it right here on my list of events for the week of May 23."

"Shoreline High School will be participating. They will have a music phenom named Devon Rockingham with them. He is playing in two events."

"That's on my list, too. He has a solo at one o'clock and an ensemble event around two. It's all on our computer."

"Good. Devon witnessed a murder in Shoreline, Michigan, about a week and a half ago. My intuition tells me that his being at MSU puts him in a prime location for abduction. I'm predicting that the murderers of the principal would like this young man silenced."

"They've threatened him?"

"Not that I know of. I'm just thinking that they'll want him quiet and having him in this different environment may give them the opportunity to entrap him, coerce him someplace, get him off campus, and potentially harm him. If not physically, certainly emotionally."

"Sounds plausible, Lou."

"My partner, Maggie McMillan, and I are going to be on campus Monday. We'll be shadowing Devon. I'll have my cell phone with me at all times. What I'm hoping is that your office will be on alert, and

212

immediately step in to apprehend any person or vehicle attempting to take Devon away from the festival."

"We'll help any way we can. Who has jurisdiction over the murder that Devon witnessed?"

"The Shoreline Police. Detective Dan Mallard is heading the investigation. We've been working with him. Last night a second murder took place in the same location. We feel that it is related to the principal's murder. My fear is that Devon is next, and my gut tells me that he may meet that fate on Monday on your campus."

"Are there any warrants out for arresting the suspects?"

"No. We, along with Detective Mallard, are holding on to a lot of circumstantial evidence that links a couple members of the Shoreline High School staff, but we have no solid evidence. I'm fairly certain a prosecuting attorney would not authorize an arrest based on the circumstantial evidence we have, even as convincing as it appears to be."

"Why don't you touch base with us when you arrive on campus and we'll coordinate our activity at that time? I'm assuming you don't want our plainclothes officers to be involved, since you are going to be doing the shadowing. Sounds like you just need vehicles standing by and human intervention if this young man is kidnapped or enticed away from the music festival."

"That's right. I'll be on foot all the time, watching and following Devon. If a car pulls up and they take him away, I'm helpless. That's where I need you to pursue or spot with a helicopter."

"Are there any suspects whose mug shot we can pull up from our files to share with officers who will be working security for that music festival on Monday?"

"Our major suspect is Heidi Simpson; she's the one we've got a lot of circumstantial evidence on. She's expected to be there to support Devon, as his special education teacher. At this point, I don't know if Heidi could be a potential threat to Devon. Another potential suspect is Rick Bolt, the school's athletic director. I doubt you'll have file photos of these two. Both are teachers. I don't think they have criminal records."

"We've got a lot of surprises in our scrapbook, Lou. We've got grandmothers in there with stories that would cause their children and grandchildren to faint."

"Oh, yeah. I wouldn't be shocked."

"Anyone else who could be a threat to Devon?"

"She's not really a suspect yet, but we're trying to see if Phyllis Weaver of Kalamazoo is involved in any way. You probably have her in your files because she's been picked up often for DUI."

"I'll check and see what we have."

⌇

Duck Mallard had clearance to meet with Mrs. Hines. He invited Lou and Maggie to go along. The three went in Maggie's van because it was accessible. They went up to the door of the two-story older wooden frame home on Shoreline's south side. Mrs. Hines' sister, Agnes, let them in and showed them into the living room. Lucy Hines was still very emotional about the death of her husband. Her sons were at their grandparents' home. The police had been constantly at the site, searching.

"We only have a few questions, Mrs. Hines. We know this is a difficult time for you and we'll try to be brief."

Lucy Hines sat in a worn dark blue upholstered wingback chair, her eyes were red from continual crying. She clenched her handkerchief and looked down at the floor during the entire period of questioning. Mallard began, "Did Tom give you any idea that he was in any danger?"

"Last Thursday or Friday he was very upset about a window that had the paint scraped off of it. He kept saying, 'I might pay for that, Lucy. I might pay for that.' I got so sick of hearing him say that all last week! I told him to stop talking like that. He just seemed so obsessed with the window being scraped."

"Did he say who was upset by it?"

"He kept saying 'she,' but never gave a name. He said, "She's upset, she's furious. She'll get me for this."

"Did you know what he was referring to when he talked about the paint being scraped from the window?"

"Yeah, the death of the principal. Tom found him floating in the pool."

"But, he never mentioned a name or hinted at a name? Do you have any idea who he was talking about?"

"I think it was either Heidi Simpson or Phyllis Weaver."

"Why do you think it was one of them?"

"Well, because Tom was saying that Heidi wanted the principal dead; apparently he mistreated kids, teachers, and parents. Phyllis was hard on Tom, especially when his bills weren't paid."

"What bills aren't paid?" Mallard asked.

"Tom has a problem with gambling. Not a big problem, but a problem nonetheless. I got suspicious when his paycheck seemed to disappear and we had bills to pay. I confronted Tom and he admitted to it. He got into quite a debt with this Weaver. She would have nothing but cash, and it needed to be in her hand on time or heads would roll. When he was killed, the first thing to come to my mind was this Weaver woman. I thought maybe Tom got in debt and refused to pay. Then I thought this Heidi may have killed the principal and she was mad at Tom for scraping the window that allowed someone to see her commit the murder."

"I see. Did Tom seem unusually nervous when he left for work yesterday?"

"No. I don't think so."

"He didn't mention that he might be home late or anything like that?"

Lucy began sobbing again.

After a few seconds Duck continued, "I'm sorry Mrs. Hines. I know it's difficult for you, but we need to get as much information as possible, so we can hopefully apprehend the person who did this."

"I know. I just don't have my Tommy anymore. He was a good father, a good husband. This shouldn't have happened to him."

The room became silent. Duck thought a woman's voice may be

more consoling during these questions so he nodded to Maggie, inviting her to comment.

"Lucy. I've been through tragedy myself. I know that it is all very painful now, but with time you will find strength to heal."

"I know. I know. It's such a shock and so sudden. Oh, my Tommy, my Tommy." The sobs continued.

Lou asked, "Mrs. Hines, did Tom say anything about talking to anyone at the *Herald Palladium*?"

"That's another thing. He said someone kept bugging him about the Otterby drowning. Tommy said he told 'em what he knew and that he would probably get into trouble for that, too."

Duck, Lou, and Maggie looked at one another knowingly. They gently informed Lucy that they would be going and asked that if she had any more information later, to call. Agnes showed the investigators to the door. On an intuitive hunch, Maggie thought of a potentially new source of information. Maggie asked, "Excuse me, do you know if your brother-in-law kept a diary?"

The heavyset woman thought for a second. "I think he did. He enjoys writing for a hobby, and he would often read the events of various days to my children. They would pick out a date and Tom would turn to that page in his diary and read the happenings to the children."

"Could I see that diary?" Maggie asked, realizing that an event such as the death of a principal would certainly merit mention in the diary of a committed writer.

"I'll ask Lucy. There may be some pretty personal things in that journal. She might not want strangers to see it," Agnes said.

"Sure, I understand."

Agnes reappeared a little while later. Lucy says you can read the journal. The diary is in a room that Tom used for writing. It's a bedroom on the second floor." She laboriously climbed the stairs and returned holding a red diary. She handed the diary to Maggie, who immediately turned to May 12.

She read to herself, "Terrible night. Our principal was murdered in the school pool. I almost got sick in the heat of the pool area talking to the cops. Warren had to pay for his shortcomings. Lessons sure come with a price! I wish now that I hadn't agreed to participate by giving information. They were so convincing telling me that it was the perfect crime and that there was no way we could get caught. I was convinced that they were right and I went along; gave them information and played dumb when the cops came."

Maggie turned the page and continued to read, "No school today, the police are investigating the murder. My afternoon TV program was interrupted to announce that Otterby had killed himself. That suicide note typed on his typewriter with gloves on my hands worked."

Maggie found no entries for Saturday or Sunday. On Monday she read, "I learned today that the balcony pool door window had been scraped by our staff earlier in the day that Otterby died. My heart sank and beat rapidly for a long time. There's still no question about Warren killing himself, but there's an outside chance that someone could have witnessed the murder. After all, there were people in the school at that hour. I remember seeing the Rockingham boy leave school shortly after Otterby would have been killed. He looked upset. If he saw the murder, my goose is cooked and could be cooked even if he didn't."

Tuesday's entry read, "Rumors are that the Rockingham boy did see something, and now there's a question that the suicide did not happen. There's a good chance I couldn't live to see the weekend. Information and pool security was my job. Somebody overstepped me and took the paint off the window only a few hours before Otterby was killed. I need to be sure that my life insurance and legal papers are in order."

Maggie turned the page to Wednesday. "They want more information. I have to find out who's riding the bus to East Lansing with Devon. What's the arrival and departure time for the bus? What time does the Rockingham boy perform? Are his parents going to East Lansing? The kid's life is in danger, but as much as I'd like to tell someone, I can't. I'm dead in the water if I do. I may have a date with death as I write this. My only chance to live is to give them the information they want. I'm giving my boys and Lucy hugs. I hope they know that I love them."

Maggie continued on to the next page, Thursday. "I got a ticket to Los Angeles today. I'm taking a Greyhound west. I'm not telling anyone I'm leaving. I've given them the information they want and now I'm out of town. The bus leaves early Saturday morning. I'll call Lucy at points along the way. I've got to get out of town and lay low till this thing blows up or settles down. I'm probably a fool for writing all of this incriminating stuff, but writing has been my way of releasing what goes through my mind for years, and I can't stop now."

That was the last entry. Maggie noticed that the page for Friday was torn out. The next page was Saturday. He hadn't gone to work until four o'clock Friday, and he could have learned something, written it in his diary and then decided not to keep it. Tom Hines was dead in the pool late Friday night or in the early morning hours of Saturday. He didn't get out of town on the Greyhound as he'd planned.

Maggie asked, "Could I take this for a day? I'd like to photocopy a few pages. Would that be okay with Mrs. Hines?"

Once again, Agnes slowly walked into the living room where Lucy remained in mourning. Maggie quietly said to Lou and Mallard, "Wait till you hear what Hines has written in this book!"

Agnes returned with the news that Lucy agreed to her taking the diary. "I'll get it back to you soon. Thanks," Maggie said.

⌘

While the three sat in Maggie's van, Lou read the journal entries so all could hear. "'Them,' 'them,' 'they,' 'them,' who are 'them?'" asked a frustrated Duck Mallard. The case is solved if he'd just tell us who 'them' are!"

Maggie sat pensively a moment before responding very simply, "'Them' are not school people. 'Them' are people not associated with Shoreline High School."

"How do you conclude that?" Lou asked.

"School people wouldn't have to get information about a bus list from a night maintenance employee. A bus attendance list would be general information, easily available from the music instructor. In fact, I saw a sign-up list outside the band room door, on a bulletin board. It also had the times that the bus was leaving and getting back. Any school employee could look at the list. It was on the wall in plain view. You don't need to ask a custodian what time Devon plays. You get that from asking Miss Whitmore. You don't need to ask a custodian if a student's parents are going to attend and how they're getting there. Tom Hines was an informant, and he gave information to people not from the school. My conclusion is that this is a stroke of luck for Heidi Simpson and Rick Bolt. I didn't say they're out of the woods, but their luck just turned."

"It could be a ploy to take our attention off the school people for the very reasons you're pointing out," Mallard said. "Simpson and Bolt could be asking Hines to get information and to leave a trail to confuse us so we're convinced it's not them. Maybe the backup plan is to convince us that they're not involved. Heidi and Rick could have killed Hines for his slip in not ensuring the window was painted. They would have been really upset because he may have talked to the media and implied that school people were involved and a student may have been a witness. With all the attention on them, Heidi and Rick would have little choice but to put him away. Now they have to kill Devon. Take out the witnesses and you've got a tight case of circumstantial evidence. I still think it's Heidi and Rick. They're smart. They needed Hines to pull it off in school." Duck Mallard's hypothesis sounded pretty convincing.

Maggie came back, "Are you telling me that you think two teachers would kill a student? A special education teacher would kill one of her pupils? Not a prayer!"

"Listen. If they killed Otterby, they have the sociopath personalities to destroy life. It doesn't matter if the life belongs to the Pope, the President or some special education kid who's good with a bassoon. We're talking about the big gamble for freedom versus life in prison. It all hangs on silencing the kid.

"Teachers wouldn't kill a kid," Maggie said. "An evil principal? It's possible, but not a kid. I won't buy it, Duck. I won't buy it."

Lou glanced at his watch. "It's ten-thirty. Let's go get a cup of coffee and plan our next steps. Devon is playing the competition of his life on Monday. We must ensure he's safe from harm. We need to protect him. Either he doesn't go to MSU, or he goes with very tight security. The questions asked of Tom indicate that something is being planned for the performance. We need to put our energy into protecting that boy."

Maggie pulled away from the curb and headed to McDonald's. Coffee and strategy go together like love and marriage.

ॐ

Heidi enjoyed an uneventful flight to Minnesota. She had plenty of time to think. She felt like a character in a bad dream. She tried to look at her circumstances in a spiritual way. Heidi told herself that she had made no mistakes, and perhaps she would learn some lesson through all of this.

ॐ

Maggie's beeper went off as she ordered a cup of coffee and an Egg McMuffin. She didn't recognize the number on the display, but knew that it was long distance. She got her tray and went to a table in the non-smoking section. She took the cell phone from her bag which hung from the wheelchair. After dialing the number a voice answered, "Mrs. McMillan?"

"Yes."

"This is Lydia at The Hair Emporium in Kalamazoo. Sorry ma'am, couldn't find any sale to a Phyllis Weaver. I also studied the photo and have no recollection of seeing anyone like that in my store."

"Thanks for checking. I appreciate it."

"Sure, sorry not to be able to help."

Maggie turned off the cell phone, put it in her bag, and turned to Lou, "That was the hair place in Kalamazoo. They have no record of Weaver purchasing a hairpiece there."

"We can check that off. It doesn't mean a wig wasn't purchased there, it just means we can't be certain Weaver bought one. We'll make note of it," Lou answered. "I just think that if Devon thought he saw Heidi, the hair would have to be identical and perhaps this Phyllis, if she killed Otterby, would need to look as much like Heidi as possible."

The three discussed the merits of having Devon cancel his performance at Michigan State University. "I'm going to try to convince the prosecuting attorney to issue warrants for the arrest of Heidi and maybe Rick," Duck Mallard said. "If I can do this, that should lessen, in my mind anyway, the threat to Devon."

"I take it that you believe the murders were carried out by Simpson and Bolt," Maggie responded.

"All the evidence points to that."

"Don't you mean, all the circumstantial evidence points to that?" Maggie was still quite convinced that the school folks were not the murderers.

"I stand corrected. We really don't have any conclusive evidence, you're right. The prosecutor will say that, too, but I intend to seek the warrants anyway. He can say no, but I'll feel better for having asked."

Lou had been quietly sipping his hot coffee up till now. "Two things seem critical at this point. The first is to find the page torn out of Hines' diary. If we can find that, we may have the answer to who killed Otterby. Secondly, assuming Devon and his parents agree to continue with plans to perform at Michigan State University on Monday, we need to have a cover watching over him to make sure that he's not kidnapped and killed. My guess is that he'll want to go ahead and perform. So, we'll need to be on-site, but not obvious as bodyguards."

"I agree," Mallard said. "Our energy goes to finding that page. I'll take the diary for evidence analysis and I'll have my officers conduct a search for that missing page at his home and in the school. I'll also contact the MSU Police and solicit their support for covering Devon on Monday and plan for any apprehension of suspects who may attempt to kidnap him."

"I've contacted Detective Robinson of the MSU Police," Lou said. "We have their support. I think from this point on you should handle that liaison since the people who died, Otterby and Hines, are within your jurisdiction. Law enforcement heads seem to work better without private investigators getting involved." Lou had laid the groundwork for the cooperation from MSU. Mallard agreed. He would call later, around noon, to establish plans.

⌇

From McDonald's, the team drove to the Rockingham home just north of the downtown district of Shoreline. They were welcomed into the Victorian three-story home with furniture from that era. Lou thought he was stepping back in time.

In the living room, Mrs. Rockingham offered her guests coffee, tea, and cookies. All three accepted her invitation and she left to prepare the refreshments. Devon came into the room and greeted everyone. He explained that his father was out of town on business.

When Mrs. Rockingham returned to the living room, the conversation, led by Detective Mallard, turned serious. "We're here because we are concerned about Devon's playing at Michigan State on Monday."

"Is there a problem?"

"It's hard to tell. Since Devon witnessed the Otterby murder we're concerned for his safety. The perception is that the crime was committed by Miss Simpson. We understand that Miss Simpson plans on being at Michigan State on Monday when Devon is there. We're concerned that the potential exists for Devon to be confronted by those who may have taken the lives of Mr. Otterby and Mr. Hines."

"Do you think he should not go?" Mary Rockingham asked.

"Well, I think this is what we need to discuss. On the one hand we're here because we're concerned that harm could come to

Devon, but on the other hand, there is no real reason to believe that anything would happen," Lou explained. "If Devon does go, he'll have state police surveillance going and coming, and he'll be constantly watched by two or three of us at all times."

Devon was listening and said, "I want to perform in this festival. I've worked very hard for this day. Not to perform would be to run from a responsibility."

"Yes, dear, but we need to think of your safety. It's much more important than a performance," Mary said, looking concerned.

"I'll always be around other kids, teachers, and other people. I don't see how I could be harmed. Mr. Searing said they would be watching out for me."

"That's a good point," Maggie said. "Devon would always be in the presence of others. That would make intimidating him very difficult."

"I suggest that Devon go as planned," Lou said. He then directed his comments to Devon. "Maggie will be in the music building and I'll be watching you outside. Detective Mallard will be working with the police at MSU to quickly respond if anything strange happens or looks like it may happen." Lou then addressed his remarks to all present: "I think these precautions are sufficient to allow Devon to perform."

"Thanks. I like that plan," Devon said. "I'll be okay."

"Devon, you need to be cautious," Maggie said. "You need to be alert to people around you and any stranger who may approach you. You need to feel free to tell me, inside the music building, or Mr. Searing, outside, if you suspect anything out of the ordinary. Do you understand?" Devon nodded in agreement.

Detective Mallard asked, "How do you feel about this, Mrs. Rockingham?"

"Of course, I'm very concerned and worried. But, if the state police will be watching him and you people will guard him, then I guess it would be okay. I mean, life has to go on, I guess."

"Will you be there, Mrs. Rockingham?"

"I'd love to be and was planning to go, but I haven't been feeling well. I really don't think my health will allow me to make the trip. Not watching Devon perform, and not being there for him saddens me deeply. Devon knows of our concern and support. But, no, I won't be able to be there. Mr. Rockingham and I are proud of Devon, and we know he'll do very well at this performance and the thousands of concerts ahead of him."

Mary Rockingham didn't want to publicly inform people that she had been recently diagnosed with cancer. The chemotherapy treatments left her feeling like she had been put through a wringer. Devon understood that his father couldn't be present because of very important out-of-state business meetings, and he certainly understood his mother's health. Devon would be without either parent, but he knew that he was loved and fully supported.

The decision had been made. Devon would go. He would be cautious. He realized that he would be in danger, but he felt comfortable knowing that the state police, Lou, Maggie, Detective Mallard and the MSU police were in his corner.

Before leaving the Rockingham home, it was agreed that all three would go to MSU Monday morning in separate vehicles. Duck planned to call the state police and request that the bus be under surveillance by an unmarked vehicle with plainclothes officers. The bus would stop in rest areas and they couldn't take any chances of a kidnapping, or harm coming to any of the other young people on the bus.

Lou planned to keep Devon in his sight at all times when on the MSU campus. He also planned a constant surveillance for any strange activity or persons. Maggie would concentrate on being in and around the music building where the festival activities would take place. The plan was to communicate with cell phones. The team knew that the MSU police would be involved in any pursuit, arrests, or intervention with suspects if the activity occurred on the campus.

As Lou, Maggie, and Duck Mallard were leaving the Rockingham house, Jane Wills and a photographer were exiting their car parked across the street. Jane was curious about the three investigators at the Rockingham home. She asked if the house had been broken into, or perhaps if they were there to talk to Devon concerning the murder of Tom Hines.

Maggie drove up and motioned for Jane to approach her van. "Hi, Jane. We've got to go and we haven't the time to talk, but give me a call when you've got a moment and I'll brief you on what we know. The case is progressing nicely. You've got my cell phone number, don't you?"

"Yes, I do. Thanks. You've got me curious, but I'll wait. Thanks for keeping me involved," Jane said sincerely.

"Sure, good luck with your story. It'll be a prizewinner!"

With the plan in place, the team wished each other a pleasant Sunday and planned to meet for what they hoped would be an uneventful Monday on the campus of Michigan State University.

࿇

Lou drove home, cleaned up, and went with Carol to Spring Lake to spend the evening with friends, Jerry and Rosemary Retsen. The friends sipped soft drinks and ate hors d'oeuvres as they travelled around Spring Lake on a pontoon boat. The evening was warm and delightful.

As the pontoon boat was headed for the Retsen's dock, Lou's pager beeped. He saw that Maggie was calling. "Excuse me, but I need to take this call. We're in the final stages of an investigation and this may be important."

"What do you have for me, Maggie?"

"I've got some news for you. Heidi didn't go to Minnesota after talking with us like she said she was going to. She was in Shoreline the night Tom was murdered. She can't back up her statement of where she was and what she was doing around the time Tom was believed to have been drowned. She left early Saturday morning for Minnesota. Mallard tried to get a warrant for her arrest and it was denied. This means she's free to travel without being apprehended by law enforcement."

"Very interesting. The next time we see her will be at MSU on Monday for Devon's performance."

"Correct."

"What about Rick Bolt?"

"He said he was on the east side of the state at a meeting of school athletic directors. He played golf after the meeting and left for Shoreline after the golf outing, about ten something. He slept about four hours at a rest area along I-94 and arrived back in Shoreline around 6 a.m. So, once again, no witnesses exist to verify his presence when Hines was murdered."

"These two should get the bad luck award if they're telling the truth."

"Mallard's convinced that both are viable suspects. I think not, but I've got to admit that it sure sounds convincing given what we've found during the last week and a half."

"I know. Well, thanks for the call. We'll still go ahead with our plan and meet in East Lansing on Monday. Call me if anything else develops and I'll do the same with you."

"Sorry to interrupt your evening with friends, Lou."

"Not a problem. Call whenever."

"Oh, Jane Wills called. I let her know that we're concerned for Devon's safety and that we'll all be at MSU on Monday."

"Good. We promised to keep her in the loop. And, I never complimented you on asking for a diary this morning. Where did that brilliant idea come from, Maggie?"

"When we interviewed Tom, he had a book with him. The title was *How To Be Creative With Your Diary*. I noted that, and it occurred to me that maybe he writes in a diary. There was certainly enough going on to have something to write about."

"Great work, Maggie. Very perceptive. That may have been the break we've been looking for!" Lou's joyful exuberance showed.

"Thanks. I feel pretty good about it. See you tomorrow."

Lou put his phone away and apologized to his host and hostess: "Sorry for the interruption."

"This new life of yours is much more exciting than being in the Michigan Department of Education!" Jerry said.

"Much more exciting, Jerry."

Once back on shore, the Searings and the Retsens enjoyed salmon cooked to perfection on the outdoor grill. Jerry managed the grill while Rosemary was inside preparing the salad, new potatoes, and a variety of sautéed vegetables.

The tasty and healthy meal brought many compliments to the chefs. Conversation drifted from Rosemary's computer business to Jerry's new job in special education administration at the Muskegon Intermediate School District. Carol talked about her grandchildren, Benjamin, Nicholas, and Hannah. She also announced her pending retirement after 37 years in education. Lou listened and enjoyed having his mind taken from the specifics of the Otterby and Hines cases. His brain needed the break.

After dinner the friends returned to the pontoon boat for a sunset cruise. They enjoyed coffee and angel food cake covered by berries.

CHAPTER 12

Sunday, May 22

In church, the Rockinghams were sitting in their usual pew. Dr. Wheeler delivered another thought-provoking sermon to his flock. As the parishioners filed outside into a beautiful Michigan spring day, Dr. Wheeler saw the Rockingham family coming toward him. He had not called Devon nor spoken to his parents.

As he greeted Mary Rockingham, he realized that she and the family had recently received the shocking news of her cancer. He was certain this was what was on Devon's mind. "How are you doing, young Rockingham?" asked the pastor. "Everything okay with you? Anything especially bothersome these days?" Posing this question would allow him to fulfill his promise to Laughton Lancour, to see if he could help the young man.

"No, sir. I'm concerned about Mom and my music competition tomorrow at Michigan State. I guess that might be considered bothersome."

"Well, I'm quite certain that your mom is going to be well. Medical science has come a long way, and I feel very good about her future. You'll do wonderfully tomorrow. Your discipline and hours of practice will pay big dividends. I'll be looking in the paper to see how you fare."

"Thank you, sir." Devon had been taught to be respectful of persons in authority or those who had achieved a high degree in their profession.

Reverend Wheeler then shook Ron Rockingham's hand. "Good to see you, Ron. Can I interest you in running for the church council?" "Afraid I hardly have any time for my family, Dr. Wheeler, let alone serving the church. I'll retire one of these days and then I'll give you all the attention you need."

Reverend Wheeler smiled, "Have a nice day. God bless you."

After church, Lou and Carol planned to go to Grand Rapids to visit their son, Scott, and his family. When they arrived in the early afternoon, Scott suggested a visit to the Frederik Meijer Gardens. A vote was taken and all agreed to visit the unique local attraction. The Gardens, known for a beautiful marsh, a boardwalk, and a loopwalk that allowed visitors to enjoy much wildlife in a natural habitat, was an entertaining experience.

After the visit to Meijer Gardens, all returned to the younger Searing's home for coffee and a fresh batch of chocolate chip cookies that Patti made especially for "Grandpa and Nana," as grandson, Benjamin referred to Lou and Carol. The late mid-afternoon treat provided the opportunity to get caught up on family news and to plan for a family reunion later in the summer when Amanda, her husband Joe, and daughter Hannah would be coming up from St. Louis, Missouri. A group photo would have to be taken; and if it turned out well, it could be the Christmas photo for Lou and Carol's card.

Lou knew he had a big day tomorrow. He suggested that he and Carol head back to Grand Haven. When the family heard this suggestion, they knew that they had heard Lou's first call to leave. Typically there would be two more suggestions to leave before Lou and Carol would back out of Scott and Patti's driveway on Michigan Avenue.

CHAPTER 13

Monday, May 23

Devon was up early. After a shower, he put on his clothes and prepared for the school bus ride to East Lansing. He planned to sit with a friend and enjoy the two-hour ride to the campus of Michigan State University. When he got to the parking lot of the high school, Jane Wills and the *Herald Palladium* photographer were there to take pictures and to get some quotes for the feature article.

"Well, how do you feel as you leave Shoreline for MSU?" Jane asked.

"I'm excited, but a little nervous."

"How will you spend your time on the bus?"

"It will be kind of quiet. We're all pretty nervous about performing. We'll just talk and some kids might read or sleep."

"Do you feel that your performance will be outstanding?"

"I hope so. I worked hard for today. Mrs. Whitmore says I'll have a strict judge with high expectations. So, unless I am perfect, I'll be knocked down for any mistakes."

"How does that make you feel?"

"A little nervous, but I like the pressure and the expectations. If I do a good job, my rating will be deserved and all who knew that this judge evaluated my performance will respect the final score. I'd rather have a judge with high standards and expectations."

"Is this your last public performance of your senior year?"

"Yeah. Soon they'll be paying me to do what I love to do."

"You deserve it. Have a fun trip with your friends. We'll meet you getting off the bus in East Lansing. The photographer will most likely come on board to take a few photos before you leave."

~

Lou and Carol were up early. Lou had his jog along the shore of Lake Michigan and the couple enjoyed a light breakfast before getting into Carol's Jeep Grand Cherokee for the two-hour drive to East Lansing. Carol had permission to take the day off. She had accumulated several hours working at a weekend conference and attending some evening meetings with parents. Carol planned to meet friends at Jacobson's for a shopping spree in downtown East Lansing. Lou's plan was to stay near Devon. He expected to be a shadow to Devon and to keep his eyes and ears open.

Carol slept for the early part of the trip. As Lou passed the 28th Street exit east of Grand Rapids, Carol woke up and joined the living.

"Where are we?"

"Just past the 28th Street exit. Have a good nap?"

"Yeah. I guess so."

"It should take us about an hour and a half more, with one rest area stop."

"Okay. I told Jane and Sue that I'd meet them at nine-thirty in front of Jacobson's. Will we be there by then?"

"Not a problem. You're going to have a few minutes to spare, according to my calculations."

"Good. Now brief me again. What are you expecting to have happen today?" Carol asked.

"Devon Rockingham, from Shoreline High School, is performing at a high school solo and ensemble competition on the campus of Michigan State today. Devon is the young man whom we suspect witnessed the murder of Warren Otterby at Shoreline High School a week and a half ago. There's a chance that his life is in jeopardy, and I have this gut feeling that Devon could be in danger today."

"Well, if Devon's in danger, that means you'll be in danger too. Right?"

"Yes, I guess that's true."

"Well, you be careful. I don't want to be paged in some East Lansing store because you're on the way to Sparrow Hospital," Carol said with concerned affection.

"I don't expect to get hurt. There'll be so many people around. I think we're taking adequate precautions. It would be very atypical for any type of gunfire or a hostile confrontation. But, you never know in this business."

"Please be careful, Lou. Promise me you will."

"I promise," Lou said, thankful for Carol's concern.

"Well, I'm going to have a great day with my friends and shopping."

"Driving Miss Daisy could be the highlight of my life today," Lou said smiling. He broke into a chuckle that caused Carol to smile and shake her head from side to side.

An hour and a half later, the Searings pulled into a city of East Lansing parking lot. Lou and Carol agreed to meet back at the car at three o'clock. Lou knew that the school bus would be leaving to go back to Shoreline at about three-thirty, so if Devon were on it, Lou would feel comfortable about driving back to Grand Haven.

It was a beautiful spring day. The Red Cedar River wound its way through campus. The grass was green, trees leafed out, and tulips were fresh and colorful along walkways and in flower beds scattered throughout the campus. Even if his day were spent just people watching and being with nature, it would be great, Lou decided. What would make it extra special would be a chocolate chip ice cream sandwich from the Melting Moments Ice Cream Store on Grand River Avenue. Lou had enjoyed this ice cream treat when he attended MSU basketball games when he and Carol had lived in Haslett.

Lou walked over to the parking lot. Buses were beginning to arrive from around the state of Michigan. Nervous musicians poured out of cars, vans, and large school buses. Everyone headed to the music building to get schedules, sign in, and prepare for performances.

Lou was on hand when the Shoreline High School bus pulled into the parking lot at nine-forty. A vehicle was close behind, and Lou figured it was the Michigan State police surveillance vehicle. The state police officers would now turn over the security detail to the MSU police, and Detective Mallard, now that Devon was on campus.

From a distance, Lou watched the students exit the bus. Devon was one of about 35 students stretching and obviously glad to be off the bus. Devon was carrying a long, narrow, rectangular shaped black box, his instrument case. He also had a briefcase which held his music, a tuner, his reed tools in a small leather case, a water container, a swab, a reeds case, and a pencil. Devon walked with a chaperon and the other 34 students to the music building. His solo performance was about three hours away. He glanced at his watch and seemed content with how his morning was progressing. Lou followed the group from a distance. He looked around to see Maggie's wheelchair about a block away. Two sets of eyes were on the boy and everything going on around him. Lou called Maggie on the cell phone to touch base.

"Looks like all's going according to schedule. Do you pick him up?" Lou asked.

"Yes. I have him. I can also see Jane Wills and the photographer."

"Okay, just wanted to do a phone check and to make sure as many eyes as possible were on Devon," Lou said. "Mallard is also watching at some point, and he should be in constant contact with the MSU police."

Ȝ

It was five minutes to one. Devon was outside the door to the room where he was to perform his solo. Through the window he could see

Miss Whitmore and several of his friends. There were also some other bassoonists from around the state whom he had met at various events. Devon noticed the *Herald Palladium* reporter and photographer not far away. In the second row he saw Miss Simpson. He felt pleased and somehow comforted to see her, and he was appreciative of her efforts to drive all the way to East Lansing to support him.

At precisely ten minutes after one, the moderator for the bassoon solos rose, "Our next performer is Devon Rockingham from Shoreline High School. Devon has chosen to compete in Proficiency III. His solo will be "Concerto in F Major" by Carl Marie Von Weber. After the solo he will play his scales followed by sight-reading. Ladies and gentlemen, Devon Rockingham." Devon entered, wearing a dark suit and looking very polished and professional. There was a loud round of applause.

As Devon was about to sit down to perform, he glanced out the second floor window. His eye caught sight of a figure, the same figure he had seen the night that his principal died. The woman was about the same distance away as she had been the night of the murder. She pointed up at a bird or something in the sky. The profile, the figure, the clothes, the arm extended upward, all looked so familiar. Devon flashed back to the figure holding the gun pointed toward Principal Otterby. Devon was shocked. For an instant he couldn't understand how Miss Simpson could be in the room with him and outside the music building at the same time. He quickly looked over to see Heidi Simpson smiling at him. He returned to look at the woman outside. He was certain she was the same woman who had been in the pool area. She was standing the same way, facing the same direction, the body form was the same, her hairstyle the same.

Devon sat on the chair, positioned the bassoon, prepared his reed and tried to concentrate. He tried to put the woman out of his mind for the few minutes he would need to play the piece to perfection. He had yet to nod to the pianist that he was ready to begin.

In an unusual move, Devon stood and began to speak, "Before I begin, I'd like to thank my teacher who is here to support me. I also want to thank Mrs. McMillan for being here. We both have a disability. Hers is visible and mine's hidden, but we both are learning to cope, to adjust, and to adapt. Recently I referred to the Bible in regard to a shared problem we were having. Even now as I look out the window and see people walking around, I'm reminded once again of the Gospel of Matthew, chapter 26, verse 52. Devon looked out the window, looked back at Maggie and nodded. Devon concluded his remarks, "Miss Simpson and Mrs. McMillan, and to all of you who are here, thank you for your support. It's now my pleasure to perform my last piece as a student at Shoreline High School."

There was a round of applause as Devon made his final arrangements to perform. As the love of an admiring audience was coming toward him, through smiles and prolonged applause, Devon was momentarily relieved to know that his teacher did not kill his principal. That realization in itself helped him relax as he prepared to tackle a very challenging piece by Weber.

Unbeknown to others in the room, Maggie had just received an important message. She powered her chair out of the door. Twenty feet down the hall, she used her cell phone to call Lou. "Lou, Devon gave us a big clue just now. Before his performance I saw him glance outside and hesitate. He was obviously seeing something or someone. Then before performing he stood up and gave a speech thanking people for their support. He then repeated his reference to the Bible, as if to tell us that what he saw in the pool was being seen again, outside the music building. See if you can pick up on a Heidi look-alike. She should be on the east side of the music building. Call, if I can help. I'll have to stay outside the room where Devon's performing, but I'll see this woman if she comes up to the room. These next several minutes are critical."

Lou called Duck Mallard immediately and passed along the message. Duck in turn alerted the MSU police.

When Devon was comfortable, he began to progress through the very complicated piece. He played it to perfection. On that particular day in East Lansing, there wasn't another bassoon player on the face of this earth who could have matched Devon's performance.

When he finished, the entire audience rose to their feet and gave young Rockingham a prolonged standing ovation.

The judge spoke glowing words of praise for the performance, "We've just heard a performance by a young man who is destined for musical stardom." He looked proudly at Devon. "A masterful job, young man," he said. Devon figured that he had missed a few notes in the sight-reading portion of his performance and that would cause him to lose a point or two. Devon, if he survived the afternoon, was to become a bassoon phenom in the country, if not around the world.

Devon felt pleased that the performance went well. The support of the audience was thrilling. Devon bowed three times and even managed a smile. He realized that he had met the intent of the composer, and he had played the piece exactly as it had been written and intended to be played. The audience remained standing. Devon left the room and was met by his teacher, Miss Whitmore, who gave him a hug and told him how proud she was of him for doing such a masterful job. Other admirers joined her. There were many handshakes and pats on the back.

Heidi Simpson was in the crowd. She, too, approached Devon and hugged him. She looked him in the eye and said, "Remember our ice cream date after your ensemble performance." Devon smiled and nodded his head.

As Jane Wills was writing her perceptions in a small spiral notebook, Maggie drove her wheelchair up to her and said, "We promised to bring you into the investigation as it was being concluded. You're at the right place at the right time. Be alert. Things could happen quickly. While Jane was listening to Maggie, the photographer snapped pictures, including one of Miss Simpson giving Devon a hug. The byline would surely be, "Teacher is Proud."

※

Lou located the woman indicated by Devon. There was a resemblance to Heidi Simpson. Of that, there was no question. She was talking with someone. She seemed to fit in as a chaperon, parent, or a music leader at the festival. Lou didn't recognize her, but kept her in his sights.

Back on the second floor of the music building, someone handed a note to Heidi and disappeared. She read it and saw that it was a message for Devon to talk to his mother. He was to go to the Student Union. The call could be taken at the information desk. The message read, "This is an emergency. Please get Devon to the reception/information desk in the Student Union. His mother's very ill and wants desperately to talk with him."

Devon was talking with a few friends. Heidi immediately interrupted, "Devon, excuse me. I need to talk with you."

"Sure," said Devon, as he excused himself from the small group of friends.

"We have to go to the Student Union. It's the first building north of here. Your mother is holding on the phone for you. Sounds like an emergency related to her illness. We should leave immediately. Come with me."

Figuring he would be back in a matter of minutes, Devon left his bassoon and briefcase of personal items behind and quickly exited the building, with Miss Simpson leading the way. They headed down the walkway between the two buildings. Maggie missed their departure from the building because of where she was located and the exit route Heidi chose to use.

Once outside, Lou saw the two moving quickly toward the Student Union Building. He glanced back to the woman suspect and saw her get into a black car. Lou used his cell phone, "Duck, Heidi and Devon are moving quickly north of the music building, heading toward the south end of the Student Union. They're approximately 50 yards from it. The woman suspect has gotten into a black car heading east from the music building."

Mallard and Detective Robinson got the message and directed unmarked cars with plainclothes officers to proceed to the Student Union. Lou followed, to keep an eye on any activity.

A one-way street from east to west, West Circle Drive passes between the Student Union and the music building. As Heidi and Devon were about to cross West Circle Drive, a black Lincoln Towncar pulled up and blocked the crosswalk. The driver rolled down the window as Devon and Heidi came up to the road. "Devon, take the call from my car phone. Your mom's very sick and needs to talk with you."

Devon quickly jumped into the front seat of the Towncar. The car door was slammed. Heidi was pushed back onto the grass and the car sped away. Lou saw the whole thing and reported it on his cell phone to the MSU police: "A black Towncar is heading west on West Circle Drive...." Luckily the Towncar did not turn immediately to the right, which would have meant an exit from the campus at Abbott Road. Instead, it went straight, allowing the MSU police to get to the major campus entrances and establish a roadblock.

Heidi stood at the roadside, shocked. She realized what had happened—Devon Rockingham had been kidnapped. Heidi took off her shoes and ran toward the band practice field to catch the Towncar as it turned south. As she ran, she took her pistol from her purse. Using a tree for protection, Heidi caught her breath and fired a shot at the left rear tire. She hit the tire on the third shot. It popped, and in a matter of seconds the luxury car was crippled.

Four MSU police cars converged on the slowed vehicle and forced the driver to stop. The police got out of their cars, using their doors for shields. One officer demanded the occupants of the car exit with hands up. The male driver emerged from the car. The back doors opened and two more people exited, a man and a woman. The police ordered all three onto the ground. Heidi ran up. Disregarding the orders of the police to stay back, she opened the passenger door and helped Devon out.

The police, with revolvers pointed toward the vehicle, immediately checked to see if anyone else was in the car. Lou, who had seen the drama unfold from a distance, came upon the scene and joined Duck Mallard and MSU Detective Robinson. An officer escorted Heidi and Devon to one of the MSU police vehicles. Both were safe, and although shaken by the incident, were going to be fine.

Lou used his cell phone to call Maggie. "All are in custody, Maggie. Devon was kidnapped outside the Student Union. Heidi was with him. She fired a shot that crippled the vehicle and allowed the MSU police to converge and apprehend the kidnappers. Three suspects were on the ground and are now being handcuffed and frisked for weapons. The woman looks like Heidi's twin. I don't know if she's Phyllis Weaver or not. That's the story from here."

"I'm glad Devon's safe," Maggie said with a sigh of relief.

"Thanks for catching Devon's clue about the woman outside. Good work as always, Maggie."

The three suspects were taken to the MSU Public Safety Office for booking and interrogation. Maggie had experience with police procedures. She knew the case backward and forward, so she went with Mallard to handle all of those precise and legal details.

Once the police were certain that Devon was unharmed and he had told Mallard and Robinson what happened in the car, he was free to go with Lou and Heidi. According to Devon, once in the car the woman who looked like Heidi said, "The scare about your mom was our ploy. There was no phone call from her. We needed you with us, that's all."

و

Lou, Heidi, and Devon went to a public phone in the MSU Public Safety Office and called Devon's mother. Lou did the talking before handing the phone to Devon. "Mrs. Rockingham, I want to assure you that Devon is just fine. We had an incident where Devon was kidnapped. He's shaken, as he should be, but the ordeal is over. He's safe and seems to be handling it quite well. In fact, he seems quite relieved. I'll put him on."

"Oh, I'm so thankful Devon's okay. I've been concerned ever since he left this morning." Lou sensed that Devon's mother was about to cry.

"Yes, he's okay. Here he is."

"Hi, Mom. I'm okay."

"Thank God, Dev. I'm so thankful."

"I saw the woman who killed Mr. Otterby outside the music building. Mrs. McMillan picked up on a message I gave in a talk before my performance. She, Mr. Searing, and the police caught the people soon after I got into their car. Mom, they said you were sick and needed to talk to me. That's why I got into the car. Are you all right?"

"I'm very thankful, Dev, and I'm fine. You sure you're okay?"

"Yeah, Mom. I'm okay. The truth has made me free. I can really say that now."

"I'm anxiously waiting for you to come home, Dev."

"I'll be there in a few hours, Mom."

"I love you, son."

"I love you, too, Mom."

Lou got back on the line to once again assure Mrs. Rockingham that Devon was safe and that the ordeal was over.

Once the phone call was complete, Heidi, Devon, and Lou went over to the Melting Moments Ice Cream Store on Grand River Avenue, across from the MSU campus. "How about a chocolate chip ice cream sandwich?" Lou asked.

"Sounds good to me," replied Devon. It was the first moment of true relaxation since the day began.

"That stuff will go right to my hips," Heidi said. "I'll have a small cup of frozen yogurt."

They sat at a small round ice cream parlor table. "You all right, son?" Lou asked.

"Yeah, I guess so. I'm glad it's over. It's probably been the worst two weeks of my life."

"I can imagine. You know, you had me confused. I couldn't figure out why you didn't tell anybody about what you saw that night. You are such an upstanding citizen, and active in your church. Such a fine young man as yourself, I'm confused that you didn't confide in someone, a parent, a minister, a counselor, us, or somebody, but you didn't."

"Sorry, but you see Miss Simpson felt quite sure that I saw what happened in the pool. I heard a sermon last Sunday and the theme was, 'The truth shall make you free.' Well, the newspaper said the police had determined the death a suicide, and I knew that wasn't the truth. I told people lies myself, when I said that I hadn't seen or heard anything. I had to figure out a way to communicate that I had seen something without hurting Miss Simpson. She has been such a good teacher and friend to me."

"So, you told us the scripture reference."

"Yeah, and you got it. I also hoped that the amount of time I spent looking in the window would help. Nobody would spend that much time looking at nothing at ten-fifteen at night. I may have a significant learning disability, but I'm not crazy."

"We got it. Great clues, Devon."

"I couldn't believe that Miss Simpson would kill somebody, but the woman looked exactly like her. I was really torn up about that."

Heidi said, "You handled it well. You were honest, you treated me with respect, and you followed your conscience in letting people know what you experienced."

Lou added, "You were sure high on the suspect list for a long time, Heidi. You had so much circumstantial evidence working against you that you could have been put in prison for it. I've seen people with far less circumstantial evidence put away for a long time. The past week hasn't been lucky for you. You don't realize it, but it was Tom Hines' diary that gave us the biggest clue that you were not the one who killed Otterby. Also, you might learn how to spell principal. That mistake didn't help you any either."

"Principal? Let's see that's P-R-I-N-C-I-P-L-E. Right?"

"That's right if you mean, "A set of principles. But, the leader of the school is..."

"Oh, I know, the principal is the students' pal and it's P-R-I-N-C-I-P-A-L. Except Otterby wasn't the students' pal or the teachers' or the parents' or the state's or the fed's or anyone's pal for that matter."

"That misspelling put you high on our suspect list!"

The three chuckled, finished their ice cream and prepared to leave. "I let my ensemble down," Devon said. "We were supposed to perform at two. I hope they did okay without me."

"I'm sure they did."

Lou and Heidi escorted Devon back to the music building to be interviewed by Jane Wills and reunited with his friends and admirers.

Heidi stayed with Devon until the bus left for Shoreline. Miss Whitmore was on the bus also. She said that she'd be responsible for seeing that Devon got safely home.

Lou and Maggie made their way to the MSU Public Safety Building. The kidnappers in the car were identified as Phyllis Weaver and two of her friends from Kalamazoo, Don Overton and Gene Emmer.

The whole case came to a dramatic conclusion when Detective Mallard received a phone call. The call was from the State Police Crime Lab in East Lansing. Mallard had dropped off the diary for analysis and the technician said that with their new technology they were able to study the indentation of the page following the torn-out Friday page in Tom Hines' diary. While the page was blank to the eye, the indentation created when Tom Hines wrote on the page was very clear. There, in telling detail, the mystery was solved. The three listened as Mallard read what Tom Hines had written: "Warren Otterby was killed by Phyllis Weaver. She was assisted by Don Overton and Gene Emmer, her friends from Kalamazoo. There were two other people who guarded the locker room doors, but I don't know who they were. I assume friends of Phyllis. Otterby died because he didn't pay his gambling debts to Weaver. Phyllis is an old friend who asked me to give her a lot of information about the school and the people who work there. From all of this information she was able to craft a plan for Otterby's murder. To be honest, I crafted the plan. Phyllis couldn't put a light bulb in a socket without help. Unfortunately, I agreed to help her and I'm guilty as well. If I don't get out of town, I'm a dead man."

THE PRINCIPAL CAUSE OF DEATH

Heidi stopped at the MSU Public Safety Building before she left for Shoreline. She found Lou and Maggie chatting in a conference room. "I wanted to thank you for all of your work in solving this mess."

"You're welcome," Lou said. Maggie nodded and smiled.

"There are a few things I wanted to explain before I leave. First of all, the lie about using my phone in the school. I was scared and wanted to do whatever I could to diminish any belief that I was involved in the death of Otterby. For some reason that I can't explain, I thought it best that I give the impression that I was alone and talked with no one."

"That little lie did a lot to ruin your integrity in this case. We couldn't trust any of your answers from then on," Maggie said.

"Yeah. I can understand that. The light went on in Mrs. Norton's office, right? I didn't think of that."

"Yes, that's how we knew someone was in your classroom. The three of us were meeting in Lorraine's office when the light from your phone went on," Lou explained.

"Sorry. The second thing I want to explain is Mothers for Justice."

"Yes, please do. They were an unnecessary negative force," offered Lou.

"Well, I had been working with Harriet Haskins for some time. We were trying to get Otterby to come in line with state regulations. Mothers for Justice is a good group to put pressure on difficult administrators. I told Harriet she had a challenge in Otterby and that motivated her to see that change occurred. We were working together about the time that Otterby was killed. When she learned that you were investigating the murder, she feared that I'd be a suspect and she didn't want anybody looking into the cause of death. She was trying to be supportive of me."

"Once again, Harriet's actions only added to the impression that you had something to hide. Her help wasn't help after all," Maggie explained.

"I guess I made a mess of things all along the way. Thankfully, you two got to the bottom of it. I can't thank you enough!" Heidi gave each a hug.

"You can thank us by getting some professional help for your gambling problem. Nothing would please us more than to learn that that problem has been put to sleep."

"I will. It's been a problem most of my life. Maybe that's the lesson I'm to learn through all of this."

"I hope you and Rick will have a better week, now that you're clear of all charges and rumors."

"I think it'll be an easier row to hoe from now on. Anyway, I'll be on my way. Thanks again. I'll be thankful to you both each day of my life."

"Oh, Heidi, the spelling of 'principal.' Tom Hines typed the notes to Otterby and to Rick. Like you, he didn't know that 'principal' is spelled 'al.' Phyllis Weaver, the woman whom Detective Mallard and also Tom Hines, in his diary, said could not plan a meal with a refrigerator full of food or screw a lightbulb into a socket, wrote a note to Tom Hines. She spelled 'principal' correctly in it."

"So, the lesson is that bookies can spell?" Heidi asked with a chuckle.

"My sister's from Texas and I'm fairly certain her comment would be 'go figure,'" Lou said with a smile.

"Oh, Lou, I'd like to write a note to Mrs. Rockingham," Heidi said. "Do you have a piece of paper? You know a piece of S-T-A-T-I-O-N-A-R-Y."

"You're hopeless, Heidi. Go home and enjoy your new lease on life!" Maggie said, shaking her head and smiling.

"You mean I misspelled that homophone, too?"

೨ෆ

Late that evening, Lou, Carol and Samm walked along the shore of Lake Michigan. "Another one finished, Lou?"

"Signed, sealed, and delivered."

"I'm proud of you, Sweetie. Scares me having you out there in harms' way, but I guess I'll have to get used to it."

Lou threw a stick out into the lake. Samm took off with a mission to get the stick and brought it back to her master. "As long as conflict exists in education and I can help, I'll go after every challenge. Just as Samm brings the stick back to my feet for another toss, Maggie and I will bring the evidence back and hope it solves a murder."

Carol squeezed Lou's hand. They stopped and turned to watch the sun slip into Lake Michigan. The sky was peaceful and full of magnificent pastels. They lived the moment. They were thankful to share their lives.

CHAPTER 14

Tuesday, May 24

The citizens of Shoreline read the headline in their morning paper, "Principal Otterby Murdered by Kalamazoo Group: Local Teachers Cleared." Jane Wills was commended for her marvelous job of reporting the story and for explaining the heroics of Heidi Simpson, and the teamwork of Detective Daniel Mallard, and private investigators Lou Searing and Maggie McMillan.

She wrote a second piece about the remarkable young man, Devon Rockingham, who in addition to performing to his potential at the solo and ensemble competition had played a significant part in solving the murder. She ended her article with words of praise for all: "Our youth are served by excellent educators under the leadership of Dr. Donald and Mrs. Norton. Devon Rockingham is one of hundreds of young people in our community who give us plenty of reasons to be proud of our schools and the accomplishments of our youth."

༄

Lou's tee time was 10:17 a.m. at the Spring Lake Country Club. Life was good.

Epilogue

Phyllis Weaver was arrested for the murder of Warren Otterby and Tom Hines. She also was guilty of kidnapping. She was sentenced to life in prison without parole.

Don Overton, Gene Emmer, Larry Leys and Tina Lewis were arrested and found guilty as accomplices in the murder of Warren Otterby and Tom Hines. Don and Gene were also guilty of assisting in the kidnapping of a minor. All four were sentenced to 20 years in prison with the possibility for parole based on good behavior.

Heidi Simpson was given an award for heroism in assisting in the apprehension of the murderers of Warren Otterby and Thomas Hines. She got control of her gambling. Heidi became the recipient of the Learning Disabilities Association of Michigan's Teacher of the Year award.

Rick Bolt began a courtship with Heidi. During a Labor Day picnic, Rick asked Heidi to marry him. She accepted. Rick asked Devon to play at the wedding and reception. He accepted.

Lorraine Norton enjoyed many years as an exceptional principal at Shoreline High School. In fact, she was named Principal of the Year by the Michigan Association of Secondary School Principals. Parents, teachers, and the community grew to respect, love, and admire her as a leader.

Dr. Donald was asked, by the State Board of Education, to accept an appointment as Superintendent of Public Instruction. He accepted and became a significant force in leading Michigan's public education system.

EPILOGUE

Devon Rockingham attended the Julliard School of Music in New York City and went on to a nationwide concert tour. He appeared on "Oprah" and other talk shows to relate how it all began for him at Shoreline High. America, and eventually the world, loved him. So did Wendy, and their friendship blossomed. Marriage at some point seems like a real possibility.

Jane Wills did break the news of the principal's murder. She also won a Pulitzer Prize for her feature story about Devon Rockingham.

Lou and Maggie relaxed a bit. Lou spent time writing his novels, playing golf, enjoying the beach, and being with Carol. Maggie worked on her insurance claims investigations. Her husband Tom, when he wasn't yanking molars, was visiting and trying to conquer the world's greatest golf courses. Maggie was constantly on the watch for a phone call from Lou and the opportunity to work on another education case with him.

Order Information

To order additional copies of *The Principal Cause of Death* or *A Lesson Plan for Murder* visit the website of Buttonwood Press at www.buttonwoodpress.com for information. Or, forward the following information to:

Buttonwood Press
P. O. Box 716
Haslett, Michigan 48840

One copy of *The Principal Cause of Death* or *A Lesson Plan for Murder* costs $12.95 (this includes MI sales tax, if applicable, and shipping and handling).

Number of books requested:

_____ *Principal Cause of Death* @ $12.95 each

_____ *A Lesson Plan for Murder* @ $12.95 each

Total Enclosed: _____

Mailing Address:

Name: _____

Address (include zip code):_____

_____

Autograph requests: To _____

Questions? Call the Buttonwood Press office at:
(517) 339-9871.

Thank you